*When Buffy got a firm enough footing,
she came up again, hard, swinging her bone-weapon
in a neat semicircle across the area
directly under the jawline.*

There was no roar of pain.

This time, there wasn't any sound at all.

With its airway and main artery severed, the creature wobbled soundlessly where it stood for an overlong ten seconds, opening and closing its mouth as if it couldn't believe what had just happened. More blood—Buffy had never seen anything bleed this much—fountained from the upper part of the wound, spraying everything in its way. Buffy felt a line of it cross her face, warm, wet, and utterly disgusting.

Finally, the thing lay lifeless in front of them.

"Piece of cake," Buffy quipped, but she didn't mean it.

Oz, covered in grit with a bruise along one pale cheekbone, raised an eyebrow. "I'm glad you think so," he said gently. "But . . . where's the other one?"

Buffy the Vampire Slayer™

Available from ARCHWAY Paperbacks and POCKET PULSE

Buffy the Vampire Slayer adult books

Available from POCKET BOOKS

BUFFY
THE VAMPIRE
SLAYER™

PALEO

YVONNE NAVARRO

An original novel based on the hit TV series created by Joss Whedon

POCKET BOOKS
New York   London   Toronto   Sydney   Singapore

Historian's Note:
This story takes place during the third season.

An *Original* Publication of POCKET BOOKS

POCKET BOOKS, a division of Simon & Schuster, Inc.
1230 Avenue of the Americas, New York, NY 10020

ISBN: 0-7434-0034-8

First Pocket Books printing September 2000

10 9 8 7 6 5 4 3 2 1

Printed in the U.S.A.

For
Jeff Osier,
who first fired my interest
in dinosaurs years ago.
Thanks.

Acknowledgments

A book about vampires and dinosaurs is just too much fun, and you can't have something like that come into being without having a whole bunch of people to thank. So, in no particular order, get ready . . . set . . .

Go!

Lisa Clancy, Howard Morhaim, Nancy Holder, Chris Golden, Jeff Osier, Don VanderSluis, Micol Ostow, John Platt, Sephera Giron, Martin Cochran, Matthew Woodring Stover (I stole his word. Again.) and Bob Eggleton.

Prologue

"ALL RIGHT," DANIEL ADDISON SAID. "WHERE DO WE start?"

No one answered, of course, because no one else was in the basement storeroom; it was just him, the dust, and the mousetraps surrounded by wooden crates that hadn't been looked at in years. He ran a hand through his hair and was reminded that he needed a haircut, then belatedly realized how grimy his hands had gotten from pushing everything around down here. Ridiculous grunt work, but the task wasn't as bad as he'd imagined it might be. Daniel knew he could've fared much worse when his supervisor at the Sunnydale Museum of Natural History had doled out the grad student assignments. While he tended to think of the man as a dried-up old prune, somewhere in Professor Rami's shriveled chest apparently beat a heart: he could've just as easily assigned Daniel to the Herpetology Department. Going over an inventory of snake skins might make the day for some people, but Daniel's interest in reptiles ran to a *much* larger scale.

The boxes were stenciled with dates and he'd arranged them chronologically; now it was time to pry them open and see what was inside and how it ought to be entered in the museum's computer files. The crates went back more than sixty years, to when the museum had first been built, and he was looking at about forty-five boxes. Whatever was in these things had long ago been cycled out of past exhibits, and prior to 1960 the contents hadn't been added to the data banks. Now it was time to rectify that, and what better slave labor than one of the local college students?

"Banzai," Daniel said, just to hear his own voice, but he only sounded annoyed and resentful. He picked up a crowbar and set to work on the lid of the earliest-dated crate. It was eerie down here in the basement, a good fifteen degrees chillier than on the first floor. Occasionally he could hear sounds, but the museum's heavy construction muffled the noise above him beyond recognition. Daniel doubted he could tell the difference between footsteps or something being dropped. He was fairly disoriented, but he thought he might be at the back of the huge building; the only windows down here were made of two-level heavy glass blocks, so there was no way to tell without a floor plan.

The lid of the first box, marked 1939, suddenly came free with a screech and a jerk that sent him stumbling backward. The scent of mildew drifted out, undercut by something else that Daniel hadn't expected—a smoky smell that brought to mind the image of burning paper. Glad he'd thought to wear work gloves and, wishing the light down here was a little better, the young man began lifting things out of the crate. Professor Rami had assigned him one of the Paleontology Department's laptop computers, and the idea was to unpack each crate's contents and enter everything on the data inventory form, then carefully repack every box. Tedious but not so complicated, and Daniel tried to convince himself that it was worth it—he might find a cool item or two, something forgotten or that, out of lack of knowledge at the time, had been thought unimportant. Anything like that he would return to the Paleontology Department for examination.

While he wasn't sure what he had expected to discover in these crates, the items he lifted from the first one were already oddly out of place. He'd anticipated records of old digs, photographs, and maybe broken fossils—really good finds would still be on exhibit—but certainly not this. Perplexed, Daniel sat back and surveyed what he'd uncrated. No bones here; instead, he was looking at the scorched remains of someone's tool kit: hammers, saws, chisels, brushes with no bristles and the head of a small spade, what was left of a leather hat and pair of gloves, a canteen, and a primitive pair of half-melted goggles. There was a beat-up metal clipboard, a ragged roll of plasterer's scrim that had escaped the as-yet-unexplained flames, even a still half-full sack of plaster, all of it charred and covered with a fine layer of black soot. Stuffed to the side was a blackened leather saddlebag, and when Daniel looked inside, he found a mound of ashes that might have once been paper.

Tucked beneath a twine-encircled stack of papers and files whose edges were burned to a mottled brown was the final item in the box of gear: the shredded pieces of a heavy, army-style canvas tent. When Daniel spread it out, the skin at the back of his neck crawled. It looked like an entire side of it had been destroyed and there wasn't nearly enough left to provide shelter. Worse, it was obvious from the smoke stain pattern that the fire had been on the *inside* of the tent.

Daniel shivered and sat back, again surveying the crate's contents for a moment before reaching for the files. He cut the old twine encircling them with his pocketknife and began to separate the stack carefully, wincing as some of the dry, fire-damaged pages crumbled in his hands. It took him nearly an hour, but he finally had a name and enough information to combine with the 1939 date so that he could lose the gloves and do a search of the museum's data files on the laptop.

Nuriel, Gibor (Professor). B. 1891 / D. 1939—Dept. of Paleontology. Hire Date: 2/14/13. Termination Date: N/A. While on a dig at a Big Bend, Texas location on July 2, 1939, Gibor Nuriel was killed by an explosion and fire inside his tent. The explosion was attributed to a faulty camping stove. There are no known surviving family members. Material recovered from his tent was deemed irreparably damaged and of no use, and was relegated to chronological storage. Per orders of the Probate Court, Prof. Nuriel's personal estate was liquidated and the resulting funds (total $658.00), were donated to the Museum.

Frowning, Daniel finished reading the entry, then rubbed the goose bumps on the back of his neck. There was something unaccountably . . . *depressing* about the notion that this middle-aged scientist had died a horrible death in what back then had been the center of nowhere, and this was all that had been recorded about his life: a stupid accident with a camping stove that should have been outside his tent, no relatives, and his whole life had been worth $658.00. It was just made worse by the way some thoughtless clerk had called Nuriel's final work "of no use." *The man died out there, for God's sake. There has to be something worthy of note in these files and papers. All a person has to do is dig a little, and isn't that what paleontology is all about?*

Forgoing the gloves, Daniel went back over to where he'd spread out the contents of the 1939 crate and knelt on the floor in front of the three stacks of paper he'd lifted out of it. Working carefully, he flipped through the sheets, stubbornly checking every single page before laying it aside. Cracked and stained with water, the edges were ferociously prone to disintegrating no matter how gingerly he handled them, and Daniel had to admit that what he saw wasn't encouraging. He could imagine the whole scene: the explosion of the stove fuel that probably—and hopefully—knocked Nuriel unconscious, the flames sweeping over everything inside the tent while the other members of the team ran for buckets of water to try to put it out. And they had. The proof was on every page where the professor's blocky handwriting, which at one time had probably been quite easy to read, was now water-smeared and mostly illegible.

Daniel began going through the last stack but didn't expect the results to be any better. He'd been involved here for almost two years while he went to the local university, but outside of the occasionally semi-interesting tasks like this one, the museum was still assigning him the same old grunt work; all the really cool projects went to the people who'd already graduated. Shoot, he was just as smart—smarter—than any of the others doing post-grad work here. *Most of them couldn't find their way out of a wet paper bag unless someone else ripped it open.* But they were still the ones who were chosen to go on the digs during the summer months, while Daniel was forced to stick around and mop up the slop.

Somehow he'd never pictured the start of his paleontology career as being like this. He might be young, but he knew his stuff just as well or better than any of the staff here. Why did he have to paw around the museum's dirty basement while other people got to go out on digs and get hands-on experience? His big coup so far—and it wasn't much—was that out of a half-dozen candidates, Professor Rami had chosen Daniel to go over and give a talk on dinosaurs to one of the senior classes at Sunnydale High School next Tuesday. Daniel had probably been elected only because he'd graduated from there. It sure wasn't where someone with his level of intelligence deserved to be—out in the field with the rest of the real paleontologists—but at least it would get him away from this dirty, lower-level drudgery. He—

"Whoa," Daniel said. "What's this?"

There'd been a bulge at the bottom of the last stack, a place where the papers didn't line up evenly. He hadn't paid any attention to it at first—everything here was water-warped and a mess—then he'd lifted the next two sheets of paper. Underneath was a leather notebook, the cover split so badly that it was almost torn in two, while the stitching at its edges and spine was blackened by the fire and left smudges of soot on Daniel's fingers. *Wow,* Daniel thought reverently. *Professor Nuriel's dig journal.* Could he really hope to find anything inside, or would it be as washed away as all the other information?

As carefully as he could, Daniel opened it.

Pay dirt! At first glance it looked like Nuriel's chunky writing still filled a number of the pages. Daniel scanned it eagerly, but his delight soon did a fast fade. Yeah, there was info here, but way too much of it; the bottom half of nearly every page was obliterated. *Too bad.* There had been so much here that he could have learned, overlooked information that could have helped him get ahead in a department that a lot of the students called "Department of Dinosaurs" under their breath. The older people here at the museum were stodgy and unyielding, with no time, patience or interest in the fresh concepts or new questions the younger students raised. Some of the theories that the dead professor hinted at might, had all the information been there, have been atypical, but how would Daniel—or anyone else—ever know?

Fascinated, Daniel forgot about the damp basement air and the chilliness of the concrete floor beneath his crossed legs. Even though so much was gone and lots of the entries were probably just preambles to things that were proven in later decades by other paleontologists, he could still tell that some of Professor Nuriel's entries were . . . well, unique, that he'd had an open mind rarely found in the older members of the field. Written in a diary-like style and filled with cross-outs, the last couple of pages in particular caught Daniel's attention. He read them, then read them again, nearly unable to comprehend the words on the pages:

28 July 1939 Wednesday
I've made the most ~~amazing~~ strangest discovery of my entire career, and this in the midst of the locals' efforts to make this area into some kind of a national park——they are calling it "Big Bend National Park."

I can only hope this place remains hidden inaccessible, but I doubt it——the trading post they are setting up at Lajitas will take care of that. Mankind spreads upon the most precious areas of our world like fleas on the back of a stray dog. Someday the roads here in South Brewster County will be paved and it will be much easier for the common people to visit and ultimately destroy the wondrous things that nature has preserved.

Speaking of which, while Jimmy and the rest of the crew were working on freeing what appeared to be the femur of an iguanodont in the main part of the site, I had gone off behind a large outcropping to attend to the ne

Like all the other pages in the journal, the rest of the words smeared into the watery equivalent of a Rorschach test, but Daniel was able to pick it up on the opposite side of the journal:

old leather saddlebag. The papers inside are written in what I believe is a Romany dialect, but I can translate enough of it to theorize that it is a spell ritual of some sort. It's very strange peculiar and seems to postulate that something dead can be brought back to life, but it's also very specific with regards to what that object is——no people, only animals "such as large lizards or the petrified remains of their spawn."

Interestingly enough, there's a reference in the text that might pertain to ancient Greek mythology. Roughly put to English, this is the incantation:

Hear this call, spirits of Ladonithia
Awaken and return from your abyss to this
 frozen host
First of four, to then combine
And grant to he who resurrects you
A single wish fulfilled.

Another chunk of the writing was destroyed at the bottom, but Daniel expected this. Again the text picked up on the other side of the page, and here the young man's eyes widened with every paragraph he read:

Wednesday and so I must wait for the Mexican workers to leave. They will stay through Saturday afternoon, then return to their families for Sunday worship. There's no logical reason to try this except for curiosity, but I am a scientist and so must investigate even that. "Petrified remains of their spawn"—could that not refer to, perhaps, a fossil? There's precious little entertainment in this dismal location, and so I've selected the small (though regrettably incomplete) skeleton of a young hypsilophodont. Reanimation? Impossible!!! I do this only for amusement's sake, of course, and so must hide my foolishness from the

There the entry stopped, and Daniel was disappointed when the next pages were blank. Weirdness, but then it had been sixty years ago, at an isolated dig site and, as far as Daniel was concerned, it might as well have been ancient history. He knew nothing about Gibor Nuriel, of course, but still . . . he was surprised that a mature man of science would even waste his time on something like this. The last part of the journal was sturdier and not so badly damaged, and Daniel flipped idly through the blank pages. *Really, what had Nuriel hoped to gain from—*

"Hey, what's this?" As he stopped at a page near the end of the journal with writing on it, the loudness of his voice startled him. He'd forgotten, again, that he was alone down here, had been for several hours. The light through the glass blocks had dimmed and the shadows in the dusty room had gone several shades darker despite the fluorescents; if he wasn't careful, he'd lose track of time and end up locked in the museum for the night. While he wasn't afraid of the dark, the notion of being stuck in here with everything from a life-size replica of a Ceratosaurus to the remains of an Incan mummy princess just didn't rock his socks.

Daniel squinted at the journal in the growing darkness. More of Nuriel's crude handwriting, but this was haphazard and blotched, scrawled at an angle across a random page as if the man had been in a terrific hurry to get it all down:

This was a terrible error in judgment—I should have NEVER said this incantation aloud. I thought it was a joke, but I am the one who is the fool, the puny man at whom the universe laughts laughs. A living, breathing hypsilophodont—my God, who could have ever imagined?? But it's WRONG . . . how was I to know? The dinosaur creature is missing half its spine and two limbs, also part of its skull—yet still it thrashes and screeches—yes, it's actually reanimated somehow ALIVE. I don't know if it's in pain or just . . . evil. I think that's it, because it "speaks" to me inside my thoughts, demanding that I continue, bellowing commands into my mind that I must do more for it. God forgive me but I don't think I can hold out—I'm not strong enough. What have I done? To save myself, to save everyone, I must dest

And that was it. Intrigued, Daniel sifted through the rest of the journal but the pages were blank. Finally, he checked out what little remained of Nuriel's files, but hardly anything in there was legible, and there was certainly nothing to do with the far-fetched claims set down by Professor Nuriel in the notebook. What had caused them—too much heat? Texas in the summer could be brutal and there sure hadn't been any a/c in the old man's tent in 1939. Still, it seemed a bit detailed for a sun-induced fantasy. Could there be a touch of truth in there somewhere?

Daniel glanced at his watch, then stood. Time to wrap up the drudge work for the day, although he had to admit that it wasn't as dull as he had anticipated; finding Nuriel's journal had made things a bit more on the edge of interesting. In fact, he wouldn't mind taking another, more thorough look at it in his spare time. Who would know, or even care, if he took it out of the museum? Hey, no one had thought about this stuff in fifty years or more, maybe since the day they'd packed up the old professor's desk. The suits—that's what he called the administration and the teachers and all the rest of the hard-nosed older people—didn't think about the feelings of any of the people they ordered around. They just wanted the work that the little guys like him did so they could turn around and trade it for the almighty dollar.

Well, I'm not that dumb.

Sunnydale, he thought as he wiped his hands and carefully tucked the journal inside his backpack, was a pretty darned abnormal place. His first instinct had been that the dead professor should have dismissed his findings, but then he thought more about it. The incantation Gibor Nuriel had discovered might have seemed unbelievable to most people in 1939 Big Bend, Texas. But here? *Not.* There was something slightly . . . *off* about Sunnydale, and maybe it had been so even back then; after all, Nuriel had been from Sunnydale. Daniel hadn't been here all his life like most of his friends, but as far as he could tell, not growing up here was a *good* thing. People—kids, teenagers, everyone—*disappeared* here with a regularity that as an outsider he'd noticed right away. He wasn't sure what amazed him more—the downright weirdosity that oozed out of everything Sunnydale, or that the people of Sunnydale accepted this, and the disappearances, without so much as blinking.

Daniel tidied up the stuff he'd uncrated and decided he'd finish cataloging the contents tomorrow. It was getting late, he was hungry, and he'd had a lot on his mind before finding the journal, which itself added a whole arena of potential to things. Walking through the nearly empty museum on his way out just reminded Daniel of how much of an uphill struggle it had been for him over the last two years. The museum was so full of politics—he hadn't expected that. Everything was seniority and who you knew, who threw the best parties and had published umpteen papers full of boring, much-reprinted facts disguised as educational literature. Who wanted to sit in front of a computer and peck out hundreds of pages that no one would read anyway? Not him, that's for sure.

Outside it was a beautiful spring night, the kind that reminded him that he ought to have a date with a real live girl instead of a bunch of textbooks. Better yet would be if he was making plans for the next dig the museum was sponsoring, the one in Dinosaur Cove, Australia, over the summer. Like they would ever include him. Fat chance. He knew his dinosaurs, he could sketch, he could write, and he could dig, but with the kind of back-slapping that went on here, he'd be as old as Nuriel before he even got to help *clean* one of the finds they brought back. To his supervisor and the rest of the suits, he was nothing but disposal sludge.

But maybe, with a little help from the incantation in Nuriel's journal, he could change that. He'd only scanned it a time or two, but if he tried, he could just remember how that last line had read:

And grant to he who resurrects you
A single wish fulfilled.

That was certainly something to think about, wasn't it?

Chapter 1

LET'S SEE, BUFFY SUMMERS THOUGHT. *WHERE WOULD I rather be? Here in the dark, standing by a dirty and disgusting headstone—cracked on one side and covered with mold and something else I don't even want to identify, or—*

A branch snapped behind her.

She did a neat, tight spin, ready to fight, with the fingers of one hand curled comfortably around a wooden stake, but there was no one there. Buffy scowled, yet didn't drop her guard. It might be a bird or a raccoon, even someone's pet cat; what it would *definitely* be the instant she slipped up was some ugly bloodsucker trying to make her into a midnight snack. There was something out there—she just *knew* it. It would be so much nicer if they'd just get it over with so she could go home. It was Sunday night, for crying out loud. All good people, children, and monsters, should be put away for the Sabbath . . . or something like that.

She heard another snap, not quite muffled by a line of waist-high bushes separating two sections of the cemetery. Friend or foe?

Foe!

Instinct made Buffy leap to the left. She twisted in midair and when she landed she was already facing the thing that had just pounced on the spot where she'd been standing only a split second before. It was a girl, no more than seven or eight years old and done up for a proper burial in a white lace dress adorned with ribbons and tiny, pink satin roses. Red hair divided into what should have been perfect braids, except now they, and the rest of her burial outfit, were full of dirt, leaves, and bits of sod. Damn—the grown-up ones were bad enough, but Buffy hated it when the night's vamp turned out to be a child.

"Okay," Buffy said in a reasonable tone of voice. Did vampire kidlets listen any better than real ones? "We can do this the easy way, or the hard way. Your choice."

The little girl grinned at her, showing pointed white fangs beneath the classic twisted brow and glinting, yellow eyes. She took a step forward and Buffy tensed—

—then yelped in surprise as someone else grabbed her shoulders from behind.

Fetid breath stung her nostrils—she *hated* that—and a second, older vampire tried to fasten its mouth on the right side of her neck. She scrunched up her shoulder and slammed her head sideways simultaneously; the creature howled and let go of her as it took the hit along its eyebrow. It stumbled back at the same time as the childish bloodsucker darted forward and tried to spring at her, but Buffy swatted the girl away as though she were nothing more than an annoying mosquito. The adult vamp growled and lunged, but Buffy slipped sideways under its outstretched arms and came up behind

16

it, burying her stake deep into the center of its back. Her weapon found the heart-point inside the creature's body and rewarded her with a midair explosion of black-brown dust.

Great, Buffy thought. *One down, one-half to g—*

"Hey!" she said in surprise. "Where'd you go?"

A quick scan and she saw the little girl crouching behind one of the larger tombstones about twenty feet away—even full of graveyard dirt, it was hard to camouflage that white dress in a cemetery near midnight. Buffy covered the distance in a heartbeat and hauled the snarling vampire-child out into the open, trying to get the little monster into a position where she could be staked. It was like fighting with a wildcat, the girl's size and flexibility making her movements a lot more energetic than Buffy expected, but finally the Slayer managed to straddle her. Holding the vamp-kid down with her left hand, Buffy raised the stake in her right.

"Time to go to sleep," she said as gently as she could.

"I don't want to!" the girl wailed. "The boogey-monster is down there!"

Buffy started to retort that the girl *was* the boogey-monster, then decided against it. Bad enough the child was going to die for the second time. The girl bucked and nearly threw her off as she clawed at the ground and tried to sit up. "Be still and let's just get this over with!" Buffy grunted.

"No!" the vamp screamed in a high-pitched voice. "I want to stay *awake!*"

Her voice cut off as Buffy slammed her down yet again. Enough of this. The stake was on its downward swing as she heard the small vampire's next words, and Buffy couldn't have pulled her strike if she'd tried.

"You'll see!" the child shrieked. "It's just about to wake up—"

Dust.

Buffy's backside hit hard-packed soil as the mini-bloodsucker disintegrated beneath her. The air went out of her with a little *whuff* sound and she blinked and frowned at the breeze-blown pile of nothingness that a second before might have been telling her something she needed to know. *"What's* going to wake up?" she demanded uselessly. Like dust particles could speak.

She stood and brushed herself off, automatically checking the shadows surrounding her. She brought the stake up defensively when one shadow amid the trees at the end of the walkway disengaged itself from the rest, then relaxed as Angel, his skin as pale as the moon, strode silently over to stand in front of her. Dark clothes, dark hair, dark eyes . . . he looked handsome enough to make her heart ache.

"Better late than never?" she said a little sourly. She hoped she didn't have vamp dust in her hair.

His calm expression didn't change. "You were holding your own."

They stared at each other for a few seconds, then Buffy forced herself to look away from him. She needed to think about something else—*anything* else—besides how badly she wanted to be in his arms, so she grabbed for the most recent thing floating inside her brain. "Did you hear what that vamp kid said?" she asked. "Right before I skewered her? Something about a boogey-monster waking up."

Angel shrugged. "She was a kid. She could've been talking about anything."

But there was a catch in his tone that made Buffy

look at him hard. "What?" she demanded. "You're not telling me something."

"Only because I don't know," he said as they began following the path that led out of the cemetery. "I've heard a few whispers, but nothing specific."

"Whispers about what?"

"That's the thing," Angel told her. "For all I know it could be a new prophecy or some weird way the planets are aligning this week. Nobody will say. But there's a kind of general . . . anxiety going around, like something big is coming."

Buffy thought about this for a few moments as she walked next to him. "Like something big is coming," she repeated softly. "Or . . ." She looked back to where the vampire child was now nothing more than a memory blown apart by the night wind.

"Or something's *waking up*. . . ."

Chapter 2

THE WINDOWS IN THE EARTH SCIENCES DEPARTMENT of the ninety-year-old building were tall and stately, multi-paned and topped with wide, fan-shaped decorations. Dark, heavily varnished wood surrounded the glass, and the window sills were wide enough to display everything from plaster casts of bone to the real deal: segments of prehistoric dinosaur spines to a sampling of Jurassic teeth blackened by millions of years of aging. Sunlight spilled through the glass panes, warming the high-ceilinged room on what otherwise would have been a Monday morning too chilly for the old heating system, set to late spring temps, to combat. Dust motes spun lazily in the sunbeams, striping the desks and the long row of display cases along the back wall. The case to the far left, the one containing the meticulous paleontology display he'd set up, was his favorite. In it, he'd—

"Mr. Sanderson, do you think you could give us the benefit of your attention anytime soon?"

Wait . . . wrong classroom.

Kevin Sanderson swallowed and grimaced as everyone in the classroom turned to stare at him, then he nodded at his teacher, Mr. Regis. "Sorry." He looked down at the earth sciences book on his desk and tried to focus on the words, but he was bored bored bored. He was way beyond the level of what was being taught here—the curriculum, the room itself, the *school*—none of it could compare to what he'd been involved in at Lane Tech back in Chicago. Plus, this place couldn't come close to the spirit or the character of the classrooms at the University of Chicago, where he'd spent untold hours poring over paleontology texts and samples and taking pre-college courses for extra credit. The bright Spanish style of Sunnydale High School—arches, lots of palm trees, the breezy Quad—were really pretty but just didn't do it for him.

Kevin sighed, then felt someone watching him. When he looked up, he saw it was the guy at the next desk, Oz. Kevin remembered him because his nickname was so cool, plus Oz had this way about him, like he was the King of Understatement. As if confirming this, the other teenager regarded him with calm green eyes from beneath a thick cut of spiked-out reddish hair, nodded, then looked away.

Kevin slouched over his textbook, wishing he could think of something to say that would get a conversation going. He could use a friend here, but Oz probably wasn't interested. He'd seen the guy in the hallway with his friends, had even picked up on the group's names—after all, paleontology was a lot like detective work and he trained himself to catch the details. Oz's girlfriend was Willow, the redhead sitting on Oz's other side and who had a sweet smile and simple beauty that

Kevin really appreciated. The rest of Oz's circle, at least what Kevin knew of it, included a fellow named Xander who had dark hair and whose humor had a sharp edge of desperation that made Kevin uncomfortable—too much like the way he himself had felt on a daily basis since arriving in Sunnydale. Now and then Cordelia Chase drifted in and out of the group, and everyone seemed to know her: high-class, high-money, and the elevated attitude to go with it. The last person in the main quartet was Buffy Summers, who looked to Kevin to be the embodiment of the California high school girl—blond, pretty, and totally fashionable. Oddly enough, everyone around here, including the jockjerks, seemed to have an unspoken respect for her, and there were rumors that she had an older boyfriend no one wanted to mess with. Maybe there was more to Buffy than just appearances.

Mr. Regis was droning on about something—marsupials and placental mammals—and Kevin glanced at the clock for the hundredth time since this torturous period had started. Only fifteen minutes to the bell and freedom, but it felt like a lifetime. He couldn't believe this was what his existence had turned into: grinding through the days, waiting for period one to be over, then period two, and three, ad infinitum. Had his parents even considered his future when they'd decided to move here from Chicago? Sure, he was as concerned about his father's health as anyone, but couldn't his dad have just retired from his position at the University of Chicago and then stayed put? Or, if he really couldn't deal with Chicago's harsh climate, made the move with Kevin's mother but let Kevin stay behind in the care of his uncle? *Only one more school year until I grad—*

"Mr. Sanderson."

Kevin blinked as Mr. Regis's voice broke into his reverie, then realized that once more everyone in the class was staring at him. Drat—caught again. "I'm . . . sorry," he had to admit. "I didn't hear the question."

"I said, perhaps you'd like to stand up and tell us about the evolution of mammals."

Great.

He dragged himself to his feet, feeling the gazes of a couple dozen kids on him, their expressions ranging from interest to boredom to utter spaciness. Did anyone here really care, or was Regis just aggravated because he could see that Kevin thought the teacher's middle name was Dull?

He cleared his throat. "Mammals came from early reptiles," he said. "About two hundred million years ago during the Triassic."

Mr. Regis looked at him expectantly. "And?"

Kevin pressed his lips together. Just how deep did the teacher want him to go? "Well . . . now Artiodactyla—animals like cattle and sheep—are considered to be the peak of evolution for herbivores because of their digestive system. Carnivora, such as lions and bears, are the epitome of carnivorous mammals."

"Yeah," someone hooted from the back of the room. "That's like us humans. We rock."

Kevin turned and automatically responded before Regis could get the words out. "Actually, humans are primates, not carnivores."

He wasn't sure who'd made the comment until a prim-looking girl at a desk in the next to the last row turned to the sloppily-dressed boy beside her and lifted her chin. "I always *knew* you were a monkey." Howls of laughter resulted and Kevin faced the front of the room again, a corner of his mouth lifting despite the fact that he so desperately wanted to be somewhere, *any*where, else.

Regis shook his head ruefully. "Thank you, Mr. Sanderson." He clapped his hands to regain the students' attention. "Okay, put a lid on it so we can wrap this up."

Kevin sat down, then felt a tap on his shoulder as Oz leaned over. "Nice save. Sanderson, one; Regis, zero."

"I'm not trying to win anything," Kevin said.

"Some of us maintain differently," Oz said and sat back, clearly through with the conversation.

Kevin frowned. *Maintain what?* Status, perhaps. Oz might have a point—maybe Kevin had yapped more knowledgeably than he should have just to get Regis to leave him alone. But that was a potshot; some teachers might call on you less if they thought you knew your stuff, others would single you out and expect you to perform. He wanted to be singled out, but not because he knew a bunch of tedious science facts. The problem was that what was most important to him, paleontology, got precious little recognition in the halls of Sunnydale High. Heck, he didn't even *look* different here. Back in Chicago, his blond ponytail and earring, skin that was consistently tanned from going on digs with the teams at the University of Chicago, and the tattoo of two battling Velociraptors that wrapped around his upper right arm made him special. He was cool with the guys, and the girls thought he was tall, blond, and hot; here in California everyone seemed to have a tan, long hair, and earrings, and tattoos were practically second nature.

In Chicago, he'd had stuff to do, even during the school year. Why, last October he'd run in the same marathon as his idol, Professor Paul Sereno. It had been a fund-raiser to help reconstruct the bones of a 130-million year old sauropod that Sereno had brought back from the Sahara Desert. There was nothing, absolutely *nothing,* in Sunnydale that could compete on the awesome scale of something like that.

"Listen up, people," Mr. Regis was saying. "Tomorrow we're going to have a guest speaker from the Museum of Natural History." The bell rang and the class exploded with activity as students snatched up their books and backpacks and hightailed it. Kevin stood very still, listening intently. Regis raised his voice, trying to get the rest of the info into their brains before they escaped. "His name is Daniel Addison, and he's from the museum's Department of Paleontology, so come armed with questions about dinosaurs."

Kevin grinned as he made his way out of the classroom, feeling something that might have been happiness for the first time in his so-far miserable term at Sunnydale High, a "short" week that seemed to have begun at the start of the Cretaceous about 144 million years ago.

Finally, something to look forward to besides the breezy palm trees and sunshine his mother constantly crowed about.

Chapter 3

W*HERE WILL WE ALL BE TEN YEARS FROM NOW?*

Buffy sat up a little straighter and clutched her history book, wondering where that thought had come from—heavy stuff to just pop into your brain while sitting at a table on the Quad on a sun-filled afternoon. She'd have much preferred keeping her mental load on the light side; as the Slayer in Sunnydale—the Chosen One whose responsibility it was to fight the vampires and stop the spread of evil—she felt she had enough to deal with. More, in fact, than any self-respecting teenager deserved; when one added geometry, English lit, and the politics behind the Battle of Hastings, she was headed toward overload.

The question zinged through her thoughts again and she scowled. Why couldn't she be thinking about makeup, shoes or clothes—like buying new ones—or which movie was coming out next week? She could definitely do a romance flick, or a good comedy. She certainly didn't want to think about school, and the future—that wasn't a happy thing to contemplate since Sunnydale was on the Hellmouth, a portal to the underworld that was apt to yark up all kinds of demonic nasties with zero notice. While Buffy knew that oh-so-annoying doorway had probably existed for hundreds, even thousands of years, sometimes she thought that the universe had created it just to make her miserable. It was hard not to take stuff like that personally when, through no fault of your own—no *desire* of your own—you were appointed Slayer status with all the accompanying benefits, minor perks like staking vampires, killing demons, and having the guy you love turn out to be almost two hundred and fifty years old. The Slayer's litany—*"As long as there have been vampires, there has been the Slayer. One girl in all the world . . ."*—was something that had a tendency to run through her mind with bummer-level regularity.

But she was what she was. As much as she struggled against it on the outside, sometimes to the point of unabashed rebellion, somewhere deep inside herself, where no one else could touch, Buffy *knew* that fact, knew about *all* of it. Her life, her future, what tomorrow and next week and next year would bring, and the ones after that—she was the Slayer and slay she would, for all those years to come.

Well . . . provided she lived to see them, of course.

Buffy didn't know that much about previous Slayers, except that they were all dead, including Kendra, who'd been "called" only because of Buffy's—temporary—death. Perhaps Buffy would be luckier than the others; after all, she had friends who had pitched in with the battle from practically the first day she'd walked into the halls of Sunnydale High School. It was kind of a give and take; they'd saved her a dozen times, she'd done the same for them times ten. Willow was her best friend and total confidant, a soul sister in whom she entrusted nearly everything she had to hide from everyone else. True, there'd been an exception or two along the way—Angel returning from Hell came immediately to mind—but Willow had done a secret dance or two of her own, and occasionally Buffy would have a feeling that there were things the redhead still wasn't telling her. But that was all right; if the world was meant to know what Willow was all about, it would eventually come out. In the meantime, Willow had a perfectly matched boyfriend in Oz, a laid-back guitarist with a local band called Dingoes Ate My Baby and an interesting secret of his own.

Then there was Xander, who like Willow had grown up in Sunnydale. Despite his wackiness, Buffy had no doubt that she'd have been vamp meat if not for Willow and Xander, and she'd never forget that it was Xander who'd given her CPR and another chance at life after she'd drowned fighting an ancient vampire, The Master—which in turn had brought about the later appearance of Kendra. There was more to Xander than his obnoxious surface—free-spirited, sarcastic, always looking for the easy way out—and as much as Buffy felt like a traitor for thinking it, Xander really needed a little sit-up-and-take-notice from his parents.

The future. For some reason, the concept nagged at Buffy today, and she wished she could swat it away like the annoying little mind-gnat it was. Should she apply the question to her friends and family, the forecast wasn't so hard to figure out. Willow and Oz were both almost frighteningly high on the smart-charts. Willow was sure to end up being something like a nuclear physicist or the female equivalent of Bill Gates, only nicer. Oz . . . well, he was more enigmatic. Smart and a musician, he might go either way; he and Willow had been the only two students during Career Week to be approached about high-tech computer jobs, yet the laid-back Oz seemed to prefer the occasional gigs that he pulled with his band to anything with more white-collar, high pressure possibilities.

Xander . . . well, he was just Xander, and hopefully he'd work stuff out. And as for Cordelia—who knew where she was headed? Beauty and no brains had pushed a lot of people up the road to stardom; Cordelia had both, with a load of self-confidence to boot.

But for the details of her own future, Buffy could use a little assistance from someone's crystal ball. Because no matter where the others went, she was the only one who could fight the vampires.

Sure, her friends helped. But there were . . . *fundamental* differences between her and them, the most obvious of which was strength. Add to that agility, speed, the fact that she needed only a fraction of the sleep a normal teenager required, way too much courage, and a much keener sense of when danger was lurking around the corner, and it was obvious she was who she was— The Slayer—and her friends were . . .

Well, they were just her friends.

Buffy sighed and smoothed the fabric of her skirt, momentarily marveling that outwardly some things about herself seemed just as normal as anyone else. For instance, pretty soon it would be time to go in for her history period, and if the teacher threw a pop quiz at them about that whole Hastings thing, she was doomed. She could remember the year—1066—but she had to reluctantly admit that was probably because it sort of sounded like an IRS tax form. Her own career profile had come up "law enforcement," and if that's where she was headed, why did she need to know about the Duke of Normandy anyway?

"Hey."

She looked up and smiled at Oz as he dropped onto the bench across the table from her. "Hi," she said brightly, grateful for anything that would turn her mind away from the various forms of bleakdom spinning around in her head today. Well . . . okay, it might have been a stretch had it been Cordelia waltzing up to the table, but fate was smiling on her and Queen Cordy was nowhere to be seen. For now. "What's shaking?"

"The earth, actually." When she looked at him blankly, a corner of Oz's mouth lifted. "Give or take, there are about twenty thousand earthquakes a year around the globe."

"Ah." Buffy looked down at her history book again. The Battle of Hastings, earthquakes around the world, Queen Cordelia. Not really high on her interest scale. "I was thinking more about local vibrations."

Oz shrugged. "Not much. Devon and I have a meeting set up with someone about managing the band."

Buffy's eyes widened. "Not *much?* Oz, that's great—have you told Willow?"

"There's nothing to tell yet," he said calmly.

She leaned forward, shoving her books out of the way. "Well, sure there is. Like who does he manage now? Will you get gigs in Los Angeles? And has he ever signed anyone to a major label?"

"It's a 'she' and I don't know," Oz answered. "To the third power."

Buffy sat back, disappointed. "Oh. So, when's the big pow-wow?"

"Sometime Friday evening. We're scheduled to play at the Bronze that night and she's going to come by and talk to us during one of the breaks." Oz's gaze lifted to somewhere over Buffy's shoulder and while his expression didn't change, something in his eyes brightened, so Buffy wasn't surprised to hear Willow's voice.

"Hi, guys," Willow said. Oz slid over so she could sit next to him. "Who's coming by the Bronze?"

"A woman who might manage the band," Oz explained.

Willow's smile was dazzling, and Buffy had to grin. Her friend was wearing a scooped-neck jumper with horizontal red and purple stripes that should have totally clashed with Oz's green bowling shirt. Despite the color extravaganza, the two somehow managed to complement each other perfectly. "Well, that's excellent!" Willow exclaimed. "A breakthrough for Dingoes, a step toward fame and fortune—" She broke off and looked at Oz, suddenly uncertain. "It is, right? Good, I mean?"

He nodded sagely. "It could happen."

Willow's smile returned. "Great," she said again. "And we'll all be there." She glanced at Buffy, who nodded. "To give you support. For morale and friendship. And . . . stuff."

"Definitely," Buffy added and picked up her books expectantly.

Before Oz could say anything else, the bell rang. It was as though someone had flipped a cosmic switch; students sprang to their feet and zipped in all directions. Oz and Willow were a little slower—maybe their smarts gave them more confidence—while the realization that her afternoon date with the Battle of Hastings was about to become a reality made Buffy want to seriously drag her feet.

"Come on, come on, come on!" Xander called from a few feet away. "We wouldn't want to miss our afternoon classes!"

"And what makes you so eager to return to Learning Central?" Buffy asked as the three of them caught up.

"Brain fever," said Oz.

"Au contraire," Xander said with a lopsided grin. "A hunger for knowledge, the unquenchable desire for—"

He jumped as Cordelia passed him on the sidewalk, then reached over and snatched his notebook out of his hands. With a withering look at him, she read from the semi-mangled class schedule crammed into the front inside pocket. "'Health and Human Services 1.02,'" she said, and rolled her eyes. "'An in-depth examination of the female reproductive system.'"

Oz's expression didn't change. "Like I said."

Buffy chuckled. "Why am I not surprised?"

Xander managed to look offended. "Hey, I'm just trying to learn here. About important things that have an impact on my future happiness."

"You are an absolute fool," Cordelia said distastefully. "I can't believe I ever let myself be seen with you in public."

"I am the shadow that makes you shine brighter," Xander said glibly.

"You'd make a mud puddle look good," Cordy shot back.

"Doesn't say much for you," Willow observed.

Buffy elbowed Willow as Cordelia paused, scowling, and Xander looked surprised as well as perversely pleased. Oz, however, must have decided it was best to guide Willow to safety before Cordy could fully process the jab. "Later," he said and smoothly turned Willow in another direction. "The exciting world of algorithms awaits."

"Hey, wait a minute," Cordelia said. "She——"

"Gotta run," Xander said happily. "Wouldn't want to miss it when Ms. Tischler has to say those V-B-P words. It's really funny when her face gets that particular shade of scarlet."

He hightailed it, leaving Buffy to be the recipient of Cordelia's reflections. Luckily, Cordy had already lost the thought that connected her to Willow's insult. "V-B-P? What's that?"

Buffy sighed and picked up her books. Even the Duke of Normandy was preferable to this; Cordelia was in the same class, but at least then she'd have to be quiet. "Think female–male anatomy. As in the basic parts."

The dark-haired girl followed her, but only for the few steps it took to catch up and move slightly ahead of Buffy, who didn't bother to protest. "Oh," Cordelia said suddenly. "I get it. Men and women . . . *body* parts." She shook her head then. "Xander can be such an idiot sometimes."

Buffy just looked at Cordy and followed her to class. It was going to be a *long* afternoon.

Chapter 4

"I'm OUT OF HERE, MOM!" KEVIN YELLED. HE SHOULDERED his backpack and headed for the door.

He didn't make it.

"Wait, please," his mother said evenly from the dining room doorway. She regarded him with quiet brown eyes nearly identical to his own. "Your father and I would occasionally like to *see* our son before he leaves for school."

Rats. Why couldn't they have done this yesterday? Today was the day that guy, Daniel Addison, was scheduled to come in from the Department of Paleontology at the Natural History Museum, and his talk had been all Kevin was able to think about ever since Mr. Regis had told the class about it. He wanted to get to the school early, see if he could get into the classroom and talk with Addison. If he could show this man that he knew the difference between a Dilophosaurus and a Deinonychus, maybe there would be a place for him at the museum, a step in so that he could start building something here. It would never come close to what he'd known in Chicago, of course, but—

"Earth to Kevin, come in please." His father's rasping voice made him realize that both of his parental units were now standing in front of him, regarding him patiently. Looking at them made him wince inside. His dad's hair was thin and his skin seemed to just hang on a suddenly fragile frame; he looked old and tired, the emphysema really taking its toll. Standing next to him, Kevin's mother, with her carefully coifed white hair and pleasantly plump physique, appeared almost obscenely healthy.

"What—oh, sorry." Kevin glanced longingly at the door. "I just . . . really have to go. There's a lot going on today."

"At school?" Rebecca Sanderson looked first at her husband Bert, then at her son. "Things there are starting to pick up, right? You're making friends?"

Kevin started to retort, then swallowed the harsh words before they could take form. What was the use? He could complain all he wanted, but it wouldn't change anything—the move was done, the school transfer was effective, and this was where they lived now, period. Laying a guilt trip on his mom and dad would accomplish nothing but make them miserable, and then Kevin would feel guilty for doing that. His mom . . . well, she just wanted everyone in her life to be happy and, as she had always done, she tried to prioritize, deal with the most urgent situation first. And there was no denying that his dad's lungs, ravaged by too many years of smoking cigarettes, just couldn't take the summer humidity and the frigid winters of Chicago's climate anymore.

"Yeah" was what came out of Kevin's mouth. "I'm, uh, getting to know a few people." His dad's perpetually haggard expression seemed to lighten, and as furious as he still was over the cross-country relocation, the sight made Kevin feel a little better. He added, "In fact, I'm going to talk with someone from the Paleontology Department at the Museum of Natural History today." He shuffled a step or two closer to the door. "That's why I'm kind of in a hurry. To get to school."

"That good," Bert said. His blue eyes closed briefly, then he gave a short cough—the kind he used to stave off an upcoming longer fit for a few moments—behind one fist. When the older man drew a breath, Kevin could hear it wheezing into his lungs. Ouch. "Once those folks at the museum find out what a treasure you are, they'll be falling all over everything to get a slice of your time. You'll see." Another cough, this one a little stronger, and above the plain button-down shirt and tweed jacket that the former mathematics professor still wore every weekday, his face began to redden.

"I really have to go," Kevin said hastily. He loved his dad but he hated to see him cough like that, couldn't stand the helpless feeling he got as the old man's body spasmed and seemed determined to spit out pieces of his lungs.

His mom stepped forward and straightened Kevin's collar where the backpack had smashed it, then gave him a quick kiss on the cheek. "You go on then," she said. "Have a good time, and good luck with the museum people."

"Sure," Kevin said. "Thanks." He turned and pushed open the door, then hesitated and looked back into the kitchen. His mom was patting his dad gently on the back, trying, in her own way, to somehow soothe him. "Dad, don't forget your medicine."

His dad looked up and it pained Kevin to see the

gratefulness on his face. Was he really so bad that his own parents had to be thankful he cared about them? Scowling, he hurried outside and strode down the walkway, hearing the slam of the door behind him and remembering too late that he shouldn't have let it go like that. But his mom would forgive him; she'd always said that was the curse of an intelligent mind—the absorption of so much heavy-duty stuff left no room for the trivial details of everyday life.

Trivial details—those were the things that were getting to him the most these days. For instance, look at the weather here. Lots of people would think it was nice—warm and sunny most of the year, and the air had a dryness to it that had really helped his dad's breathing. In the winter, you barely needed a coat, especially if you were from somewhere frigid like Chicago. And snow? Be serious. The sky wouldn't dare do something so outrageous.

But where were the winter sports, the ice-skating or even the everyday, no-equipment kind, like pelting your friends with snowballs and building a blocky, ridiculously proportioned T. Rex out of the snow in your front yard? And there was nothing like a season of good old-fashioned blizzards to harden up those back, shoulder and arm muscles à la that most versatile of tools, Ye Shovel. If you wanted to ice-skate in Sunnydale you had to go to an inside rink—was it even open any season other than winter? Kevin was used to neighborhood parks where the Chicago Park District would come around and flood the playgrounds with water, letting each layer freeze until thick, city-sized ponds were formed, the kind that never cracked and drowned some poor shmuck because of an unexpected thaw. Back home a kid's biggest fear was doing the high-dive on a curve and smacking the edge of one of the benches along the side, not something that was really up there on the odds scale.

Everything here in Sunnydale was . . . well, it was *perfect*. Manicured lawns, well-kept sidewalks, Spanish-style buildings all stuccoed and bright, like a department store catalog. And while it was true that he hadn't seen the "bad" part of town, c'mon—in a place this small, just how bad could that be? The entire town of Sunnydale would fit *inside* a few parts of Chicago into which no one who wanted to see the next day would venture—even in broad daylight. Sunnydale just didn't seem very *deep* to him, like the whole thing was a box covered in glitzy wrapping that held nothing at all interesting below that bright, ribbon-encircled surface. Surely there had to be more to this place than palm trees, desert-toned paint, and sunshine.

At school, it was the same thing: fresh-faced students with tanned and healthy-looking bodies streamed endlessly through the halls of Sunnydale High. Hardly anyone was even interestingly Goth. This was California, for crying out loud—wasn't it *supposed* to be the land of individuality? As far as Kevin could tell, there were only a couple of jocks who occasionally tried to act like bullies. To his experienced eye they were just no contest to the real thing. There was no *excitement* in this relatively small town. It was total American suburbia, *Leave It to Beaver* in the nineties. If they had problems, the kids here kept them well-hidden, and what could be troubling anyone here in the land of milk and honey anyway?

He knew that a big part of his difficulty was that he had come out here predisposed to dislike everything—the school, the climate, the people—and that was exactly what had happened. A negative attitude generally brought negative results, and Kevin was smart enough to know that. His resentment and feelings of being different, of just not wanting to *be* here, were hard to disguise, and so far most of the other students had made it a point to avoid him.

Kevin hurried to Mr. Regis's classroom, vaguely wishing he could dump all the anger he'd built up into one of the trash cans along the way. He'd had a couple of pre-college psych classes at Lane Tech, and he'd learned that people did stupid things when they got bent out of shape about situations. Yeah, there was the obvious stuff, like the sickos who went to work armed and then blew away a half-dozen co-workers, or the mental cases who relieved their rage by beating on hapless spouses or elderly family members. But there was the not-so-obvious, too, the insidious kind of poor decision-making that could ruin a career or a relationship, or even a life, in the blink of an eye. Kevin didn't think he was that bad yet, and he sure didn't want to get there.

He swung around the corner into the room and saw that Mr. Regis, a short stocky man with a gray-flecked buzz cut, was already there and talking to someone he didn't know. Was this Daniel Addison? A younger guy, maybe only three or four years older than Kevin himself, with curly dark hair and striking light blue eyes—the girls in class would probably sit here and drool over him the entire time. Disappointed, Kevin glanced at the clock. He'd thought getting here twenty minutes early might give him the edge he needed, but he should have expected the teacher to be setting up for the day already, especially since he'd lined up a guest speaker. Kevin knew he really should've zipped in an hour or more ago, but he hadn't been sure if the doors to the school would be open; back home everything was locked up tight during off-hours.

Instead of going back out in the hall to wait with the rest of the cattle, Kevin grabbed a seat a couple of rows from the front, then pulled out a fresh notebook. If he couldn't talk to Addison before class, he'd take all the notes he could and find out later, if possible, when was a good time for him to get over to the museum and—

"Kevin," Mr. Regis said, startling him. "I'm glad you came in a bit early. Would you step up here, please?"

Kevin nodded, trying to appear nonchalant, and walked up to Regis's desk. When he got there, Regis inclined his head toward the other young man, who was studying Kevin with interest. "I'd like you to meet Daniel Addison, the guest speaker from the Museum of Natural History I told the class about yesterday afternoon." As Kevin and Daniel shook hands, Regis continued, surprising Kevin with his words. "Kevin comes from Lane Technical High School in Chicago, and he was also very involved with the paleontology studies at the University of Chicago. He's just transferred here and I suspect he's got a genuine desire to be involved with the museum."

"Really," Daniel said. "What did you do at the University?"

"Well, my father was a mathematics professor there for most of his life, so when I was interested in dinosaurs as a kid, he started introducing me around," Kevin eagerly told him. "I knew all the members in the Paleontology Department and was pretty deep into studying the field. The last couple of years, they took me on a few of the summer digs." He paused, not wanting to sound like he was bragging. "I learned a lot," he added. "They're really great people, unbelievably smart."

Daniel nodded, then all three of them glanced at the door as several students barreled into the room and found seats, chattering and laughing. It would only get noisier from here on out. "I'd definitely like to talk about this some more with you," he said to Kevin. "Do you have a free period next?"

The temptation to lie was immense, but Kevin didn't dare. One small thing—a skipped class, for instance—could screw everything up. Sometimes the agenda was hidden, like finding out how responsible a student was by dangling a trap in front of him. He wasn't so green he'd fall for that. "Not until one o'clock," he admitted.

"Okay." Daniel pulled out his wallet and took a card from it, then handed it to Kevin. "The rest of today is shot for me, but I'll be at the museum until probably six or seven tomorrow night. Why don't you come by after school and we'll see what we can do to get you involved in the paleontology arena here in the exciting town of Sunnydale." He smiled. "The scale is a little smaller, I'm afraid. But we still have our moments."

Kevin took the card and grinned at both men. "Thanks. I'll be there." He went back to his seat as more kids filed into the classroom, but he barely heard the racket they made. He couldn't believe it; he'd heard that the faculty in smaller towns could be close-knit and difficult for newcomers to break into, and he'd thought it would take more time, maybe a few donations to the museum accompanied by carefully worded cover letters from his parents. Kevin knew his parents were prepared to go that route because he'd heard them talking about it one night when they hadn't realized he'd gotten up to scrounge around the kitchen for a late-hours snack. Still, he knew it would be better if he could pull it off himself, and it seemed that because

Regis really had looked over Kevin's student file, that he *cared*, Kevin might finally be on his way.

Awesome.

Willow could hardly keep her mind on what the guy from the Museum of Natural History was saying. Yadda yadda yadda—frankly, dinosaurs were more Oz's field of interest than hers. And speaking of Oz . . . criminy! A *manager* for the band? Jeez, and he didn't even seem excited while here she was, practically bouncing around on her seat like a Slinky at the top of a flight of stairs. How could he sit there so calmly and mull over dead dinosaurs at a time like this?

As if he could sense her thinking about him, Oz suddenly glanced at her and smiled slightly before refocusing on what their guest speaker was saying. Willow smiled back, then mentally smacked herself for not paying attention in class. If he could do it, so could she . . . but then, he was a guy and guys were like that about the strangest things. Unbelievable how they could simply tune out the rest of the world when the subject turned to dinosaurs or cars or guitars. On the other hand, there were a few who tuned out everything but girls, too, so maybe it all equaled out.

"Most people are familiar with dinosaurs such as Tyrannosaurus Rex, Stegosaurus, and Triceratops," Daniel Addison was saying as he stood in front of the pull-down slide screen. The guy was definitely in the eye-candy category and Willow mentally shook her head at the way some of the other girls were focusing on him with exaggerated attentiveness. "Those are good examples of the ones that get mentioned a lot on television and incorrectly used in fiction, where the time periods in which they lived get swapped around for convenience. If we can get someone to lower the lights, I'd like to show you a few illustrations and give you an idea of what they were *really* like, outside of the make-believe realms of *Jurassic Park* and *Dinotopia*."

Someone off to the side did as Addison asked while another student stood and lowered the shades on the windows, sending the classroom into a semi-darkness that Willow found reminiscent of places she'd have preferred not to associate with school. Up at the front Addison hit the button on the hand controller and the too-bright white of the screen was bathed in color as something huge and yellowish stretched across it from end to end. The thing Willow found herself staring at had a long neck and snout with a curved form to its mouth that made her think of crocodiles. Dinosaurs weren't her thing—computers, thank you very much— but Addison's next words made her realize that her initial impression hadn't been far off the mark.

"This is a reconstruction of what Baryonyx, a kind of meat-eating dinosaur first discovered in an English clay pit in 1983, might have looked like immediately after it died. Note that in the structure of the jaw there's a strong resemblance to modern-day crocodiles, not only in the length but in the number of teeth—sixtyfour, which is twice as many as in other meat-eating dinosaurs. While the paleontologists weren't able to recover the entire skeleton, they did find about sixty percent of it, which enabled them to come up with this reconstruction. They also found the fossilized remains of a prehistoric fish in the area where the Baryonyx's stomach would have been, confirming their theory that it was probably a fish-eater."

Someone's hand shot up and Addison paused before

hitting the button to change the slide. "You have a question?"

"It doesn't look so big and tough," said one of the guys down front, a jock named Peter. "Like a good kick could take it down." Various friends around the room hooted in support.

Addison smiled, and his good-looking face seemed to go slightly sinister in the shadowy space between the slide projector and screen. "I guess you could say the slide makes it look a little out of proportion. Baryonyx weighed two tons and stood somewhere between nine to thirteen feet tall." His gaze went up to the ceiling. "That would make a big one taller than the ceiling in this room."

Willow's jaw dropped open in surprise as the rest of the class murmured and considered this, looking from the screen to the ceiling. She was *so* not into the entire dinosaur thing; anything that looked like a snake or a reptile was bad because, frankly, they generally ate small fuzzy animals and she just couldn't find anything right about that. But thirteen feet tall? Sure, she'd read plenty of facts and figures: T. Rex, up to fifty feet long; brontosaurs, basically as big as a building; et cetera, et cetera. Despite all the artwork and movie special effects, and even the skeletons she'd seen in museums, nothing had ever brought it home to her as much as the color slide now visible at the front of the room. She didn't know why—maybe it was the way it looked so lifelike, or rather, "deathlike," the skin wrinkled and pulled along what could have truly been the muscle structure of a once living animal. The long, tooth-filled mouth was slightly open, showing short, sharp teeth and a moist-looking pink tongue. Even the glazed-over eyes, half-closed and sort of . . . squinty, looked way too real. Here in Sunny-dale, almost anything could come to life—statues, mummies, dead bodies, you name it. Say, they didn't have anything floating around in town that looked like that thing, did they?

"It'd make a cool model," Oz said into her right ear. "A really *big* one. Of course, since we're talking Creta-ceous, it'd also be about a hundred and twenty million years old."

Willow felt herself smile a bit as he leaned back again, and she forced herself to chill out. See, now could Oz have been any more perfect a boyfriend? Lean in, lend a little reassurance, lean out. Sometimes it was like they were psychic.

The slide machine clicked and a different image filled the hanging screen, but Willow was dealing now. She was All Right. "Now this one," Addison continued, "is called Allosaurus. Not to be confused with Tyran-nosaurus Rex, Allosaurus was smaller and no doubt faster, with teeth that have been found to be six inches in length." Addison paused, then regarded the class. "If that doesn't quite sink in, pull out a ruler and take a look at it." He pointed back to the screen. "Note the fully functional front limbs where the infamous T. Rex of *Jurassic Park* had forelegs that were so small and slender that they were rendered nearly useless. As a side note about the Tyrannosaurus Rex, also contrary to what most people think, they were probably more prone to be carrion eaters than true hunters, which is not to say that a T. Rex wouldn't have grabbed the op-portunity to take down prey. When you're talking about animals in this size range, however, moving around means burning massive amounts of energy. Not only did they likely have to consume huge quantities of flesh from already dead dinosaurs, it's also probable that they spent a lot of time lying around as opposed to rampaging through primeval forests."

Oz sat back and contemplated this theory. He'd always assumed Tyrannosaurs had actively hunted, using their massive leg muscles to chase down prey on a regular basis. What Addison was saying made a lot more sense though; even lions, as small as they were compared to dinosaurs, spent a lot of time just lying around. Interesting life.

The new guy, Kevin Sanderson, was sitting one row up and a couple of seats to Oz's right, and he seemed a little weirded out, overexcited for a class in the earth sciences. Right now, Kevin was nodding his agreement with Addison and scribbling hastily in a notebook that Oz could see was already crammed with writing. Still, if Kevin's interest level in this was pretty high, then this Addison dude showing up here was probably the event of the week for him. Although he didn't know any more about Sanderson than he knew about Addison, it was hard for Oz not to view this as a good thing; being the new face in a school where almost everyone had been around for a while could make it a real pain in the neck to make new friends. He thought he'd heard somewhere that Kevin had transferred in from Chicago, and Windy City to Sunnydale equaled major adjustment. If Kevin had an interest in dinosaurs and could hook up with dino-guy from the museum, that would be most excellent. Addison would be like a made-to-order mentor.

Oz glanced over at Willow again. Speaking of hooking up, he had to admit he was a little more jazzed about this band manager thing than he was letting on to her or the rest of their friends. He had more info than he'd shared, too, but what was the sense in getting everyone all high on the concept when he and Devon didn't know if anything was going to happen?

They did, however, know a few things about the woman. Her name was Alysa Bardrick, and while they'd never seen her, the guy who did the band scheduling for the Bronze said she did the calendar-dance for three or four of the bands he regularly booked. They were lesser known ones, but still; the number of bands on the music scene that had started out playing local gigs was astronomical. In this biz, everyone had to start on the bottom rung and claw his way up, and the members of Dingoes weren't stupid enough to think they'd be any exception. There wasn't anything easy about it.

So if this Bardrick woman could help pave the way, why not? She might be just the person they needed, with contacts in the industry and in L.A. Oz still wasn't sure being in a band was *the* thing he wanted to do with the rest of his life, but what if as their band manager she showed up with a contract for them to sign with a major label or something? Who knew how he would feel then?

Sometimes, Oz thought as he studied the play of emotions across Kevin Sanderson's face while the guy listened to Addison turn his subject more toward the concept of paleontology as a career, all a person needed in life was the right guide.

"So, Kevin, how'd you like the talk? Was it interesting or just all info you already learned in like fourth grade?"

On his way out of the classroom with the rest of the students, Kevin stopped and turned back when he heard Daniel Addison's question. "Dinosaurs and paleontology are always interesting to me," he answered honestly. "It doesn't matter if it's about sections I've already studied. I could still listen all day."

Daniel grinned and looked pointedly at Mr. Regis, who smiled faintly as he gathered up a pile of class papers. "Spoken like a true young paleontologist." The dark-haired younger man swept his own materials into a fabric briefcase. "I know you told me you have classes, but would you mind if I walked with you for a minute?"

Kevin blinked. Would he *mind*? In what lifetime? "Not at all," he said.

Daniel nodded, then he and Regis shook hands. "Thanks for having me," he said to the teacher. "It's always fun to come back to your roots now and then."

Regis nodded solemnly. "Yes, it is. And it wasn't so long ago that I forgot when I had you in my class."

Daniel nodded back and waved good-bye, then he fell into step next to Kevin as the teenager pondered the expression he'd seen on his science teacher's face. He could have sworn it'd been disapproval, but then, what did he know? He'd only been at Sunnydale a little over a week; Regis might scream like a gorilla when he got angry and Kevin wouldn't have a clue it was coming until he saw the man actually in the act.

"So these digs you mentioned," Daniel said, cutting into Kevin's thoughts, "where were they?"

"A few in Montana," Kevin told him, smiling at the memories. "Short ones sponsored by the university. I guess you'd call them summer field trips, a couple of weeks each. The full team stayed out there all summer, and then I got to camp out with them for about a month the year before last." He hesitated, wondering again about the fine line between boasting and stating actual fact, then decided Daniel would want to know more.

"Last year I really got lucky and they let me go on the dig in Australia with them."

But Daniel's eyes were bright with interest and he sounded anything but put off. "Australia—no kidding. Did they come up with anything good? What was it like being out there?"

Kevin nodded. "Oh yeah, they found plenty. The Australia dig was a heck of an experience, a lot different from Montana or anywhere in the States."

"How so?" They maneuvered around a gaggle of cheerleaders.

"Well, they were both exciting, of course—especially when you actually find something—plus hot and pretty uncomfortable. But being on one in another country gives you this kind of . . . nervousness. It takes away the safety net of 'home' and makes it sort of dangerous, like everyone walks around fueled by adrenaline all the time. And this was in Dinosaur Cove, in Otway National Park. I can't imagine how it would be in someplace like Mongolia or Argentina, where there's a history of not being able to get equipment or supplies."

"I'll bet it was great," Daniel said, clearly impressed. "The museum's sponsoring a dig in Dinosaur Cove this summer. So what did your team come up with in the way of fossils?"

"More of what's been found previously in that area—pterosaurs, plesiosaurs, a few incomplete Allosaurus skeletons, some . . . other stuff." Was he running at the mouth too much, or—

But the older guy was still listening closely, ignoring the students streaming around them. "That's excellent." He nodded, as if to reinforce his own words. "I bet you could be a big help to me, and contribute a lot to the museum. You've got a lot of hands-on experience."

"Yeah," Kevin said, and this time he let his eagerness show. "I think I could. Plus I got . . . I mean, they let me keep a few souvenirs, from the, uh, dig." Drat. He hadn't really meant to say that, but he'd been so pleased at the good impression he was making on Daniel that he'd blurted out the recollection without thinking. He hoped the older guy hadn't noticed the way he'd fumbled over his choice of words. "Let him" keep? That was way beyond a stretch.

But Daniel was totally cool. If he'd picked up on Kevin's hesitation, he gave no sign of it; instead he ran a hand absently down the front of his tee shirt and for the first time, Kevin noticed the design, a fleshed-out pterodactyl separated from a proportionately-sized man by an italicized *VS*. Beneath the picture floated two straightforward words: *No Contest.*

"That's great," Daniel said now. "So what are they—the souvenirs?"

Kevin swallowed, then decided to go for it. "Well, from the Australia trip, I really only got one thing worth mentioning," he hedged. "An egg—small, of course. Nothing that remarkable."

"What kind?"

"Timimus," Kevin said, his heart suddenly pounding. Daniel Addison wasn't a stupid man. He had to realize that . . . well, Kevin had swiped the fossil from the dig site. It was no big deal, really; there had been a nest of the things, almost a dozen unbroken ones in the pile. No one had seen him do it so no one had cared, and now he had a memento of the trip that would last well beyond his own lifetime.

Next to him, Daniel smiled widely. "Kevin, that's excellent. Could I take a look at it? I could send someone by your house to pick it up—"

"I'd rather keep it with me," Kevin said quickly. "Just because it's so rare."

Daniel held up a hand. "Of course. What was I thinking? But when you come by the museum—you're coming by tomorrow, right?" Kevin nodded and he continued. "Good. Bring it so I can take a look, all right? I wasn't aware they'd ever found a nest for that genus."

"It's not something they ever made a big announcement about," Kevin admitted nervously. "The Australian team's discoveries kind of got eclipsed by a trip to the Sahara by the head paleontologist there. Still, we thought it was pretty good and they put up an exhibit in the department highlighting the trip. I'll bring the egg with me."

"That'd be super," Daniel told him. He seemed a little distracted for a moment, as though he were thinking about something else. Then his gaze refocused on Kevin and he smiled. "Yeah," he said, as though making sure Kevin had understood him. "Definitely bring it. And, hey, in return, I've got something I'd like to show you that I'll bet you never even thought existed."

"Really?" Kevin was fascinated. "What is it?"

Daniel shook his head, then glanced at his watch. "Nah—I don't want to spoil the surprise. And anyway, you'd better get to your next period. I wouldn't want old Regis accusing me of leading his students astray. You just come by tomorrow like you said, okay?" He clapped Kevin companionably on one shoulder, then turned and headed in the other direction.

Kevin stared after him, even more excited about tomorrow than he had been at the start of class. What could Daniel have to show him that he believed was so different? Either it was something truly spectacular, or Daniel had no idea the range of stuff that Kevin had seen in his past involvement in the realm of paleontology.

Kevin's grip tightened on his books and he double-checked his class schedule before hurrying to his locker to pick up his completed geometry homework. At first he'd felt stressed about admitting that he had the Timimus egg, but now he was okay with it, totally chilled. In fact, he actually thought he might have just made his first real *friend* here in Sunnydale. Daniel's slap on the back definitely pointed in that direction. The fact that Daniel was someone with whom Kevin had so much in common was nearly too excellent to be true, but he wasn't going to complain if for a change the universe wanted to smile down on him a little.

After all, it was about freakin' time.

Rupert Giles recognized Buffy's footsteps as she entered the library before she actually came into his view. She might be the Slayer, but as her Watcher he had a few talents of his own, all utterly unappreciated, of course. She was standing there expectantly when he glanced up, looking quite charming in a lightweight pastel sweater and skirt and probably thinking she'd sneaked up on him. Not hardly. Still, the summery outfit gave him a pang. Was it really that warm outside already? What had happened to the bulkier jackets of winter? Sometimes he felt like he stayed inside this library as much as Angel stayed inside the night.

"Good morning, Buffy," he said, and closed the *Glossarium de Vespertilionis et Daemonis* that he'd been skimming—boring stuff anyway. He already knew most of the text and frankly, he'd just been looking at the etchings. Repetition and all that. Still, he mustn't look distracted or, God forbid, sound uninterested. Buffy Summers was a teenager, and as her

Watcher, he needed to present a steady figure, a constant role model for her. Sometimes, Giles knew he fell abysmally short of recognizing the problems she had to deal with; the truth was, without children of his own, he found most of the so-called difficulties of teenaged life exceedingly trivial. Ridiculous clothes, abominable music, patently obscene dancing—really, what was the point? There was also Buffy's relationship with Angel, which existed in a realm of the complicated that even Giles found mind-boggling and, at times, had had devastating consequences to all concerned. Still, he liked to think of himself as intelligent, and therefore Giles recognized that admitting his thoughts on any of these matters probably wouldn't win him any points with his Slayer.

"Anything happen on your patrol last night?" he asked now. "Difficulties, or . . . ?"

"Two vamps," Buffy replied cheerfully. "If anyone wants them, they'll have to pick 'em up with a Dustbuster."

Giles frowned. "A what?"

"Think of it as a motorized dustpan." Buffy glanced around the library, her gaze touching on the piles of books and papers scattered here and there, the general chaos that always seemed to happen anytime the librarian was left alone with his books too long. "Maybe I'll get you one for Christmas."

"No, thank you," Giles said. "You may not realize it but I know exactly where everything is in this room."

"Really." Buffy put her hands on her hips. "*Face Odyssey.*"

"I beg your pardon?"

"*Face Odyssey,*" she repeated. "By Howard Alberts."

"I . . . well, what kind of book is it?"

"Hairstyles," Buffy said perkily. "I believe it was called a 'coiffure collection.' "

"Yes," Giles said. A book . . . a *real* one, of hairstyles? Good Lord, Americans would immortalize anything. "Hairstyles. Well, I imagine that would be in Modern Culture, or perhaps Photography—"

"Actually," Buffy interrupted, "Cordelia found it in the Careers section."

Giles grimaced. "Careers?"

"Modeling, Giles."

He must have still looked blank because she tilted her head to one side, her expression one of exaggerated patience. "You know, that thing where women paint their faces and put on pretty clothes, and then get paid massive green?"

Giles folded his arms and regarded her. "Really. I always thought that was the ritual before tribal warfare."

"Touché!" chortled Xander from across the room.

"Don't you have class?" Giles asked sternly as Xander swaggered up to them, then dropped onto one of the chairs at the nearest table. The librarian looked back at Buffy. "In fact, don't you *both* have class?"

"Of course we do," Buffy said, "but the entire class thing is way overrated."

"Class as in of the educational variety," Xander put in. "Not to be confused with the upper and lower—"

"—type of Cordelia's imagination," Buffy finished smartly.

"That'll be enough," Giles said. "I don't have Principal Snyder breathing down my neck again, claiming I'm setting a bad example. Buffy, I'm well aware of your schedule, and I believe you're late for English literature, isn't it? I don't know what your morning looks

54

like, Xander, but I'm quite convinced it doesn't include lounging about in here."

"Wow," Xander said, sounding hurt. "Check out the taskmaster."

"Off you go," Giles said briskly. "Believe it or not, there is knowledge out there meant for the spaces in your brains. In addition, I have actual library duties to which I must attend."

"Duties?" Xander asked. "Here?" He seemed completely befuddled.

"Yes," Giles said. "Sunnydale High School does actually require something of me, for which they even occasionally reward me with a paycheck." He slipped off his glasses and wiped at them with a handkerchief. "You may have even heard of it—the checking in and out of books?"

"Oh." Giles frowned when all Xander did was shoot Buffy a lopsided grin. "Does that include guessing what Sunnydale's evil-of-the-week is?"

"Xander—"

"All right, all right." The teenager held up his hands and slipped off the chair. "You're right. I just know Mr. Regis can't wait to pump *something* into my head!"

"Out!"

Xander scurried toward the door as Buffy picked up her book bag and prepared to follow. Giles saw him pause and allowed himself a mental sigh; he should've known the boy wouldn't be able to resist a parting shot. And never one to let down a potential audience, Xander fairly beamed from the doorway. "I'm his favorite student, you know."

Giles took a step toward the door, but Xander was gone before the older man could say anything more. Instead, he turned back to Buffy and raised his eyebrows. "English literature, am I correct?"

"Got it," she said, looking chastised. "Go forth I to England. Figuratively speaking, of course."

He nodded as she left, then looked up just as she started to push out of the library. "Buffy?"

The Slayer turned back. "What's up?"

Giles opened his mouth, then shook his head. "It's nothing. Go on to your class."

She studied him. "Are you sure? Because you've got this huge blinking question mark hanging over your head."

He frowned at her. "Buffy—"

Buffy grinned. "Would you look at me? I'm not even here!"

The door swung shut behind her and Giles stared at it blankly for a few moments, then turned back to the library counter and began sorting through the book returns that had piled up through the morning. He'd wanted to ask Buffy if she'd thought he was doing a good job in his guidance of her, but really, what kind of a question was that for the teacher to ask the student? The recipients of knowledge always seemed to want to gain it the easiest way possible, without realizing that easy wasn't always best.

He couldn't admit it, but sometimes he felt totally overwhelmed by this job. With him, there was no hidden agenda, nothing personal to be gained such as riches or power or, heaven help them all, immortality. He just wanted to be the best Watcher he could, for her and for . . . well, everyone, himself included. Thanks very much, but he'd like not to see the world end in a blaze of fire as much as the next bloke.

But *was* he truly a good leader for her, the best example he could be? He tried to get her to do her studies, but the slaying seemed to always interfere; the girl barely got any sleep or time to read beyond poring over demonic research. He also tried to present a model figure as far as motives and moral standards, so that even if her friends were stumbling a little, he hoped Buffy would always see the path to right, or as close to it as he could illuminate.

Feeling rather depressed about the entire thing, Giles sat on the chair Xander had vacated and looked around the library. Others might call it dim, but he liked the way the room was never truly bright. To him it always kept a kind of warm, golden glow about itself, a beauty carried through every nook and cranny by the abundance of natural wood banisters and shelves and, of course, the thousands of books. Where there were books, on *any* subject, he believed there would always be a soul; surely no vampire could ever take that away. Books gave life and instruction. There was even the *Watcher's Manual,* which told him, and others like him, how to properly perform their duties. And there were other Watchers he'd contacted on occasion.

Still, Giles wished there was a living, breathing example of a Watcher *and* surrogate parent for *him* to follow, a mentor for the Watcher, so to speak, so he could at least have a clue if he was doing this correctly.

Chapter 5

IF THE MEMORY OF THE TERRIBLE DAY THE MOVERS HAD come to their house in Chicago and loaded up his family's belongings hadn't still been fresh in his mind, Kevin would have thought that today was the longest day of his life.

It wasn't Mr. Regis's fault, of course; there were probably plenty of people who thought that the evolution of mammals was the most interesting thing next to the truth behind how they made blue M&M's. And maybe it was, but he had covered this a long time ago. It wasn't that he was any smarter than anyone here; it had to do, obviously, with dinosaurs. If you wanted to know about them on the level that Kevin did, about how they'd evolved and existed and ultimately become extinct over the course of millions of years, you had to cover the biological arena of the theory of evolution early, a long time before the rest of your friends and classmates.

Another bright and beautiful day here in California

and Kevin hardly noticed. Regis might ask him a question at any moment, but the teenager wasn't worried. Despite his excitement, he'd done his studying last night—more of a brushup really—and he felt fairly confident he could handle himself no matter what the science teacher threw at him. For most of the class he just sort of sat there, taking up space, doodling in his notebook, and thinking about the end of the day, when he could finally head over to the Museum of Natural History and spend some time with Daniel Addison. Tucked safely inside a shoe box in his locker was the Timimus egg, and if an inanimate object really could "burn a hole" in something—like money supposedly burned a hole in some people's pockets—he was surprised that the prehistoric fossil wasn't blasting through the metal door out in the hallway right now.

A quick glance at the clock—for maybe the hundredth time since class had started—and he was pleased to see there were only a few minutes left. Kevin made an effort to pay attention, following along on Regis's quick review of the class and writing down the homework assignment for the next day. When the bell rang, he rose with the rest of the students and headed for the door, then heard his name called.

"Kevin, may I speak with you for a moment, please?"

Reluctantly, he paused at the sound of Mr. Regis's voice. Much as he wanted to just keep going, he had to turn back. "Sure."

Regis kept an extra chair at the side of his desk and he pushed it toward Kevin and motioned for him to sit. When Kevin did, the older man pulled his own chair out from behind his desk and sat where he could face the teenager. Kevin waited, trying to figure out what was going on and what he'd done to merit a heart-to-heart from a teacher he barely knew.

"I'm sure you realize I went through your file from Lane Tech, which is how I discovered you have a serious interest in the paleontology field—and an excellent academic record, by the way." Kevin nodded, but didn't say anything. Regis glanced away for a moment, his expression unreadable. "Am I right in understanding that you're going to be dealing with Daniel Addison?" he finally asked.

"Yes, sir," Kevin answered. "I'm going over to the museum today after school."

"I imagine you've got a lot of hope tied up in getting involved with the Natural History Museum here," the science teacher said. "We don't have the extensive programs that the University of Chicago has, of course, but don't short-change us too soon. College brochures are starting to pile up, and you'll find that the University of Sunnydale has—" He broke off, then smiled faintly. "But of course, you'll probably end up heading back to the Midwest."

Kevin shrugged. You bet he was, but he didn't see any sense in crowing about it or putting Sunnydale down. It was . . . well, *Sunnydale,* and lots of people here probably lived happily ever after. It just seemed like that kind of place.

"Well, I guess what I wanted to get across to you," Regis continued, "just between the two of us, is that I wouldn't recommend you getting too involved with Daniel Addison." When Kevin looked at Regis in surprise, the older man leaned forward with his elbows on his knees and clasped his hands, looking for all the world as if he were Kevin's dad having a birds-and-the-bees conversation with him. "If this seems out of bounds, I'm sorry. But you're a bright kid, Kevin—a lot brighter than Addison. I had that young man in my class for four straight years. I *know* him, and I know how he works. And how he thinks." Regis hesitated, then plunged on. "When Addison looks at you, he sees a tool, Kevin. On the surface he's all smiles and friendship, but he won't ever think of you as a person. For him you'll either be a thing he can use to further his own career here, as quickly and as easily as possible, or you won't be worth his time. He's willing to work, but not as hard as he should. He'd much rather have someone else do the hard stuff for him—that's the way he's always been." Regis stared at the floor. "I think you've got an exceptional future ahead of you, and you might think the transfer to Sunnydale just stands in the way of that. The truth is it's only a temporary delay. But even for a short time, it would be a shame to see you turned into a stepping stone for someone else. Get the picture?"

Kevin nodded. He didn't know if he bought the story, but this entire conversation was sure making him uncomfortable. Daniel Addison was Kevin's only way to get involved with the museum here in Sunnydale. Was Regis actually recommending that he *not* do that? "Absolutely, Mr. Regis," he said out loud and stood. "I'll definitely keep what you just told me in mind."

The science teacher rose at the same time, pushing the chairs back into place. "You probably think I'm crazy," he said. He smiled briefly, then the expression was lost behind a frown. "I'm really just recommending that you be cautious. I know you'd never consider scrapping the idea of being friends with Daniel, so I won't even suggest that. But sometimes in a small town, in *Sunnydale,* people aren't always . . ." He hesitated. "Well, they aren't always what they seem. So all I'm saying is, watch your back. All right?"

Kevin nodded again. Man, he couldn't wait to get out of here. "Sure."

Regis's eyes searched his and Kevin felt vaguely guilty when he thought he saw defeat flash across the older man's gaze. "Well," Regis said, "good luck." The teacher turned his back, dismissing him.

More than ready to amscray, Kevin hurried to his locker to switch books. *Watch your back?* What the hell did that mean? But only a child or an idiot would completely ignore a warning like that, especially when they didn't truly know what they were getting into. For all Kevin knew, Daniel Addison could be a serial killer, some pervert who collected the bones of kids in a sub-basement vault at the museum. Of course, he didn't know much about Mr. Regis either, but as much as kids tended to rebel at advice tossed at them by adults, if you took the time to think about what was being said, it was usually because they didn't want you to screw something up. It wasn't always the greatest advice, but most of the time the intentions were honorable. At best, they knew something and they were desperate for you to know it, too; at worst, it was easier to listen and get it over with than fight.

Regis and Daniel Addison. Kevin thought about this. Could there be some connection beyond the student/teacher one that Regis had brought up? Four years was a long time to deal with someone on a nearly daily basis; you got to know a person and how they thought. But could Regis be jealous of Daniel over something about which Kevin knew nothing? There was an old saying about how the truth was somewhere in the middle of what two people would tell you, and Kevin was the new person here, the odd man out who had to learn everything from scratch and build from it. Even if he found nothing at all to fault about Daniel Addison, it wouldn't hurt him to watch his step.

"Hi," Willow said.

Her boyfriend turned at the sound of her voice and smiled at her. "Hey." Without saying anything else, he fell into step beside her as she headed toward the Quad.

"So, what's on the lunch menu for today?" She pointed at the paper bag he had crumpled between one arm and his books. "Anything yummy?"

Oz pulled it out and opened it one-handed. "Apple," he said, peering inside. "A sandwich of some indeterminate type of processed lunch meat, probably low fat. No candy bar or chips." He scrunched the bag shut again and shrugged. "Health kick."

Willow nodded in understanding and patted her backpack. "My mom's on one, too. Cucumber and sprout sandwich on wheat bread with Thousand Island dressing—there wasn't a piece of turkey to be found in the house."

"It's like a disease," Oz said ominously. "Healthitis."

She grinned and he stayed next to her as they made their way to their favorite table beneath the shade of a tree on the Quad's far side, where Xander was already slouching over a mass of rumpled plastic wrappings. On the other side, Buffy brightened considerably when she saw Willow and Oz coming. "Hi guys," she said. "Please tell me what's new and exciting. Sunnydale is having a serious lack."

"What, you haven't had your daily quota of bloodsuckers?" Oz asked dryly.

"I'm not complaining," Buffy said quickly. "Just

making an . . . observation that since Sunday night, absolutely el-zippo's been happening around here."

"Ah, another serious absence of toothy pals on your midnight stroll last night." Xander nodded and crammed a huge cakelike wad of dark chocolate into his mouth. He tried to say something else and white filling began to ooze out the corners of his lips.

Willow groaned. "Xander, that's disgusting."

"Oink," he mumbled around the food.

Buffy giggled. "Look out, it's the chocolate vampire!"

"Actually," Willow noted as she and Oz sat and began to unwrap their lunches, "it kind of looks more like foam. You know, like in a dog—" Oz glanced at her and her hand flew to her mouth. "Oh! Not a wolf-type dog or anything, or . . . one with rabies, just one that's . . ." Her words stuttered away.

"Hot," Buffy said, jumping in with a neat save. "You know, like they get in the summer."

Xander studied Oz. "He doesn't drool, doesn't he?" he asked around a mouthful of cake.

Willow looked shocked all over again, but before she could respond Xander started coughing violently—a little *too* violently. Buffy pounded him on the back until it seemed like he could breathe again. When he found some air, he gave her a grin filled with enough chocolate cake to rival the teeth inside a rotting corpse's smile. "Thanks," he wheezed.

"Chew. Swallow." Oz looked at him over his own sandwich. "Simplicity itself."

"I guess you would know," Xander shot back.

"Eating is pretty much required of all life forms," Oz said in an even voice.

"Yeah," Xander said. He started to reach for another

plastic-wrapped snack cake, then stopped. "In fact, some things consider us humans nothing but items on the Sunnydale Restaurant menu." He looked up when no one said anything. "Uh, that was a joke?"

"Ha ha," Willow muttered crankily. She took a small bite of her lunch, then decided to change the subject. "So," she said to Xander, "did you hear the latest? Dingoes might have a band manager."

Xander's eyes widened. "No kidding? Are we talking stardom here? Rock 'n' roll and babes—"

"Careful, Xander," Willow grinned. "You're starting to hyperventilate."

"They say the cure for that is to shove a paper bag over the person's mouth," Buffy said. She sounded way too gleeful, and Willow chuckled.

"You can use mine," Oz commented, and this time Willow just laughed out loud.

"Play your little word games if you must, but seriously inquiring minds need to know," Xander said with a sniff.

"There's nothing to talk about yet," Oz told him.

"But—" Xander began.

"Friday night," Oz promised. "From her mouth to ours to yours."

"Now that's sharing," Xander marveled. Then he realized what Oz had said. "'Her'?"

"The opposite of 'him,'" Oz affirmed.

For once Xander seemed out of comments. "Oh."

"We're all scooping on this," Buffy told him. "And it looks like we'll all just have to wait it out."

"Maybe she could use an assistant," Xander said suddenly. "I can type."

"In what universe?" Willow asked without thinking.

"I have fingers." Xander shoved away the mess of used wrappers. "I can use two of them. Maybe I don't have the lightning fingers of you, Little Miss Computer Brain, but I can hold my own."

Willow snorted. "Hold thi—"

"I hate to break up a good fight as much as the next Slayer," Buffy interrupted smoothly, "but we've got like two minutes before the bell to finish our food and for Xander to clean up the nuclear waste dump he's made of this portion of the school grounds."

They all groaned, remembering how Snyder had come down on them last week because he'd imagined they were the cause of a stray plastic bag he'd found jammed beneath the leg of the table they'd used during lunch. The decrepit grocery sack had obviously been stuck there for weeks, but that hadn't stopped His Rattiness from instantly envisioning the foursome as Mother Earth's new Number One Mortal Enemy. There had been a lot of words flying around that day; interestingly enough, most of them sounded a lot like "detention."

"I'm on it," Xander said. "Got it covered, it's co-pacetic, under control—" He reached for a fistful of plastic and it went flying, lifted neatly out of his reach by a breeze that was obviously put there to torment him.

Or, Willow saw with dread, to bring down doom upon all of their pathetic heads. "Here comes Principal Snyder," she announced. But bless Buffy, who with a quick lean to the left and a swoop of her hand, saved the day. Or at least the trash.

"I see you kids have taken my previous warning to heart," said the principal as he stepped up to the table and saw Buffy deftly tuck the last of Xander's lunch debris back into his bag. Willow fought a giggle as she saw her friend glance at her fingers—smeared with chocolate—and make a *eeeew* face before hiding her hand under the table.

"Right to the heart, yes, sir," Buffy said with false brightness.

Snyder, his beady-brown eyes hard, glared at each of them. "Environmental criminals spend entire lifetimes in prison," he said in a rigid voice. His gaze cut to Willow's and she felt herself wince. "Aren't you going to finish your lunch, Miss Rosenberg?"

"N–no, sir," she said, and shoved her half-eaten veggie conglomerate back into the paper sack. "I . . . guess I've lost my appetite."

Xander perked up immediately. "Can I have it?"

Before she could respond, Snyder yanked the bag from her hand and thrust it at Xander. "Wastefulness is just as bad, you know," he snapped into her face, then jerked his finger at Xander. "And you, young man. See you don't leave the remains lying around."

"We never do," Oz said, with absolutely no inflection in his voice. Snyder glowered at all of them a final time, then stalked off. For a few seconds, they all simply stood by the table, too fatigued by the encounter to comment.

"Wasn't *that* fun?" Xander said, then without warning he stuffed the entire second half of Willow's sandwich into his mouth. "Sthee? Nuyo waphsft," he said in a garbled voice as bits of greenery sprayed in all directions. He chewed a few token times, swallowed, then made a face. "Hey—where's the meat?"

"Roll call," Buffy said. Right on cue, the bell rang and the Quad broke into a frenzy of students heading in all directions. The four of them snagged the rest of their trash and after a short detour to the trash bins, made for the building.

"How do you *do* that?" Willow demanded of Buffy. "You don't even wear a watch!"

"Raw talent." Her friend slung her bag over one

shoulder, then stopped and gave her a sly grin. "Actually, it's an evolutionary thing that us non-bookheads are developing. It gives us advance warning of when we should run."

Willow laughed as Buffy gave her a high sign, then hurried off in the other direction. Xander had already zipped away and now Oz touched her arm. "Tuesday afternoon means sociology," she said, knowing what he was going to ask before he bothered.

He nodded. "Then I'll catch you later. Chemistry awaits."

"Oh!" She always seemed to forget about Oz's chemistry class. Maybe it was a form of self-denial, a safety stop. "Don't . . . you know. Blow up anything."

"How about any*one?*"

"Well," she said. The way he looked at her—like now—sometimes made her a little breathless. "I guess that depends on . . . who."

Oz gave her a little grin, then shook his head. A quick kiss—too quick—and he was strolling away. She watched him for a few seconds, then cut across the sidewalk and toward her classroom. Why couldn't she be more like that—calm and cool? Absolutely nothing—well, except for the werewolf-thing—seemed to get to him. Maybe that was *why* Oz was so calm: whatever anger he built up during the month or how deeply someone got under his skin, he kind of had this monthly built-in valve that allowed him to let it all out. Even though he had to be locked up in the library for those three nights, he just seemed so *lucky* to be able to cut loose like that.

Willow caught a glimpse of Xander at the far end of the walkway. Was she really annoyed at him? No more than usual, she supposed. It was the whole band manager suggestion making her sort of edgy or something. She ought to be as happy for Oz on the inside as she acted on the outside, but she couldn't quite pull it off. What if . . . what if this unknown woman really did have enough connections to get Dingoes signed to a label, or send them on some kind of music tour or something?

And what if they . . . well, kind of flubbed out?

Willow shook her head and wrapped her arms around her books, then realized a couple of geeky-looking kids had caught her movements. Jeez, she must look like a spaz or something. She stepped up her pace and left the gapers behind, her thoughts spinning around—again— the concept of a manager/agent for Dingoes. Someone who could line up places to play for them, who knew people in the music business and might get them noticed. This was supposed to be a good thing, right?

Then why, every time Willow thought about it, did whatever food was in her stomach want to claw its way up and out?

Sunnydale's Museum of Natural History didn't have the grandeur and imposing presence of the gigantic Field Museum of Natural History in Chicago, but it was still better than Kevin had expected. In fact, it looked pretty good. Three stories high, the roof consisted of three domes—a huge middle one flanked by two that were only a third the size of the main one. The entrance was in the center of three fifteen-foot high arches, and the whole thing was surrounded by an expanse of lawn that was lush and green, even in very early spring. A strip of scarlet petunias already blossomed down the center of the lawn, while marigolds and sculpted bushes followed the fence and trees that bordered the grounds and parking lot, flora that the Chicago area wouldn't see bloom for another three or four months. Below the brilliant blue of the California afternoon sky, it looked quite lovely.

Kevin stepped into the huge main foyer with a sort of childlike reverence. He'd been so angry at everything that had to do with the relocation and so furious over the loss of what he'd had in Chicago that he hadn't even considered visiting the museum on his own, much less exploring Sunnydale. Their house was still half boxed-up anyway, entire roomfuls screaming to be unpacked. He'd expected to hate what he'd decided was an undersize museum, to criticize every aspect of it right from the start; instead, he found himself filled with excitement and an odd sense of adventure at the thought of starting over. And really, for a dinosaur lover, how much fault could he find with a place that spotlighted the immense skulls of a Tyrannosaur and a Triceratops in the center of its main hall?

He glanced at his watch and grinned as he hurried past the skull exhibit. He wished he had more time; he'd love to spend the evening exploring the museum, all of it. How many hours had he logged in at the Museum of Natural History in Chicago? But tonight exploration would have to wait. He'd given Daniel a call just to confirm the meeting, and the other man had told him to be there no later than five-thirty. That, he'd said, would give him enough time to take Kevin on a quick, informal tour of the dinosaur exhibits and show him behind-the-scenes in the Paleontology Department. He'd made it clear that if Kevin liked what he saw, there would be more opportunities in the future.

He made his way straight back, then turned right and went down the hall. The restrooms would be on his left, the fossils exhibit straight ahead; as instructed, he took a left before he got to either and found himself facing the entry foyer to the dinosaur exhibits. The light overhead was golden and rich, the typical go-for-the-drama mood that museums favored. Kevin liked it; he'd spent so much time in the Field Museum that encountering the same ambience here made him feel comfortable and secure, the last sensation he had expected. Beneath his feet was a floor made of huge old-fashioned granite tiles that picked up the shine of the lights and diffused it, giving the whole place an aura of class and shine. Life, at least for the current slice of time, was fine.

Daniel Addison was waiting for him just inside the high, arched entrance to the dinosaur exhibit, standing beneath a tropically-designed sign that read WELCOME TO PALEO-VIEW! "Hi, Kevin, how are you?"

"Good," Kevin responded automatically, and was privately surprised when he meant it. Despite the importance of this meeting and his need to get to know this man, and even after all the time he'd spent around dinosaurs, Kevin couldn't help it when his gaze slipped past Daniel and went to the exhibits. Some were skeletal reconstructions of the expected variety: a Stegosaurus in a defensive posture against a Ceratosaurus raiding its nest; a browsing Pelorosaurus; an unexpected but extremely interesting depiction of a group of Cynognathus feeding on a downed Kannemeyeria; another Ceratosaurus that had mostly been left in skeletal form. Kevin's practiced eye recognized immediately that the rendition of an Hypacrosaurus nest contained fiberglass components, well-made but impossible for the knowledgeable eye not to detect. More striking were the full-flesh reproductions of lesser known species like Typothorax, Euparkeria, and Oviraptor.

And even though they weren't true dinosaurs, at the far end of the hallway near a less obvious exit was what he immediately considered the dinosaur exhibit's crowning achievement: a life-size simulation of Pteranodon ingens in flight. They'd chosen to portray the skin tones in varying shades of red and russet browns, and the model of the creature soared overhead like some kind of massive flying devil, its wingspan easily twenty-three feet. Backlighting shone through the fragile-looking membranes covering its skeleton, highlighting the lengthened thumb that had enabled the pterosaurs to glide through the air. The long triangular jaw was filled with sharp, tiny teeth, while the reproduction's dark eyes glinted unpleasantly. Guttural roars, screams and growls, man's best guesstimate as to how these creatures would have sounded, blared intermittently from speakers hidden among the fake foliage.

"Pretty damned realistic, wouldn't you say?" Daniel grinned next to him, and Kevin recalled the *No Contest* tee shirt Daniel had worn while giving the class presentation. "It's my favorite exhibit."

Kevin nodded. "It's excellent," he said with his own smile. "I'll bet this scares the beans out of the kids."

Daniel laughed. "Yeah, it does. When they first set up the exhibit, it was up by the front in the showcase spot, and they came up with this awesome idea for positioning the thing where you couldn't see it until you were all the way inside. Then you looked up, and *wham!* There it was, looking like it was going to swoop down and snatch you right up. The reaction was great—from the parents and the teenagers. The little ones were terrified, though. They ended up with nightmares, a few of 'em actually upchucked on the spot—not a pretty sight. The parents were calling and complaining about how freaked out their kidlets were, so we decided to move it to the far end." He shrugged. "You can see what you're getting into now, so the reaction isn't as strong. If you ask me, that takes all the fun out of it. The surprise was key."

"Definitely," Kevin agreed. "But it's still a great scene."

Daniel looked pleased. "Come on," he said. "I'll take you upstairs and show you the cubbyhole that I call an office. They hide the academic types on the third floor, as far in the back as they can."

Kevin nodded and followed him, listening as Daniel chattered on about the exhibits along the way, everything from African Mammals to California History to something called the Douglas Perren Memorial Room. Not a bad setup for a small-town museum, and again Kevin was pleasantly surprised. It looked like Sunnydale had more to show beneath its bright but rather generic-looking surface, and like Daniel had said, surprise was key. They went down a series of hallways that led them farther toward what Kevin thought was the back of the building, and it wasn't long before Kevin was disoriented. But that was okay; in time, given the opportunity, he hoped to know this little museum quite well.

Daniel's office wasn't exactly the cubbyhole he'd described, but it wasn't that much more. A large, rectangular closet with an L-shaped desk and bookshelves built into it might have been a better description, and it was packed to its maximum with books, papers, fossils, bits of petrified bone and boxes of God-only-knew what. The tiny area was cramped and crowded far beyond the level of comfort, and Kevin thought it was fantastic.

"So," Daniel said as he squeezed behind the desk

and dropped onto his chair. "It's time to take you from the world of Chicago's big-time paleontology to our version here in small-town Sunnydale." He glanced at Kevin out of the corner of his eye. "That *is* what you want, right?"

"Absolutely," Kevin said. He hesitated, but felt obliged to be honest. "I have to tell you, though—next fall, I'm out of here. I'll be heading back to the University of Chicago for college."

Daniel nodded. "I expected as much. With the kind of connections you've probably established there, you'd be a fool to go anywhere else. But," he scrounged around on his desktop, "I think we can keep you from getting bored in the meantime."

Kevin grinned. "That's great. What can I do around here?"

This time Daniel laughed outright. "Oh, take your pick of a couple thousand uncompleted tasks! Still, if you don't have any objection, I'm in the middle of one right now. I'll tell you what's going on with it and you can decide if you're interested. If not, we'll do the paperwork to get you in the computer files, and I know we can find something else."

"Sure." Choose something else over whatever Daniel was working on? Not likely. The man was his benefactor here, the major element in making sure he didn't spend the next eight months so mentally unchallenged that he came out of this small town with his brain atrophied and drool running down his chin. "What are you involved in?"

Daniel came up with a fistful of paperwork and offered it to Kevin. "There's a stool under that pile of folders," he said, pointing to one corner. "Just set them on the floor. You'll need to fill these out." When

Kevin looked at the paperwork curiously, Daniel began to tick off the items on his fingers. "An employment application—you'll actually get a few bucks an hour for your time—Social Security info, next of kin, junk like that."

"Got it," Kevin said. Tedious stuff, but necessary.

"What I'm doing," Daniel told him as he began filling out the forms, "is going through a huge stack of crates in the basement. My area's paleontology, of course, and there's all kinds of stuff down there that's never been cataloged, everything from field journals to supplies and files to fossils that were, for whatever reason, never recorded in the museum records when they were found. Most of it dates back to the pre-computer era, and of course someone's come up with the bright idea that now it needs to be entered into the system." He paused. "It's an . . . interesting experience. I thought it was going to be the pits when I first started, but the more I get into it, the better the stuff I'm finding. What do you think?"

"It sounds totally cool," Kevin lied. "I think I could get into that." Shuffling through storage boxes? Not what he'd hoped for, but at least it was something. Of course, if he preferred, he could listen to his new schoolmates talk about sports, bands he didn't listen to, and girls he didn't know.

Daniel leaned forward, watching as Kevin put *x*'s in the last of the required spaces on the forms, then signed his name. "I was hoping you'd say that," he said as he gathered up the completed papers and set them aside. "That has a lot to do with what I mentioned yesterday at the school and what I wanted to show you." He paused for a moment. "Did you . . . did you bring the Timimus egg?"

"Sure." Kevin picked up his backpack and pulled out

the box with the carefully wrapped fossil. He offered it to Daniel.

"Wow," Daniel said as he opened the box. There was a hint of reverence in his voice when he ran his fingers over the rough surface of the petrified shell. "Imagine, a hundred and twenty million years ago, given the right conditions, this would have been a living creature the likes of which we can only try to visualize now." He studied it carefully, gently rolling it first one way then the other, before placing it back into the box and handing it back to Kevin. "Imagine," he said again.

"Oh, I have." Kevin set the box aside but didn't say anything else, so Daniel reached under his desk and hauled out a battered gray canvas backpack, then shoved his hand inside it. When he pulled it back out, he held up an aged leather journal, and after a second, he offered it to Kevin.

Kevin reached for it without thinking, then almost recoiled when he realized that the journal's leather cover was blackened with soot, evidence of some long-ago fire. Beneath his fingers the small book felt oddly heavy, and for a second he had the absurd notion that it was filled with something—potential maybe—that he would do well to leave alone.

"What's this?"

"It's a dig journal I found when I started going through the crates," Daniel told him. "I don't expect you to read through the entire thing. I already did, so I can tell you that a lot of what's in there is just what you'd expect, although the fact that it's from 1939 does make it a bit more interesting—a look at the past from a point of view you might have never before considered. There's a chunk of every page missing though, burned or ripped away, so I couldn't get a totally clear picture."

"Really," Kevin said. He flipped through the pages, skimming parts of the stained, chunky looking writing. 1939? Missing info or not, this was completely fascinating. The digs Kevin had been on were hot and uncomfortable, alternating between the joy of discovery and the constant aggravation of inconvenience. What had it been like back then, minus even the smallest of modern inventions that Kevin and the rest of the crew had so taken for granted?

He started to turn another page but Daniel stopped him with a hand on his arm. "Kevin, before you read any further, there's . . ." He hesitated, obviously trying to decide on his next words. "There's something about Sunnydale," he finally said.

Kevin frowned. "What do you mean?"

Daniel looked at him and Kevin could see him trying to find the right words. "Well, things—*strange* things—sometimes happen here, stuff that just doesn't go on in other places."

Kevin lowered the journal but didn't let go of it. "What kind of . . . strange things?"

Daniel shrugged self-consciously. "I can't really explain it, except to say that after you've been here awhile, you'll start to notice it. And *accept* it." The dark-haired guy looked at his fingernails, at the books crammed all over the tiny room, at the floor—anywhere but into Kevin's eyes. "I can't really go into more detail than that, because . . . well, you'll think someone left the lunch meat out of my brain sandwich."

"I guess I'm not following you," Kevin said slowly. He was reluctant to admit it, afraid that Daniel would find him lacking in some way and change his mind about letting him into the museum's inner circle. The truth, however, was undeniable: he had no idea what Daniel Addison was talking about.

"And you don't have to understand," Daniel said. "I don't even expect you to. All I'm asking is that you try to keep an open mind when you read the next few pages in that journal. As utterly wacked-out as it seems, here in Sunnydale, the things that Professor Nuriel writes about? Well . . . there's a chance that here, in this town, they could really happen."

Completely bewildered now, Kevin only nodded as Daniel inclined his head toward the journal, a sign that Kevin could resume his reading. He lifted the beat-up book again and found his place, his eyes following the words as his brain automatically interpreted them. It didn't take long—seconds—before his mouth dropped open and he lifted his gaze to Daniel's. His new mentor said nothing, only sat and watched him, and waited; uncertain, Kevin tried again to process what he was seeing.

I can translate enough of it to believe that it is a spell ritual of some sort. It's very strange peculiar and seems to postulate that something dead can be brought back to life . . .

Kevin sat back. "Daniel, I—"

"So," Daniel interrupted. "You've got the egg, and I've got the journal. Let's try it."

"What?"

Daniel grinned at him. "I said, *let's try it.*"

"Try *what?*"

"The ritual." Daniel took the journal out of Kevin's hand and flipped forward a few pages. "There's a formula in here that the man who wrote this journal—a professor who at the time was a well-respected paleontologist in his fifties—claims will bring certain kinds of fossilized animals back to life. Your Timimus egg falls right into the category that's supposed to work. Are you game?"

Kevin just sat there, unable to believe what he was hearing. A spell? Like in . . . what? Witchcraft or something, maybe a game? But whatever you wanted to call it, that this was the next step was written all over Daniel's face. There was a whole bunch Kevin wanted to say right now, and high on the list was "Are you out of your mind?", but he didn't dare. He'd heard stories about small towns and how sometimes they did things . . . well, *differently*. But *spells?*

No matter what he thought, he had to go along; every instinct he had told him that if he didn't, any future he might have had with the Sunnydale Museum of Natural History was finished, strangled before it had a chance to take its first breath. Unless he wanted the rest of the school year to feel like an eternity, he didn't dare refuse.

Kevin cleared his throat. "A–all right."

"Excellent," Daniel said, beaming. When Kevin didn't do anything else, Daniel gave him a patient smile. "The egg?"

"Oh—yeah." Kevin reached down and plucked it from the box, running his fingers over the rough surface a final time before reluctantly handing it to the older guy.

"Great." Daniel stopped and looked around the meager space that served as his office, then looked at Kevin. A rueful smile played across his lips. "Look, I know you think I'm nuts. If I didn't know people who've lived in this town all their lives and would swear to it, I'd think I was as nuts as a bag of pistachios. But trust me, stranger stuff has happened here, and what have we got to lose anyway? We'll give it just that one try, and if it doesn't work, we'll swear never to tell anyone else how we were totally stupid enough to do it in the first place. It's just words, and you'll be right there the entire time. It's not like I'm going to saw the egg open or destroy it. Okay?"

Unwillingly, Kevin nodded. He still thought this was the craziest thing he'd ever heard of next to that guy he'd read about who'd attached hundreds of helium balloons to his lawn chair, then ended up floating out over the ocean before the Air Force got him down. But even that idiot had actually gotten himself and his supply of beer off the ground. On the other hand, what could mumbling a few words actually hurt, which, by the way, *he* wasn't going to do. When it came right down to it, Daniel could have the honor, and ultimate embarrassment, of that.

Daniel's gaze swept the area again and he stood, still cradling the Timimus egg. "Let's get out of here," he suggested. "It's too much like doing an experiment in a forgotten storeroom. Grab the journal and we'll go over to the lab." He laughed a little. "That way, we'll have access to stuff we might need."

"All right," Kevin said. He followed Daniel out of the room and pulled the door shut behind them, his nerves jangling. Was he in trouble here? Even Mr. Regis's words of warning hadn't prepared Kevin for this. No matter what Daniel said about it just being a lark, it was really obvious that he wanted to believe this was going to work, that they could mutter a spell or a charm or whatever over a nearly solid piece of rock and it would come to life. That was bad enough, but how was he going to react when nothing happened? Would he freak out, or just accept it and laugh about the whole thing? Well, they would both soon find out.

"We'll use the anthropology lab," Daniel said. "Follow me."

Kevin did as he was instructed, wishing he could think about anything but this ridiculous mission. There suddenly seemed to be so much to appreciate in this small museum—mummies, a pre-Columbian culture section, and he'd caught a glimpse of a marvelous-looking insect "zoo" on the other side of one of the rotundas. But even as he saw it on the way, his gaze slipped over everything and barely registered it. This wasn't the way it was supposed to be . . . this wasn't even remotely *normal.*

"Here we are," Daniel said. "Our grand experiment is about to begin." The older guy was keeping his tone light, no doubt because he could see how uncomfortable Kevin was. Maybe, Kevin thought suddenly, the whole thing was a test, one of those mess-with-your-mind things that prospective employers occasionally pulled to see how well you followed directions, or whether you were creative and could problem-solve on your own. He wasn't quite sure what arena reading incantations over dinosaur eggs would fall under, but that would explain quite a bit. The question was, of course, just what was the right answer?

The room Daniel led him into was a lot bigger and more brightly lit than Daniel's mini "office." Long, stainless steel lab tables lined the walls beneath shelves holding books, supplies, computers and the dozens of software manuals that were interspersed among the clutter. At least in here there was room to breathe and a person could turn around without smacking his nose on the wall. Daniel led him to one of the larger tables in the center of the room and found a cleared space on one end. The young paleontologist set the egg on its surface and for a moment the two of them just stood there, staring first at it, then at the journal Kevin still held.

After a second Kevin placed it next to the egg. "What, uh, do you think we need besides this?" he asked Daniel.

Daniel shrugged. "Well . . . a cage, maybe, to hold the baby Timimus when it hatches. Sometimes they do the monkey thing here so they've got a few tucked away. Hold on a sec—I'll get one."

Kevin nodded and watched as Daniel strode to one of the larger cabinets and dug around in it until he found something suitable. He couldn't help but notice that Daniel had said not *if* it hatches, but *when*—no sir, no lack of confidence there.

"Here we go." As Daniel came back with a small, wire cage, Kevin thought he sounded absurdly cheerful, more like he was announcing the date for the next paleontology dig than preparing for something like this. What a mess. He'd wanted so badly to be here, and now all Kevin could think about was getting the heck out of here and going home.

After a moment's contemplation, Daniel carefully picked up the Timimus egg and placed it inside the cage, then snapped the door shut. "Okay," he said. "I guess I'll read the words now." Daniel laughed suddenly, but Kevin thought he could hear nervousness and something else that he couldn't identify in the sound. Hope, no doubt. It looked to him like Daniel was trying really hard to seem normal, as though on the surface this were all a hoax and any minute now he'd admit that it was some sort of rite of passage that each newbie at the museum had to endure. But Kevin just wasn't buying it, and seeing the way Daniel's hand shook as he picked up Professor Nuriel's journal and opened it to the right page just hammered that home.

Around them, the museum was quiet, nearly empty. If there were security guards, it was still early enough for them not to bother with making rounds, so not a sound slipped through the duct work or was carried up on the drafts flowing along the wide staircases. Holding his breath despite himself, Kevin found he was leaning forward and mentally following along with the words in the journal as Daniel carefully read them out loud.

"Hear this call, spirits of Ladonithia," Daniel intoned. His voice was raspy, a real giveaway that he had a serious case of the jitters. "Awaken and return from your abyss to this frozen host, first of four, to then combine, and grant to he who resurrects you, a single wish fulfilled."

Kevin hadn't caught the contents of the incantation earlier, and even as the final words came out of Daniel's mouth, his eyebrows raised. "First of four, to then combine"—what did that mean? And a wish fulfilled—was that what this was all about? Greed, or something like it?

He turned his head toward Daniel's, but before he could say what was on his mind, a small, sharp sound rippled through the otherwise silent room.

The sound of an egg cracking.

Kevin's face whipped back toward the cage, and he couldn't believe what he was seeing. The Timimus egg was suffused in a hot, lavender-colored glow, the sort of unnatural hue that blared off the neon signs of cheap bars after midnight and hurt your eyes in the darkness. Running horizontally around it was a jagged crack, widening with every second that they gaped at it. "No way," Kevin whispered as they bent closer. "No *way!*"

"Oh," Daniel said happily. "I think it's definitely

way." Without planning to, they both circled the cage, trying to see the glowing egg from all angles. The light was slowly receding, pulling away like embers fading as they cool. In its wake there was nothing but the egg, and now it was definitely a lot more than a prehistoric fossil.

The new shell was a soft, yellowish color veined with darker lines of gold that reminded Kevin of butter melting in a too-hot skillet, just before it starts to turn brown. The egg was about the size of a child's football, one of those undersize toys that parents bought their toddler to try out in daycare, and where the shell was splitting, the edges were a brighter white and oozing with clear fluid like a wound that had broken open. Each successive crack that the shell made was like thunder in Kevin's ears, and when it was joined by something else—a low *chittering*—he nearly hyperventilated. A final harsh snap, and the Timimus egg broke completely in two.

He and Daniel automatically back-stepped, then both of them immediately returned to where they'd just been standing. Something was coming out of the splintered shell, tiny claws scrabbling and slipping at the edges of the sticky, slightly bloody embryonic fluid that coated the crumbling pieces and pulsed out between the cracks. The claws were followed by toes, the toes by the beginnings of young, fragile limbs in a golden skin flecked with brown that glistened with the birth moisture.

"This can't be happening," Kevin said hoarsely. "I can't—"

"I told you," Daniel said in a reverent voice. "Sometimes strange things *happen* in Sunnydale."

"Things like *this*."

* * *

I thought he'd never leave. To Daniel's annoyance, Kevin had hung around for nearly four more hours last night, and it was only the impending doom of parental disapproval that had finally pushed the younger kid out the door. Daniel had been done with him long before that, pretty much right after the Timimus egg had reconstituted itself and hatched. He'd gotten the critical thing he'd needed from him—the egg—so what use was Kevin Sanderson to him now?

This morning Daniel had come in early and let himself in through the employee entrance at the back. He wouldn't have left at all except he was afraid someone would notice his clothes and the shadow of a beard quickly building up. Now he made a beeline for his locked office, needing to know that the Timimus was still safe and sound in the small cage hidden under his desk. He'd wanted to take it home with him but hadn't been able to figure out how. Only the senior staff got to carry stuff in and out without getting stopped by the security guards, so he'd been forced to leave the baby Timimus here. Thank God it was all right.

He stared at the infant dinosaur now, and while he'd wanted passionately for Kevin to get out of his hair late last night, it was easy to understand the high schooler's fascination and reluctance to go. The small creature in the cage was a living, breathing specimen of something extinct for more time than most human minds could comprehend. End to end it was maybe fifteen inches long, and Daniel thought it was easy to see in real life the connection to modern-day birds—the birdlike beak as opposed to teeth, the rounded body and long limbs and neck that echoed the textbook speculation of its resemblance to an ostrich. Technically the paleontologists had been right on the mark.

Daniel checked his watch and tried to plan his day as he opened the small canvas bag he'd brought in with him. There was a pet shop a couple of blocks from Sunnydale Mall, a small place that held its own against the bigger chains by opening early, boarding cats and dogs, and selling, in addition to the usual boring array of mice, guinea pigs, puppies and kittens, some rather "colorful" creatures. From time to time they'd had things like cobras and poisonous South American dart frogs in there, and once they'd even boasted a Komodo dragon. Daniel didn't know how they got away with the weirder stuff, and he didn't care; right now, he was just thankful that they'd been able to sell him a cheap handful of white mice. The thing in the cage was going to need more than water, and he was hoping this would be sufficient.

It took only a moment to toss the two mice inside and shut the door—

—and less for the Timimus to tear into both of them.

Daniel gasped and instinctively stepped backward as blood splashed the mesh of the cage and splattered the paper-littered surface of his desk. The infant dinosaur ripped into its meal with a ferociousness that the young paleontologist had never expected; this was a modestly-sized species that supposedly fed on insects and small mammals. Was it supposed to be so aggressive, especially as a baby? He stared at it as it feasted, nauseated by the sight but still captivated by the way it cleaned itself after the meal, like a bird would preen its feathers. Was he imagining things, or did the Timimus already seem bigger? Clearly the meal had given it strength, but in a bizarre way, Daniel could have sworn it had already physically grown—

Daniel.

He spun and nearly knocked a pile of papers and fos-

86

sils off his desk. There was no one there, of course; it would have been impossible for anyone to slip into this cubbyhole he worked in without him knowing it, and anyway, he'd made sure to lock the door. Who—

A single wish fulfilled . . .

"What?" Daniel whispered. He scrunched his eyes shut and rubbed his forehead. Those words—he knew them from somewhere. When he opened his eyes again, the first thing he saw was the Timimus, squatting quietly in its cage; the second was Nuriel's dig journal lying next to it. That was the source—"A single wish fulfilled" was the final line of the incantation that had reconstituted the dinosaur egg. But he'd done that. Was this voice, this sort of . . . *presence* inside his mind telling him he was now going to be rewarded?

"Famous," he blurted without thinking. "I want to be famous so that everyone in the museum knows about me." Not so eloquently as he might have worded it given more time, but in his excitement over the live dinosaur birth, the wish part had momentarily slipped his mind. Maybe he should rephrase it. "What I mean is—"

You have not completed your part.

Daniel stopped, confused. "But I . . . I brought you back to life," he said to the infant dinosaur. In a way he felt stupid, like he was talking to the air, or maybe a dumb animal. On the other hand . . . well, proof of the extraordinary was right in front of his eyes, wasn't it? "What else do you want?"

First of four, to then combine . . .

"What?" he asked for the second time. "I don't understand."

Set me free, murmured the voice in his head, and Daniel saw the eyes of the small Timimus blaze with sudden fierce light.

Set me free and birth three others—

"Three others?" Daniel repeated. Of course; the Timimus was one, but he needed to resurrect three more. "But why?"

Whatever this entity swirling inside his head was, Daniel thought he actually felt it *smile.*

Do you not desire me to fulfill your wish, Daniel Addison? Do you not wish to be . . . famous?

Daniel sat back on his chair and closed his eyes, and just for a while, let the enticing words linger inside his mind.

Chapter 6

SHE LOVED HER MOTHER, BUT RIGHT NOW BUFFY WAS
thinking that a triple wisdom tooth extraction—perhaps performed by Principal Snyder using a pair of
iron pliers—might be more pleasant than Friday night
dinner.

The food was good, of course. Joyce Summers was
an excellent cook, and Buffy knew that her mom always put extra effort into the meal if she got wind that
Buffy wasn't planning to buzz out the door with her
friends or to patrol before the plates even hit the table.
While that ought to have been a sociable thing to do,
since Joyce had found out that Buffy was the Slayer
and what that entailed—lions and tigers and vampires,
oh my!—it had the skin-crawling side effect of making
Buffy feel that her mom was fixing her the Summers
family version of the Last Supper at every opportunity.
In cahoots with that was the constant talk of college
and, in complete self-imposed blindness to Buffy's

real-world situation, would her daughter please go away to a school at any other location on the face of this Earth?

"Here you go," Joyce said brightly, and set a bowl of dark-chocolate mousse topped with whipped cream in front of Buffy. Fancy, fancy.

"This is really good," Buffy said honestly after taking a spoonful. "I—"

"How about the University of Arizona?" Joyce asked suddenly. She stirred her own bowl of dessert with a little too much enthusiasm for Buffy to be comfortable. "Tucson is only six or seven hours away from L.A., you know. They have a really varied curriculum. Did you know that in 1998 their agricultural college had an Onion Weed Control Field Day?"

Buffy had been about to gripe at the way this seemed to be the conversation that wouldn't die, but this bit of trivia completely derailed her. "What?"

"I'm not saying this is a valid career path for you, just pointing out that they offer a lot of choices," Joyce said hastily. She took another swipe at the now demolished chocolate mass in her bowl. "There's also the Arizona State University near Phoenix, which is only four hours—"

"Can we close the book on college curriculums for a while?" Buffy interrupted. "Please? My brain is going into high-fry mode like that commercial about drugs, except this time it's *This is Buffy's brain on college.*"

Her mom looked like she wanted to say more, then she pressed her lips together and stared down at what was left of her mousse instead. Buffy swirled her own chocolate goo around, feeling guilty but knowing there was no way out of it. She was what she was—the Slayer—and yet how could she not understand her mother's desperation to somehow remove her from that? Didn't she herself always try to make sure Joyce was somewhere safe when the weird hit the fan in this town?

"So," Joyce said after a few awkward moments of silence, "the news reports have been saying there's a wild animal loose in town."

Ah ha—something interesting at last. "What kind of animal?" Buffy asked, her senses immediately tuning up a notch.

Her mother shrugged. "Some people claim it's an alligator like in the movies, someone's pet flushed down the toilet and all grown-up now, moved out of the sewers and onto the street. Others swear it looks like a Komodo dragon, but the truth is no one's gotten a really good view of it. The police, of course, maintain that it's just a stray dog."

Buffy stared at her, already back-focusing on the words. "A *dragon?*"

Joyce smiled slightly. "Nothing that breathes fire or flies, I promise. And having an Indonesian Komodo dragon running around Sunnydale is pretty unlikely. Not only are they nearly extinct, they're only indigenous to one part of the world." Her smile faded into a troubled frown. "Of course, they're large and they do move very fast. I understand they bite something, then follow it around and wait for it to die." Joyce looked a little sick, then she shook her head. "But we don't have any of those in Sunnydale, not even in the zoo."

"If it's not a dragon or a dog, then these are like what?" Buffy asked, her eyes narrowing. "Hysterical visions?"

Joyce tilted her head. "Well, a few people *have* actually had their pets killed in their yards overnight, then found what was left—not much—the next morning."

Buffy sat up straight, the rich dessert forgotten despite her normal addiction to chocolate. "This thing is attacking and *eating* the dog next door?"

Joyce nodded. "Not in our neighborhood, but not far away, either."

Buffy scowled down at her bowl as she considered this. She supposed it could be one of those dragon-thingies, but real-world endangered wasn't Hellmouth style. It was much more likely to be a goblin with lots of teeth, or maybe one of the faeries that she and the Slayerettes had faced a while back when they'd tangled with the Erl King and his Wild Hunt. And hadn't they been so fun, like mini-monsters with razor blade-lined jaws—ugh. Still, they didn't come solo, so maybe it really was—

Somewhere down the block, a man started screaming.

Buffy was up and out of her seat instantly, registering then leaving behind her mother's cry of surprise as she sped to the front door, yanked it open, then ran to the sidewalk. It took only a second to place the still-screaming voice—two houses up, the new guy who'd moved in only a couple of weeks ago. Buffy couldn't recall his name but she did remember that he had a neat dog, a friendly if hyperactive Weimaraner named, rather aptly, Mutzoid. *"Rhymes with nutzoid,"* he'd told her amiably when she'd stopped to pet it one evening.

And now, as if on cue with her recollection of it, the dog started howling.

She bolted toward his house and heard her mom calling to her from somewhere behind her, realized too late that she had neither stake nor holy water, although she didn't think either was going to help her out right now. She was running up his walkway within seconds, and it was easy to follow the commotion around to the back of his house, where she noticed a hole had been smashed through the wooden fence surrounding the yard.

"Get back! Go on—*beat it!*"

The harsh, panicked voice Buffy heard now was nothing like that of the man she'd previously talked to, and it was hard to understand the words above the nearly screaming tone the dog's yowling had taken on. The fence wasn't high and she vaulted over it rather than waste time running down to the gate; when she landed in a crouch, what she saw in the small backyard nearly made her fall over.

It really *was* a dragon.

Well, sort of—no wings, no fire-spouting nostrils. But the beast that had Mutzoid and his owner backed into the far corner where the fence met the garage wasn't far from the rest of what she'd always pictured, though thankfully a good deal smaller. Still, it was a good four feet long from its oddly-shaped snout to the end of a long, whipping tail, with skin coloring vaguely like a desert reptile. Worse, it moved way too much like a hundred monsters she'd seen animated in movies, snapping and lunging at man and dog, all the while making a horribly vicious *screeeee! screeeee!* sound that stabbed at her ears.

"Hey!" she yelled at it. "You're waking the neighbors!"

When the creature swung its head in her direction and she saw it full on, she hesitated. It was almost kind of cute, with a birdlike face and itty-bitty eyes—

"Buffy, look out!"

Too late she registered the blood dripping from the animal's beak, proof that it'd been trying industriously to make a meal out of the unfortunate Mutzoid. Instinct saved her when it was nearly on top of her; Buffy did a neat sidestep, corkscrewed her upper body and came around in a full-powered roundhouse kick that sent the beast sprawling nearly six feet away. But it was heavier and meatier than she'd expected—sort of like an overgrown turkey—and Buffy was not pleased to see it scramble right back up. It swung its head toward Mutzoid, then back at her, as if trying to decide which was more deserving of its attention. Buffy knew before it did that she'd be the lucky recipient. *Isn't that always the way it works out for me?*

She already had a plan when the animal rushed her. She faked to the left and saw the thing throw its body weight that way, then try to correct it when she went into a roll past its right side. Buffy came up on her feet next to a large metal garbage can with a slightly askew lid, and when the dragon-thing clawed its way upright and ran at her again, she had the lid in her hand like a gladiator's shield and she brained it with a good, heavy swat.

It flew over backward like a boxer whose opponent had landed the best of all possible right crosses. For a few tense moments it lay twitching between her and her disbelieving neighbor, then it was still.

"Buffy, are you all right?" Joyce hurried into the yard and reached for her, then jerked to a stop as she saw the beast on the ground. "W–what is *that?*"

"I think it's your Indonesian dragon," Buffy answered. She inched closer as her neighbor, holding Mutzoid's collar tightly, did the same.

"Is it dead?" he asked shakily. "Man, it was trying to kill my dog!"

"Not dead," Buffy said. "It's still breathing." She reached back and upended the metal garbage can, spilling out a couple of plastic bags of trash. "Help me get it in here before it wakes up."

Joyce stared at her. "You're going to *touch* it?"

Buffy raised an eyebrow. "I'm all out of dragon muzzles and leashes right now, Mom." Joyce looked like she wanted to answer, then she changed her mind and circled the thing uncertainly. "Feet first," Buffy decided. "The hind legs are pretty powerful; we don't want it kicking the lid off."

"My name's Russ," the guy said to her mother. Thank goodness; for a moment Buffy had thought he expected her to introduce the two of them, and she still hadn't remembered his name. The dog was whining and Buffy saw the poor thing was slashed and bleeding in a couple of places. "Let me take care of Mutzoid and I'll help."

"Mutzoid?" her mother repeated in bewilderment, but Russ had already stepped out of range. Joyce looked at Buffy in amazement. "He named his dog *Mutzoid?*"

"Mom," Buffy said, putting a sharp edge to her voice. "The dragon-thing, remember? Before it wakes up and tries to have us for dinner?" She glanced around the yard—was that voices she was hearing in the darkness? It was Friday night and lots of folks were out for the evening, but her luck might fail at any moment. The last thing she needed was for more neighbors to show up and start speculating about this creature. *Something about those eyes* . . .

"Oh . . . of course."

Buffy's mother circled the animal again, not sure about what to do next, then Russ reappeared. As frantic as he'd been just a few moments ago, he managed to give Joyce a slightly trembling smile. Buffy realized that he was a nice-looking guy of about forty, with longish blond hair and blue eyes. "What do we do?"

"You hold the head," Buffy decided. "Mom and I'll

lift it up and slide the garbage can under it. We need to move fast, and watch out for the mouth—if it wakes up it's going to try to bite."

"Don't I know *that*," Russ muttered.

The animal was heavier than it looked and cramming it into the trash can was a struggle, but the job was quickly over. As fast as they moved, it almost wasn't enough. Buffy had barely closed the lid on the container when the can began to shake; she and Joyce instinctively leaned on the lid and in another second, the beast inside began hammering against the metal with its beak—*clang! clang! clang!*—in a frantic attempt to get free.

"We need something to keep this closed!" Buffy shouted above the racket. "Do you have a belt or—"

"Hold on, I've got some rope in the garage." Russ hurried away, leaving Buffy and Joyce to hold the top in place while the dragon creature inside grew more agitated. The strikes increased in intensity and the can was starting to rock from side to side.

"Buffy," Joyce gasped, "what if we can't hold it?"

"We've *got* to," she answered grimly. *"Russ!"*

"I found it!" he called from inside the small building. He scurried back and began lashing a heavy cord through the side handles and across the top of the can, then he ran the rope around the bottom as Buffy and Joyce tilted it to give him access. As Russ tied it off, the thing inside finally quieted, as if it somehow knew its escape route had been eliminated.

"Animal control complete," Buffy announced, scraping a dirt-smudged hand across her forehead. Ugh, she needed a shower and her clothes were full of dirt. No time for that right now.

"Speaking of which," Russ said, "I suppose we

should call them and get this thing carted off. I'll give them a call right—"

"No!" Buffy said a little too quickly. When he stared at her, she tried to cover. "I mean, Mom and I will take care of it. We'll . . . drive it over. . . ."

"We have a friend there," Joyce said smoothly. "He has connections at the zoo and he'll probably want to look at it." Buffy could have kissed her.

Russ looked at them doubtfully. "But it's a dragon—"

"Oh, I don't think so," Buffy interrupted. "It's more like a . . . a big *bird* . . . thing. Isn't that right, Mom?"

"Exactly."

Russ looked from them to the garbage can, then shrugged tiredly. "Whatever. I just want it out of here."

"Trunk o' the car," Buffy said brightly. "No problem. And this way we won't have to wait around. You know how governmental agencies take hours to handle stuff. Mom?"

"I'll bring the family limo around, dear."

Buffy grinned. Pretty good comeback considering five minutes ago they'd been in the midst of dragon-battling. She waited with Russ while Joyce went and got the car, more to make sure Russ didn't just go on and call Animal Control than to guard against the creature's breaking out. Sometimes adults did impulsive things when you weren't watching them.

She was glad she'd stayed when her mother pulled up next to his garage and the three of them grunted beneath the considerable weight of the garbage can. "Are you sure about this?" Russ asked, eyeing the way the can stuck out of the open trunk. "If this thing gets loose again—"

"It won't," Buffy promised solemnly. "We have it totally under control."

"And our friend is an expert," Joyce added.

Russ folded his arms, clearly unconvinced. "Expert in what?"

Joyce looked at him blankly. "Research," Buffy said hastily. "Of the strange and animal variety."

Russ looked from her to her mother, but finally he shrugged. "Well, I—"

"We *really* have to go." Buffy grabbed her mother's arm and pulled her toward the car. "We'd love to stay and chat but the sooner we get this thing locked up, the better. And we want to catch Mom's, uh, friend before he goes home."

"Besides," Joyce reminded him gently, "don't you need to take care of Muh–mu—"

"Mutzoid," Buffy said helpfully. "You might want to take him to the vet."

Russ frowned. "You're right," he said. He held the car door as Joyce climbed behind the wheel. "Just be careful."

"We will," Buffy's mother promised. "Good luck with the dog."

Russ nodded and hurried back toward the house. Buffy felt a smidgen of the tension along her shoulders ease.

Joyce watched her as Buffy fastened her seatbelt. "All right, Buffy. Where to?"

She couldn't believe Joyce even had to ask.

"To Giles, of course."

"Gee," Joyce said dryly. "Why didn't I think of that?"

"Good evening," a woman's silky voice said from behind him. "You must be Oz and Devon."

Oz looked around from where he was squatting next to one of the big speakers on the stage, repairing a cut speaker wire. A few feet away, Devon was unrolling electrical cords; he and his friend stood almost in unison and came forward.

"I'm Alysa Bardrick," the woman said and held out her hand. "I hope it's not too early to meet. I wanted to be here at the start of your show tonight so I could get a full feel for your music."

The more gregarious and flirtatious Devon took her hand first, then Oz. Alysa was tall—nearly six feet—and whip thin, with short, spiked-out dark red hair and plenty of dark eye makeup on a face that was harder around the eyes than her age seemed to warrant. She was dressed in a chic, snug-fitting black dress that seemed more cocktail party than Bronze, but maybe that was it in a nutshell, Oz thought. Alysa knew how to make impressions with people while the well-meaning members of Dingoes didn't have a clue.

"Great to meet you." Devon beamed and looked to Oz.

"Likewise," Oz said. He glanced down at his hand and realized she'd pressed a business card into his palm without his noticing. *Slick.*

She nodded and inclined her head toward the equipment. "Please, don't let me interrupt your setup. I can give you a rundown of my services while you work." She glanced at her watch. "I'm sorry to say that I won't be able to stay for the whole performance. I have a couple of business associates to talk with here tonight, so I'll be in and out. Also, I've got another meeting in Marlow at eleven o'clock, so I'll have to leave by nine-thirty."

"Eleven is pretty late for a meeting," Oz commented, although what he was really thinking was that she'd barely hear them play three or four songs before she'd be taking off, probably to hear another group. They'd have to make them good ones.

Alysa smiled and glanced around the Bronze, her clear

gray eyes missing nothing. "It's a late-night business."

"So what's the deal?" Devon said, jumping right into it. "You can do what for us?"

"Provided I like what I hear tonight," Alysa said as her gaze cut back to them, "I can do a lot. Give me three months and I'll have you out of the small town scene and into L.A."

They both stared at her. "*Out* of here," Oz finally said. Well, duh; of course that would be the goal, wouldn't it? He glanced at a table a few feet away where Willow and Xander sat and watched them, barely containing their excitement. He'd been unable to convince them to wait until after the meeting; they'd much rather sit there and do the table jitter.

Alysa followed his glance and raised an eyebrow. "Ah," she said. "Of course. You have connections here."

"Well," Devon said, "it's still open for discussion." As good as Alysa might be, she didn't know Devon; Oz could already hear some misgiving creeping into the singer's voice and he couldn't blame him. Even for Devon, "out" of here seemed a little bold on the promised fast track from someone they'd never heard of a week ago.

"Are they band members?"

Oz blinked. "Say what?"

"Are they band members?" Alysa repeated. "Your friends at the table."

Oz shook his head. "They're more like audience."

Alysa looked thoughtful. "There are a lot of different areas to cover when a band goes on the road," she said. She pulled out another half-dozen business cards and handed them to him. "Scheduling, setup and breakdown, public relations, advertising, errand running. For close acquaintances, I could probably find a position in my crew."

"Numbers," Devon said before Oz could fully digest this. "What kind of numbers are we talking about?"

"Thirty-five percent plus expenses," Alysa said in a no-negotiation voice. "Expenses would include food, advertising, phone calls and travel. If you can't provide your own transportation to and from what I arrange for you, those costs would also have to come out of it. You provide your own equipment, of course."

Devon frowned, trying to do the math. "Doesn't leave much after the bills are paid," Oz said.

"It leaves enough," Alysa said flatly. "As your popularity grows, the clubs start doing their own advertising for the band because they know you'll draw the crowds, plus I start to charge more for your shows. It works out."

Oz wasn't so sure. Still, the idea of having a manager do it all—the pain in the neck scheduling, some promotion and publicity push—was really appealing. "What about recording deals?" he asked.

"We'll see what happens," Alysa said. "I've got a straight line to a lot of ears in the industry. If I say come listen to a group, it happens. You guys get your talents in top mode and I'll get the earth to shake for Dingoes." She gave them a pseudo-warm smile that didn't reach her eyes, then inclined her head toward the table where the other two waited. "And don't forget. There's enough space for a big family. Would you introduce me to your friends?"

Surprised, Oz nodded. "Uh . . . sure." He gestured at them and the two were on their feet in an instant. "This is Willow," he said as his girlfriend joined them. "That's Xander." Someone coughed lightly off to the side and Oz turned his head, startled. "Oh, and this is Angel."

Before the others could react, Angel reached to shake Alysa's hand. His face stayed impassive but Oz knew Angel and his facial expressions, and there was no mistaking it when the vampire's eyes narrowed a bit. "Do I know you? You look familiar."

"Oh, I don't believe so," Alysa said, smiling. "I'm absolutely positive I would have remembered someone as striking as *you*. Perhaps you've seen me in one of the clubs. Are you with the band?"

Angel shook his head and shoved his hands into his pockets. "I'm just an acquaintance."

Alysa nodded. "I see. Another friend." She scanned them all, then smiled at Oz and Devon. "My, but you do have a diverse circle of friends, don't you? No matter—I'm certain I can find a place for all of them." She tilted her head thoughtfully. "Angel, for instance, could be band security on road trips. What do you say, Angel?"

"I don't travel well," he said blandly.

"He's kind of like perishable fruit," Xander quipped. "But . . . you know people, right?" He leaned in closer. "People in, like, Hollywood?"

"Ah," Alysa said knowingly, "an aspiring actor?"

Xander's eyes widened. "Me? Oh no, but I could do . . . well, stuff."

"A roadie, then," Alysa said. If he caught the patronizing tone in her voice, Xander ignored it. "We can always use someone to help out in general."

"Yeah, just call me General X," Xander said enthusiastically. "At your service."

Before he could say anything more, Oz saw Alysa's gaze flick toward Willow. "How about you . . . Willow, isn't it?" She gazed at Willow thoughtfully. "That's a beautiful name. What would you like to do?"

Willow blinked nervously. "Me? Oh . . . I . . . I'm fine where I am. Really. Fine and . . . and dandy. That's me."

Alysa looked surprised. "You don't want to go with Dingoes? With Oz?"

"Go?" she looked at Oz. "Well, I—"

"She's a computer geek," Xander said. "A *deep* one."

"I see," Alysa said. "Well, you have my card if you change your mind. Or . . ." She paused, thought wheels obviously turning inside her brain. "Think about this: Perhaps you could create a web site for Dingoes, and for a few of my other bands. We haven't really tapped the Internet for advertising and marketing yet. The potential is huge, you know." At Willow's suddenly much brighter look, a corner of her mouth turned up before she again addressed Oz. "Like I said, I have a few people to meet with, so I'll let you and Devon get on with your gig for tonight. I'll be in and out of here over the next couple of hours, and that'll give me a feel for your music. Let's plan to meet here tomorrow night, all right?" She gave each of them an all-business good-bye handshake. "I can do a lot for you guys. You just need the right leader."

Oz and the others watched her head away, then Angel looked back at the table. "I was looking for Buffy. Have you guys seen her?"

"Why?" Xander demanded. "What do you—"

Willow elbowed Xander into silence. "She's on patrol," she quickly told the vampire. "But she might be around later."

Angel nodded his thanks, then, in the way he often did, somehow slipped into the shadows. Oz turned his attention back to the band manager, noting the regal walk, the total self-confidence as she wound her way through the tables to the exit. And why shouldn't she be that way? As she'd told them, she had the connections to make it happen. Oz stared after her thoughtfully, then glanced back at his friends. Devon and Xander were elated, chattering and laughing; his girlfriend sat quietly, listening to the other two but not saying anything, the way he so often did himself.

Oz looked toward the door in time to see it shut behind Alysa Bardrick. Was she really going to come back later and listen to them play, or was that just one of her standard operating lines? Nah—of course she'd be back. How could she represent a band if she hadn't heard them play?

Yeah, she'd be back. As for Willow, he hoped she was working this out in her head, and he hoped the results would be favorable. Because as Alysa had said, all they really needed was a leader.

"So it's like what—Baby Godzilla?"

"Hmmm," Giles said. He walked back and forth in front of the lockup where they kept Buffy's assortment of weapons, the same cage where Oz also waited out his wilder side three nights of every month.

"No, wait," Buffy said from behind him. "That can't be right. It's obviously Peter Pan."

"Hmmm-mmm," Giles said agreeably. He took off his glasses and peered at the imprisoned creature, then put them back on. The strange beast on the other side of the gate regarded him in return, looking savage but uncomfortably intelligent. He didn't like this, not at all.

"Giles!"

He whirled. "What!"

His much-irritated Slayer, muddy around the edges from her capture of the animal, was standing there with her hands on her hips. "Could you come out of Hmmmm Land long enough to *answer* me?"

"Yes, right," he said. "Of course. And what . . . was the question?"

Buffy rolled her eyes. "I asked you what it *is*. Excuse me for being tired, but it feels like you've been looking at the thing for hours. You've at least got a theory, right?"

"A theory," he repeated. "Yes, well, my theory is that . . . I don't rightly know *what* it is." He turned and stared at it again, thankful that he and Buffy had been able to convince Joyce they had it contained safely enough so that she could return home. Buffy had done a quick circuit of the neighborhood, looking for other creatures. In the meantime, he had skimmed through all the main books on demons that he could recall having something to do with animal shapes, but nothing had any resemblance. "It looks vaguely reptilian, but my knowledge of herpetology is rather lacking, I'm afraid. A bird's beak, that long tail. It—" He stopped and shook his head, smiling to himself.

"What?" Buffy demanded.

"Nothing," he said. "Utterly ridiculous. Just . . . never mind."

"Giles," Buffy said sternly. "Me Slayer, you Watcher. Share!"

"Well," he looked back at the cage and hesitated. "My paleontology background is right up there with herpetology—sorely lacking—but I . . . it's just that it rather resembles a dinosaur, don't you think?"

Buffy's eyes widened, but before she could respond, they heard another voice as the doors to the library were pushed open.

"That's exactly what it is," Oz said mildly as he

strode over to the cage. Xander and Willow followed close behind him, but only Xander dared to go right up to the steel barrier with him. "It's called a Timimus."

"Tim who?" Xander asked. He stuck his face close to the door and the thing inside lunged at him without warning. "Yikes!" Xander jerked backward and the whole floor shook as the beast hit the door, then thumped down. It was up again instantly, filling the library with more noise than the monkey house in the zoo at feeding time.

"Good Lord," Giles said, staring. "It certainly is aggressive."

"Especially for something that was supposed to feed on insects and small mammals," Oz said.

"It doesn't look right," Buffy said with a frown. "It's like deformed or something. The dinosaurs in Jurassic Park had teeth."

"It's certainly unique," Xander commented. "Somehow I don't think it came out of Bob's Pet Supply. Where'd you get it?"

"It attacked my neighbor's Weimaraner," Buffy told him.

"That's what happens when you're a weisenheimer," Xander came right back.

"What do you know about this thing?" Giles asked Oz. "You're sure that's what it is—a dinosaur?"

"Definitely dino," Oz affirmed. "From the land down under."

Xander looked at him, surprised. "South America?"

"Australia," Willow said, with infinite patience.

"It looks like a big bird," Buffy said. "A turkey, or an—"

"Ostrich," Oz finished. "It's one of what paleontologists call 'ostrich mimics.' " He stepped even closer to the metal door.

"Oz," Giles said hastily. "Be careful. For something that you say hunted rather small prey, it's quite hostile."

Oz glanced at him from the corner of his eye. "The cage brings that out."

Giles blinked. "Oh, I, uh . . ."

"What's really cool about this thing is that they believe it actually hibernated during cold temperatures," he continued. "Just like certain mammals do."

"I thought they were supposed to be cold-blooded," Giles said. "Like snakes."

"Outdated info," Oz said simply, moving over to Willow, who had backed to what she apparently thought was a still-unsafe distance.

"Ostrich mimics, huh?" Xander glared at the creature, apparently still ticked off that it had startled him a few moments earlier. "Don't they taste like chicken?"

"Beef, actually," Oz told him. "Really *rich* beef."

"You've eaten ostrich?" Willow asked. She was clearly horrified. "But they're so, so—"

"Large," Giles said abruptly. "They're rather large for birds, wouldn't you say?" He frowned at the dinosaur behind the steel cage, then stepped up behind Oz. Like so many other questions that had popped into his head over the past couple of years, he didn't really want to voice his next, yet he couldn't *not*. "Oz—"

"This is still an adolescent," Oz said quietly. He finally turned around and faced Giles and Buffy, and the rest of the Slayerettes. "Right now it's maybe four feet long. Fully grown we're talking four or five feet *tall*, maybe eleven feet from end to end."

Buffy's jaw dropped open. "Oh my God."

"The zoo," Willow said suddenly. "We have to give it to the zoo . . . or to the pound, or—"

"Hold it, kids," Xander cut in. He pointed at the Timimus. "Can we stop and sniff the DNA here? *Where the hell did it come from?*"

Giles opened his mouth, but he certainly had no answer. For a moment they all simply gaped at one another as Xander's question wormed its way home, then in unison they swung to consider the dinosaur.

"Oh, dear," the librarian said to no one in particular as they found it watching them with eyes that had suddenly gone from a dull, vaguely reptilian glint to a hot gaze that glowed with a malevolent and unquestionably unnatural light. "I believe Oz may be only partially right about this being a dinosaur."

Oz glanced at him questioningly. "Why is that?"

Giles took a deep breath. "Because I believe there may be a good deal of *demon* inside that dinosaur body!"

Chapter 7

"I'VE BEEN TRYING TO GET A HOLD OF YOU SINCE THURS-
day afternoon," Kevin said testily. However he might
sound, he was still endeavoring mightily to keep outright anger from his voice, but he didn't think he was
succeeding. *And you know what? As far as I'm concerned, that's okay. I have a right to be ticked off.* "The
reception desk downstairs said you were in but you
weren't answering their page. Didn't you get *any* of my
messages?"

Hunched over his desk and an even bigger pile of papers than when Kevin had been in here before, Daniel
Addison only shrugged. *Did that mean yes or no?* Or
that Daniel just didn't give a damn? "I've been busy,"
he said, still not answering Kevin's question. "With—"

"—the Timimus," Kevin finished for him. "Is it
okay? Still alive?"

For a long moment, Daniel didn't answer. "It . . . escaped," he admitted at last.

109

Kevin could only stare at him. *"What?"*

Daniel folded his arms and gave him a defiant look. "The cage was too flimsy," he said with a shrug. "It couldn't hold it."

"Where did it go?"

"Well, if I knew that, it wouldn't still be gone, would it?" Daniel's voice was sarcastic.

"Jesus, Daniel," Kevin said. Where he'd been angry a moment ago, now he was too amazed and dismayed to remember that. "How can you be such a smart-ass about this? That thing's a predator—it kills to eat. It'll target dogs, cats—kids, for crying out loud!"

"They'll catch it," Daniel said confidently. "Some micro-brained security officer or cop will shoot it before anything bad happens, you'll see. They won't even know what they're dealing with."

Still, Kevin was gratified to see that some of the snotty self-confidence had drained from his new mentor. He slumped against the doorway. "Seeing that thing come alive—it was incredible, *impossible.* I can't believe that now it's just . . . gone."

"Me, either." Daniel was silent for a moment, then his rigid expression softened and he rubbed his temples as though he had a headache. "Look," he finally said. "I'm sorry for not calling you back, and for being such a jerk just now. I was just so . . . flipped out when the thing got away, you know? I didn't want to admit to you that it even happened. Here you'd given me your only egg and we'd done this miraculous thing with it, and what happens? I let the Timimus get away." He sighed. "I saw all our chances for recognition and advancement here in the museum, all that *potential,* disappear with it. I acted like an idiot, and I apologize."

Kevin didn't reply for a moment. His new mentor's

earlier cold shoulder and tone of voice had stung badly, but the apology Daniel was offering now went a long way toward making him lighten up. "Forget it," he said eventually. "But what about the Timimus?"

Daniel looked discouraged. "It's gone. We'll never get the thing back." For a second he balled up one fist. "I had such *hopes* for what we could accomplish because of it." After a few seconds, the dark-haired young man leaned forward and picked up his pen. "But we can't dwell in the past, you know? So now I'm trying to find another source for some eggs to try it again. Everything here at the museum is either locked up or permanently embedded into one of the exhibits so that it's too difficult for me to get anything out. And since I can't give a feasible reason why I need it, these old farts are never going to give up one of their treasured fossils anyway." He sounded disgusted and disappointed.

"You want to do it again? After the Timimus escaped? Are you crazy?" Kevin's mouth was hanging open, but he couldn't help it.

"Of course I'm going to try again," Daniel came right back. "Wouldn't you? Hell, wouldn't *anyone?*" He looked around the small office and scowled. "Only this time I'll be better prepared. Make sure it stays safely contained. No mistakes, and no . . . escapes. I just have to find an egg, that's all."

Kevin didn't say anything, just watched the other man work for a few moments, his mind in turmoil. The whole thing was insane: Daniel, the spell, the undeniable fact that they had brought an extinct creature back to life. But wasn't Daniel right? The consequences . . . the *rewards*, could have been enormous, beyond Kevin's wildest dreams even at the Field Museum in

Chicago. Imagine the expressions on the faces of his old friends and the museum administration back home if he and Daniel could have actually unveiled—

"I have more eggs," he blurted.

Daniel's head jerked up. "What?"

Kevin swallowed. "I have more. But . . ." His voice faded away.

"But what?" Daniel stood and came toward him. "What's the catch?"

"They're not Timimus eggs," he said in a low voice.

Daniel's cold fingers closed around his forearm. "Then what are they? For God's sake, Kevin—come on! What we did with the Timimus doesn't have to be a once in a lifetime thing, something we only dream about redoing! If I understand you right, you're saying you've got the ingredients we need to make it happen all over again!"

"It's not that simple," Kevin protested weakly. "It's not the *same*."

"Why the hell not?" Daniel let go of him. Now he was practically waving his arms. "What's so different?"

"They're Tyrannosaurus Rex eggs."

Whatever Daniel had been about to say went out the window. "Wow," he finally managed. He stood quietly for a second, then twisted his fingers together and took a deep breath. "T. Rex."

"Yeah," Kevin said. "That's why we can't—"

"You don't really believe that," Daniel interrupted him. One hand snaked back out and gripped Kevin's shoulder, digging in hard. "Sure we can do it. We *have* to. We'll just be absolutely positive to take the appropriate precautions, that's all. Make sure we have containment."

"Like the last time?" Kevin demanded. "That was containment, all right!"

"A misjudgment," Daniel conceded without letting go of Kevin's shoulder. "But harmless, I swear. You know the background of Timimus—as a baby the thing'll only eat waterbugs and rats. If it's still alive at all, Animal Control will destroy it before they even realize what they're dealing with. It was just our learning curve."

"But we're talking about a tyrannosaur," Kevin said. He felt oddly tangled up in his own emotions: still desperate to please Daniel despite being ignored for the last twenty-four hours; full of sudden, unforeseen terror at the notion of bringing a Tyrannosaurus Rex to life; utterly stupid for thinking that it could even happen again; desperate to find out if it would. But they weren't considering a small insect- and rodent-eater here. They were talking about the *king* of the dinosaurs, perhaps the most feared creature that had ever lived on this planet.

But the idea that he might see one, perhaps hold a baby one in his *hand*, was just . . . indescribable.

"We'll be completely prepared," Daniel insisted. "I *promise*. A steel cage, a weapon of some kind at the ready if we need it. We'll think it through. And this time, you'll be involved in it every step of the way. I won't get . . . preoccupied with stuff like I did before. I'm sorry for that, I swear. This time, it's you and me all the way, Kev. We'll do it together. What do you say?"

Kevin felt himself weakening, tried to save himself by telling the truth, then realized too late that was the last thing he should have done. "But it's not just one," he said hoarsely. "The eggs are in a set of three, embedded in a rock base. I can't separate them."

"That's all right," Daniel said gently, and Kevin felt a

sense of unreality slip over him at the calmness he heard in the other man's voice. His stomach did an unpleasant twist at Daniel's next statement.

"We'll just resurrect all three of them."

"Did you find anything?"

Oz looked up and found Giles hovering behind where he sat at the computer in the library. Well, maybe hovering wasn't the right word. Lurking might be better because it much more accurately conveyed the sense of caution and secrecy that the librarian radiated every time he had to come too close to a monitor and CPU—the Watcher still seemed convinced that someday one of the things was going to rear up and bite him. Rue the day—not even his tweediness would save him then.

"Nothing that supports the idea of being able to grow a dinosaur à la Jurassic Park in the real world yet," Oz answered. "We haven't checked the water sponge sites yet."

Giles looked at him blankly. "Water sponge?"

"Dehydrated animal-shaped sponges," Willow explained from where she sat at the other end of the table and paged through a stack of past issues of *Scientific American*. "They're cool. You drop them in water and *poof!* Instant pet."

"Yes, well," Giles said. "I don't think those are the species in which we're actually interested right now."

Xander, positioned by the cage in self-imposed guard stance, looked over his shoulder at them. "I believe the species we're looking for would be the I-want-to-devour-your-flesh kind." As if on cue, the Timimus in the cage lunged forward and snapped viciously at him from the other side of the metal door. The dark-haired teenager skipped backward. "Heel, boy. I don't think he likes me."

No one commented, then Oz saw Buffy staring at the Timimus with a puzzled expression. "What's the deal, Buffy?"

She didn't say anything for a moment, then finally she tilted her head one way, then another, studying the dinosaur. "Am I shrinking or did someone feed dino-baby super-grow pills overnight?"

Giles hurried to the cage door. "Why do you—good Lord, you're right!"

Willow sat up straight. "It's bigger?" she asked in a small, scared voice. "Already?"

Oz abandoned his post at the computer and joined Buffy, Giles and Xander in front of the cage. It only took a glance. "Considerably."

Xander folded his arms. "Well, I certainly didn't feed it. Growing this fast with zero food?" He made a *tsk*ing sound. "I'm thinking serious weight problem."

"I think we're the ones who're going to have the serious problem," Buffy said. "I saw the damage it could do as a baby, and I'd swear Timmy here has already moved on to teenland."

Giles looked at him. "Oz?"

But Oz could only shake his head. "I'm not finding anything, Giles. So far, real live dinosaurs only happen in the movies."

"Then something else has to be the cause of this," Giles said firmly. "Or some*one*." He looked at Willow. "Perhaps you could . . . ?"

"I'm on it," she said, and Oz smiled as she settled comfortably in front of the computer and, after glancing around with a vaguely guilty expression, swiftly hacked into a few off-limits areas. "Uh . . . what is it exactly that I'm looking for?"

"Well, I'm not precisely sure," Giles admitted. "Consider someone with a scientific background, perhaps in the medical arena. Chemistry—"

"So you're discounting the Hellmouth connection?" Buffy asked. "Is that a good idea? I mean, just because *we* can't make 'em doesn't mean they can't be created using other means."

"But we went through everything already," Giles pointed out. "The history books are seriously bereft of dinosaur demons."

"What about paleontologists?" Oz raised an eyebrow. "Sunnydale's got a good-size section of that at the museum."

Giles stared at him, then looked flustered. "Well, that is rather obvious, isn't it."

"Duh," Xander muttered.

"Kevin Sanderson," Willow said out of nowhere.

Oz looked at Willow. "I know the guy. What's his deal?"

"Beats me," Willow said absently. She was totally focused on the information blinking on the screen. "He hasn't even been enrolled at Sunnydale High for a full two weeks. Here—yeah, Oz and I are in Earth Sciences with him. Wow. This guy's so deep into paleontology I wouldn't be surprised if he had dirt in his pockets."

Oz looked thoughtful. "I could tell he was high on the prehistoric, but making them from scratch?" He shook his head doubtfully. "Seems a little overboard."

"Well, I've searched on every record field I can think of," Willow told him and the others. "Besides Sanderson, I'm coming up with zip from the school."

"So he's the only lead we can dig up," Xander said. He seemed to be waiting for someone to comment, and when no one did, Oz heard him mutter to himself.

"My standup ability is totally wasted on the crowd here."

"Let's go talk to the guy," Buffy said. "Time's a'wastin'."

"Isn't that my line?" Xander demanded.

"Not something you can copyright," Oz told him. He looked at Buffy. "I'm up for tagging along. Plus it might be better if he saw a familiar face."

Buffy arched an eyebrow. "You mean as opposed to us total strangers marching up and demanding to know who the hell he thinks he is and why he brought something a bazillion years old back to life?"

"Buffy," Giles said hastily, "we don't know that he did any such thing. I'd hardly think it wise to accuse him before we have more information. As Oz pointed out, there are paleontology people at the museum—"

Xander rolled his eyes. "Earth to Giles? The museum's always been here. Now we have brand-new guy who likes dinosaurs, and vee-ola, a brand new dinosaur. Does it have to hit you over the head with a leg bone?"

Giles sniffed. "Bit explicit, don't you think?"

"When the info just falls on our heads, let's take advantage of it," Buffy said firmly. "Will can stay and keep hunting in the virtual. Who else besides Oz is going with me in the real?"

"I'm in." Xander and the Timimus glared at each other a final time. "I'd definitely like to see who's playing Jurassic creator here."

"Actually," Oz said, "he comes from the early Cretaceous."

Xander's mouth dropped open. "This Kevin guy?"

"The Timimus."

"Oh." Xander looked righteously embarrassed. "Yeah, right."

"Wait!" Willow stood suddenly, looking totally petrified. "You're leaving me here?" Her eyes were wide as she glanced at the cage and the pacing creature within it. "With . . . with *that?*"

"Giles will be here," Buffy pointed out.

"There's safety in numbers," Xander said reassuringly. "Everyone knows that."

Willow's glance at the dinosaur was dubious. "I don't think *he* does."

"We'll be fine," Giles put in. "It's safely contained and all we need do is keep an eye on it during our research." He slipped off his glasses and wiped at them with a handkerchief.

"Then we're gone," Buffy said. "We'll let you know if we find out anything." She strode toward the door and Xander and Oz followed. Oz glanced over his shoulder a final time and saw Willow settle timidly in front of the computer again as Giles began sorting through a pile of old volumes. Meanwhile the Timimus paced in its prison, back and forth, and watched them with glowing eyes.

What was it Giles had said? Oh yeah.

"We'll be fine."

Inside, where no one else could see, he grimaced.

It was like a miracle . . .

Daniel hadn't been kidding when he'd said that to Kevin, and now he thought it applied to a whole lot more than the revitalization of the Timimus egg. The fact that Kevin was standing here now, had actually gone home and returned with the chunk of rock containing the trio of T. Rex eggs . . . well, it was another part of the miracle that just kept on coming. There were other parts, too: Kevin believing the Timimus had escaped when Daniel had actually obeyed its demand for freedom, sneaked it down to the maintenance exit, and released it outside. More than that, the teenager had accepted Daniel's reasons for not taking his calls when the truth was that until Kevin had told him about the T. Rex eggs, Daniel really had no more use for him. In fact, he wouldn't have involved him in the ritual at all had it not been clear that where the Timimus egg went, Kevin went with it. The kicker, of course, was Daniel's inference that this would be the ultimate for both of them, some kind of huge advancement in the field of paleontology. For Kevin, could that be any more unlikely? The truth was once Daniel got these eggs to hatch viable baby dinosaurs, he would find a way to shake Kevin Sanderson off like the aggravating little ankle biter that he was.

"These are excellent, Kevin," he said. He ran his fingers gently over the fossilized shells, noting that what he could see of them outside the rock nest was intact. Good. "You're sure they're T. Rex? Not that it would make me change my mind about trying the spell again. I'd just be a little . . . disappointed."

"Absolutely positive," Kevin said. He sounded funny and Daniel glanced at him; the fear he saw there would've convinced him about the egg types even if Kevin hadn't said another word. "They came from a tyrannosaur site." He hesitated. "Listen, how I got these—"

"Let's just not go there," Daniel said abruptly. "I think it's better for both of us, don't you?" Another illusion; he didn't care *where* the eggs had come from, just that they *were*.

Kevin nodded, looking relieved. He glanced around the lab and spied the cages that Daniel had put together during his trek home and back again. "You're sure those will do it?"

"Stainless steel components held together by doubled-up steel clips. Obviously they won't cut it when the babies get bigger, but we don't have to worry about that right away. Let's just focus on seeing if we can bring these fossils back to life."

"And if it does work?" Kevin asked him in a low voice. "What do we do then?"

"Then, after we're sure we have healthy hatchlings, we'll bring in other experts, let the university, the government, whomever, take over the task of caging and controlling them. That way, everyone will be safe." He looked at Kevin steadily. "And we'll be set in the paleontology field forever. I'll get a boost a lot higher in the hierarchy here, and when you go back to Chicago at the end of the school year, they'll treat you like such royalty you'll practically be able to wear a crown."

Kevin didn't say anything, but there was something in his face. . . . Doubt? Suspicion? Daniel could hardly blame him; he knew he'd made a serious error in not keeping in contact with the kid after the Timimus resurrection. But how could he have known that he would need the boy again?

"Are we ready?" he asked.

Kevin nodded a final time, but his expression was anything but confident, and Daniel could see that the kid's hands were shaking. Too bad; Daniel didn't have time to play patty-cake with his baby assistant's frazzled nerves. He had things to do, dinosaurs to awaken, a contract to fulfill with someone—some*thing*—a helluva lot bigger and more important than Kevin Sanderson would ever, in his life, hope to be. Kevin might be scared but Daniel had it from good authority that he himself was going places. All he had to do was substitute the words "these last" in the appropriate place.

"Just do what I tell you, when I tell you," Daniel told Kevin. "And you'll be fine. We'll *both* be fine." The dark-haired paleontologist caressed the cover of Professor Nuriel's leather journal for a moment, then carefully opened it to the bookmark he'd placed on the crumbling page on which the old professor had written the ritual.

Hear this call, spirits of Ladonithia
Awaken and return from your abyss to this frozen host
These last of four, to then combine . . .

Kevin Sanderson's house looked a lot like Buffy's own on Revello Drive. This area of Sunnydale was slightly more affluent, the homes a little on the larger side, but the effect was the same: all-American tidy and flowered up. The split-level in front of them was a yellow brick with a brown shingle roof, and was bordered by low, neatly trimmed bushes. A couple of hanging baskets flanked the posts to either side of a nice, veranda-style front porch, but this early in the year they were bare. Buffy could imagine them holding bright red geraniums along about June.

Chapter 8

KEVIN SANDERSON'S HOUSE LOOKED A LOT LIKE Buffy's own on Revello Drive. This area of Sunnydale was slightly more affluent, the homes a little on the larger side, but the effect was the same: all-American tidy and flowered up. The split-level in front of them was a yellow brick with a brown shingle roof, and was bordered by low, neatly trimmed bushes. A couple of hanging baskets flanked the posts to either side of a nice, veranda-style front porch, but this early in the year they were bare. Buffy could imagine them holding bright red geraniums along about June.

"So what's our cover?" Xander asked eagerly as he followed her and Oz up the small riser of steps.

Oz smiled slightly but didn't answer, so Buffy took the initiative. "Our cover is that Oz goes to class with him and wants to copy his notes from yesterday's dose of Regis because he lost his."

"I did?" Oz considered this. "Yeah, I guess I did."

"That's it?" Xander looked disappointed. "No stealth or—"

"You're not Pierce Brosnan," Buffy reminded him.

"But he has the coolest toys!"

"And we don't." Oz reached past Buffy and rang the doorbell, and Buffy saw him eyeing the wreath of dried flowers on the front door. She didn't like them either— too much like dead funeral flowers.

"You're right," Xander agreed. "We are toy deprived." He peered around the front porch. "Don't mind me. I'm just looking for signs of Kevy's latest pet."

Buffy shuddered. "It's locked up, remember? Thank God."

There was a noise in front of them, then the door was pulled open by an older woman with neat white hair and a pleasant face. "Hi," Buffy said, giving her best bright-as-a-button smile. "Mrs. Sanderson? We're, uh, friends of Kevin's from school. Is he home?"

Mrs. Sanderson suddenly looked pleased way beyond proportion. "Oh, my—you're Kevin's friends? Why that's wonderful! Come in, please."

They looked at one another nervously, then the trio filed dutifully past the older woman as she waved them inside. Buffy swallowed. "We—"

"May I get you some lemonade?" Mrs. Sanderson asked. "How about some cookies?"

"Cookies?" Xander's attention was caught.

Buffy elbowed him. "Thank you, but we really can't stay very long," she said sweetly. "I'm Buffy, this is Oz, and that's Xander."

"Just call me the Cookie Monster," Xander said under his breath, earning himself another sharp elbow in the ribs.

"I was wondering if he had some notes I missed in

earth sciences class yesterday," Oz put in. "The ones about . . . dinosaurs."

"Oh, Kevin's not here right now," Mrs. Sanderson said. "But he could sure tell you about dinosaurs, all right. That's pretty much all he lives and breathes."

"That's what we thought," Buffy said. "Do you know when he'll be back? Or where he went?"

Mrs. Sanderson shook her head. "Not really. He told me he was going to spend the day with a friend named Daniel but didn't say where," she said apologetically. She looked slightly embarrassed. "We just moved here, of course, and to be honest, I was just so thankful that he'd found someone who shared his interests that I let it slide when he didn't mention where they would be except to say he'd probably eat dinner with him. But I'm sure he'll be home by nine tonight. I could have him call you." She smiled brightly again, completely oblivious to their discontent. "His father and I were afraid it would be so difficult on him, moving during the last year of school like this. But here he already has friends coming to the house. I guess it's going to work out after all."

Buffy nodded, trying to look as convinced as Mrs. Sanderson was trying to be. There was a sense of desperation around the edges of Kevin's mother's words that was creeping Buffy out, giving her a bad, bad feeling about all this. New in Sunnydale, Kevin was way too much like easy prey for an entire repertoire of evildeeders. To those in the know like her and the Slayerettes, the signs were already a'rumbling: Kevin had arrived involved neck-deep in paleontology, and now a live dinosaur had somehow poofed its way into existence. That his mother didn't even know where he was just made it that much worse. Bad, bad vibes.

"Daniel," Oz said, suddenly straightening. "That

would be Daniel Addison, the guy from the Museum of Natural History?"

Mrs. Sanderson frowned, but at the same time managed to look even happier than she had a few moments ago. "Well, I don't know. I assumed it was someone from school, but if he's with the museum . . . that would be good, wouldn't it?"

"Oh, yeah," Xander said. "Right on the money."

The older woman hugged herself momentarily. "Kevin had a solid footing in Chicago," she said. "We pulled him out of it, you know, and came here because of his father's failing health. My son had so much built up back there, but he doesn't have anyone to help him here, to guide him. If this Daniel person can do that, it would be a blessing."

No one said anything for a beat, and Buffy had to struggle not to wince. *A leader?* For a newbie in Sunnydale that could mean a whole bunch of possibilities, and most of them sure weren't the kinds of things a nice woman like this would wish on her only child. "Thanks for your time," she finally said, and motioned Oz and Xander to follow her to the door. "We'll catch up with him later."

"All right," Kevin's mother said, then looked at Oz. "Oh, pardon me, what was your name again?"

"Oz," he said from beside Buffy. "From earth sciences class."

"Oz," Mrs. Sanderson repeated. "I can remember that."

He smiled as they filed out. "Most people can."

"Remember Daniel Addison?" Oz asked Willow as they rejoined their friends at the library. "He gave that talk in earth sciences class last week. From what

Kevin's mother said, I'm thinking he's the guy we're looking for."

"Daniel Addison." Willow was already typing. "He's not currently a student," she said, without lifting her gaze from the screen.

"No." Oz perched on the table next to her as Buffy and Xander crowded around. "But Regis brought him in a couple of days ago—"

"Yeah, that's right!" Willow said, straightening. "I remember him now. He was the one with the creepy slides . . . the creepy *dinosaur* slides! But what does he have to do with Kevin Sanderson?"

Buffy leaned in. "Kevin's mom told us that's who he's hanging with today—as in *all* day."

Willow frowned. "Well, Addison comes from the Museum of Natural History, right?"

"Yeah," said Xander. "Another Paleo guy. I just don't get the attraction of rock-encrusted reptiles. Then again, this town attracts a lot of dead things, so why not those."

Buffy grimaced. "We can usually find a reason behind what crawls out of the ground around here. In this case, so far we've got nada."

"Here," Willow said suddenly. "I backtracked on Regis's requisition requests and came up with the info. Daniel Addison is doing postgraduate work at the museum in the Department of Paleontology. This is his second year there."

"Big surprise—not," Buffy said as Giles came out of his office and moved to the library counter. "Tell us something we don't already know."

"All right, I will." Willow typed furiously for about twenty seconds, then began to read from the screen. "'Daniel Addison is directionless and unwilling to work to succeed. He does not often think for himself.

For this reason, a third-year internship will not be offered. We suggest he return to the university and concentrate on his studies, and we will reconsider him at a future time.' "

"Willow!" Giles exclaimed from where he was leafing through a book. "That sounds like a comment an employer might make—are you into the museum's confidential records?"

"Of course not," Xander said smartly. "She's hacked into *Kindergarten Quarterly*."

Giles frowned at him. "Always a comment, eh?"

"Someday I'll have my own talk show."

"I'm sure it will be fascinating," Giles said, and looked back at Willow questioningly.

She shrugged. "I knock on a door—it opens. Unlike some of Sunnydale's residents, I don't need an invite to step in and look around."

Giles's frown deepened above his glasses. "At this point, I suppose it's useless to request information from my acquaintances at the museum?"

"Not necessary," Willow said blandly.

"What else does it say?" Oz asked. *Directionless?* That didn't sound good, especially since Daniel Addison had wormed his way into leading Kevin Sanderson around by the proverbial nose.

Willow squinted at the screen. "Let's see. Pretty much more of the same, except . . ."

"What?" Buffy asked. "C'mon, share."

Willow scrolled up and down a few times, then sat back. "Well, there are a lot of comments by the museum administration, but the gist of it seems to be that he'd prefer to get other people to do stuff he's supposed to be doing himself. He starts out strong, makes a good impression, then tries to get someone else to carry the load."

"Someone else as in Kevin?" Buffy suggested.

One side of Willow's mouth turned down. "Exactly."

Oz sat back and considered this. So much for the good thing Kevin's mother had been hoping for. There was a good chance her son had stumbled into a parasite pit. Oz would be the first to admit that while this was kind of Hellmouth style to begin with, Kevin seemed to have found an all-new version of the express elevator. For Kevin's sake, Oz just hoped there was an EMERGENCY STOP button.

"So what's our contingency plan?" Xander demanded. "Let's find this Daniel guy and shake him down!"

"I can give you his address," Willow said. "And there's the museum. He might be there."

"Yeah," Oz said. He looked to Buffy and she nodded. "I'm thinking Alysa isn't the person to be showing Kevin around." They all stared at him, then Oz realized what he'd said. "Freudian slip," he amended. Alysa, he realized, was still high in his thoughts, and now she was getting all twisted up with this Daniel–Kevin thing. "I meant Daniel." But Willow looked at him knowingly—amazing how she could tune into him like that—then turned back and read a residential address off the screen.

"Let's try there first," Buffy said, standing and picking up her bag. "It's closer than the museum. In all things be efficient."

"I'm with you guys," Xander said.

"What's the matter, Xander?" Willow asked, keeping her face carefully expressionless. "Do the books here scare you?"

"Actually it's the combination of books *and* dino-Timmy over there," Xander said. "The way he just keeps going back and forth is making me nervous. I feel outgunned no matter which way I turn."

"Let's go," Oz said. He bent and gave Willow a quick kiss. "We'll check in later." They hurried out, but Oz, his hearing so much more attuned even on the most moonless of nights, still heard Giles murmur to himself when no one else in the room even heard him breathe . . .

"Freudian, indeed."

"Well, this is great," Buffy said. "Is the feeling that we're getting absolutely nowhere a lonesome thing, or do you guys feel it, too?" Disgusted, she put her hands on her hips and backed up to look at the building, not that it would help anything. The miniest of complexes, there were only six small apartments, but the place was looking pretty shabby around the edges. The once-nice stucco was now covered in peeling paint the color of dirty desert sand, and chunks of the stucco had cracked away at the corners. The sad remains of a small front lawn was littered with trash and rocks, and the adjacent buildings weren't much better. One lone and sickly palm tree still struggled for life, leaning away from the building as if it wanted to pull itself up and run.

According to the info from Willow, Daniel Addison's apartment was on the third floor in the front. Easy enough. In fact, from here Buffy could see the triple length of dirty windows that belonged to his apartment on the left side of the three-story building. And every one of them was dark. "Ring it again." Probably useless, but she had to try.

At the entrance to the small apartment building, Xander leaned on the buzzer. Somewhere overhead came the faint but unmistakable sound of a bell.

"I don't think he'd be ignoring *that*," said Oz.

"Yeah—" Buffy forgot what she was about to say as

a window overhead grated upward and a woman's nasal voice shouted down at them from the second floor apartment directly below Daniel's, its owner just out of sight beyond limp-looking curtains.

"Stop ringing already, wouldja? Are you stupid? He's not home!"

"Xander!" Buffy said sharply. At the doorway, he glanced up at the crabby woman defiantly, but finally removed his finger from the bell.

"Excuse me, ma'am?" Buffy called before Daniel's neighbor could close the window again. "Do you know where he is? Or when he might be home? It's important—"

"I'm not his mother!" the woman snapped. There was a crash as the window slammed shut and Buffy scowled, wishing it would break just to teach the old bat a lesson. No such luck.

"The museum?" Xander asked as he ambled toward them.

"This late on a Saturday evening?" Oz shrugged. "Statistically, it's closed."

"We could try anyway," Buffy suggested. "Maybe we can find a back way in or something."

Xander folded his arms. "And if we do go the breaking and entering route—which I'm definitely up for— we're going to immediately know just where to find Paleo-Dude in that building? Fabulous place, by the way, which is about the size of a city block."

"The logical place to start would be around the dinosaurs, although we have to get past a doubled private security force. Courtesy of that whole Incan mummy thing," Oz added. "Still, I think what works against us most is the time. I'm betting our two boys are long gone."

"You're probably right," Buffy said, frustrated. "Could we bang into any *more* brick walls?"

"Come on," Xander said. "Let's go get something to drink and figure out what our next move is. Espresso Pump, anyone?"

Buffy nodded in defeat, but she was still irritated at their lack of progress. What if Daniel Addison and Kevin Sanderson were involved in this together, and somewhere out there they were working on taking their next dino project live? She couldn't shake the image of Mutzoid howling with pain and bleeding from where the Timimus had ripped chunks out of him. Already the Timimus was so much larger. What if there was another one like it, a brother or sister, running around Sunnydale right now, working its way across the food web as it grew? *Not good.*

As they expected, The Espresso Pump was crowded. It was well past eight o'clock by the time they got their coffees, Xander had his snack—didn't he *ever* stop eating junk food?—and they snagged a place by the wall where they could stand together. In the full onset of night, the temperature had dropped and Buffy found herself wishing for summer and wrapping her fingers around her mug to warm her hands.

"So we head back to Kevin Sanderson's house?" Oz suggested. "Addison might be able to stay out and play all night, but Kevin's parents are going to expect him back."

"Yeah, they do look like they remember he's alive," Xander said. He stared glumly into his coffee and Buffy couldn't help feeling bad for him. Suddenly, he brightened. "Hey, Buffster, did you hear that Oz's band manager says she can find a place for all of us?"

Buffy raised an eyebrow. "What do you mean, 'all' of us?"

"*Potential* band manager. We haven't hired her yet," Oz reminded him.

Xander clearly chose to completely ignore that part. "Even me. She said I could help do stuff like setup and takedown of the equipment, run errands. Stuff like that."

Buffy set her mug down and folded her arms. "Where does that fall under the 'all of us' realm?"

This time it was Oz who answered. "According to her, she's got connections we could all use, one way or another. She even wants to put Willow to work making web sites and running promo on the Internet."

"Yeah," Xander put in. "She even has a place for your vamp-boy, but he won't take it."

"Angel?" Buffy asked in surprise. "What would he do?"

"Security for the band," Oz told her. "He already turned her down."

"Wow," Buffy marveled. "Seems like she's got something for everyone."

Xander started to agree, then he must have realized that wasn't quite true, was it? Oz, Willow if she wanted it, Xander, Devon and the other band members . . . even Angel was covered here, but there was no place in the whole scenario for Buffy. He flushed. "Buffy—"

She waved him off. "No biggie." She started to say something else when a loud voice at a table about ten feet away momentarily drowned out everyone around it. Buffy and the guys looked over curiously.

"Dude, go ahead and razz me, but I am *telling* you," said a skinny teenager with long hair. He punctuated his story with sharp little jabs at the tabletop with his forefinger. "I *saw* it running down the alley next to the Bronze."

"Did you follow it?" asked his table mate with a crooked and obviously disbelieving grin. "I would have. Just like in the movies or——"

"My ass, you would've," said the first guy crudely. "You should've seen the size of the thing. It was like somebody's pet iguana on steroids."

Buffy, Xander and Oz were out the door before their coffees ever had time to cool.

Chapter 9

"So," Giles said. "Buffy briefly mentioned Oz's new band manager. Allison . . . Beadrack?"

Willow looked up from the computer with a puzzled frown, and Giles wasn't sure if it was because he'd interrupted her or because she didn't know how to answer his question. Then her expression cleared. "Bardrick," she told him, then smiled a little. "Alysa Bardrick. And . . . I'm not sure what he knows. Oz being the master of conversation that he is."

Giles pulled a chair out across from her and sat. Sometimes it was so difficult to ask these teenagers the simplest question. *Is this what parents go through?* he wondered. A day-by-day effort at trying to drag information out of their children while constantly being wary of offending them? "Well, I suppose I'm curious because of Oz's odd slip of the tongue."

Instead of answering, Willow returned to scanning

the computer monitor. "Ladonithia," she said before Giles could pursue the topic further.

"What's that?" Giles squinted over at her, more than happy to go back to familiar demonic, hellish, and historical territory. "Ladon? I believe that was a dragon in classical Greek mythology. If memory serves correctly, the creature supposedly had a hundred heads and guarded the golden apples of the tree given by Gaea to Zeus and Hera at their wedding."

"Not Ladon," Willow said as Giles stood, then came around to her side. *"Ladonithia."*

Now Giles was completely puzzled. "Some kind of derivative?"

"Looks that way." The young redhead's hands hesitated over the keyboard, and finally she folded them on her lap. "But I can't find anything more on it except for a reference to this one web page, and it dead-ends as a 'not found.' The rest of the search engines are coming up blank."

"All right," Giles said firmly. "Then we'll have to do it the tried and true way: hit the books."

She'd investigated the alley beside the Bronze hundreds of times and dusted dozens of bloodsuckers in there besides. But moving into it now, when she suspected there was something hiding in its dark length that literally wanted to eat her, gave Buffy a whole new level of creeposity. The shadows were longer and darker, as though stretched by an unseen hand to accommodate a creature so much larger than a vampire and which Buffy really didn't have a clue how to fight. If it was like the Timimus imprisoned at the library, it would bleed and feel pain like any other living creature, but what about its size? Its weight? How would she bring down something that might have two hundred or more pounds on her?

And what about its *teeth?*

"There," Xander said, making her and Oz jump. "Way in the back by the chain link fence."

"At least it's trapped," Oz said. "We—oh, so not good."

"What?" Buffy asked as she literally heard Oz swallow, then she turned her head back to the alley and saw what he saw.

Xander inhaled sharply. "Can we say *run?*"

"No," Buffy said automatically. "We can't." Still, they didn't move forward either, and luckily the beast hadn't seen them yet. "Oz," Buffy said under her breath. "What the hell *is* that?"

He didn't answer immediately, and Buffy wondered if that was because he couldn't figure out exactly what it was, or because he'd known the instant he saw it. Finally, his reply came in a strained whisper.

"Tyrannosaurus Rex."

Xander made a strangled sound in his throat, for once all out of wisecracks. Buffy stared down the gloomy alley, too terrified to take her eyes off the dinosaur. "Guess our boys have branched out," she said at last.

"Buffy, we can't fight that thing," Xander said a little desperately. "I mean, *look* at it—we're talking the size of an Oldsmobile here. Or maybe a Lincoln."

"We can fight it, and we will," she told him. She slipped off to the side and quietly pulled something she'd spied earlier, a nice two-plus-foot length of metal pipe, from its spot on the ground. "We just have to improvise."

"Are you sure about this?" Oz asked dubiously.

Buffy hefted the pipe experimentally. "No."

"At least its forelegs are too short for it to grab at us," Oz offered.

"Somehow I'm just not comforted," Xander said in a ragged voice. "Look at those teeth—can't we get a bazooka?"

"No time," Buffy said. "And no time like the present." She took a deep breath to try and squeeze out her fear, then marched down the alleyway.

The T. Rex turned and saw them.

It was green and gold and, if it hadn't been equipped with all those teeth and a big dose of murderous intent, Buffy would have thought it was quite beautiful in a grand, special-effects movie sort of way. Its skin reminded her of a snake's but was more shimmery, like glitter beneath the glowing streetlights. She could only imagine what it would look like in the sunlight, perhaps as it moved through a jungle that hadn't existed for millions of years.

But all the pretty went out of the creature when there were no zoo bars or electric fences between it and them. The baby dinosaur was easily as tall as she was, and she wasn't going to even try to estimate its length. Its movements were fluid and sure; if there had ever been a resemblance to an awkwardly moving infant, it was long gone.

The eyes beneath the protruding ridges of bone on its skull were also gold and unnaturally bright, and Buffy thought they were shining with cunning and hunger as it swayed its head first one way then another. Long lines of drool seeped from beneath a row of bright white teeth—*baby teeth,* she realized—that hung over the heavy bottom jaw, and when she took a tentative step forward, the dinosaur snapped at the air. It might have been a warning, but Buffy thought it was much more likely the forerunner to an attack from the so far eerily silent monster. Whatever the demonic thing Giles had said was inside it—pure evil forces or an actual demon spirit—it was smart enough to keep the volume down.

Beside her Xander and Oz spread out, each hunting for weapons of their own but unable to come up with much beyond a couple of weak-looking two-by-fours. This was not going to be fun.

A tilt of its head, as if there were an abnormal decision-making thing going on inside that small, prehistoric brain—

And it leapt.

Buffy literally felt the ground tremble beneath her. Infant or not, the dinosaur was heavy, powerful, and *fast,* much more so than she'd expected. The flight instinct that welled up inside her was also much stronger than she'd ever faced, way beyond anything she'd ever felt while confronting a demon or a vampire.

"We can't let it get out of the alley!" she yelled, as much to reinforce herself as to remind Oz and Xander that while running might suddenly seem the best course of action, it was *not* an option. "I'll go for the head. You guys aim for the legs!"

"I'd settle for not letting it eat us!" Xander squeaked as it closed the distance in a frighteningly short flash of time.

Then it was right in front of them, lunging forward and growling, low and viciously. Xander and Oz went in opposite directions, each swinging as hard as he could at its meaty back legs while Buffy ducked under a bite that filled the air above her scalp with the dinosaur's foul-smelling breath and a spray of saliva.

"Might as well be trying to slap a cow's butt with a twig!" Xander exclaimed.

"Look out!" Oz yelled. "It's coming back around! Watch out for the tail—"

"Wha—" *Smack!* The ground fell away from Buffy, then came back with a dismaying return to reality as she landed hard on her left shoulder. Her upper right arm instantly began to throb nastily and a three-inch welt raised where the tip of the T. Rex's tail had cracked across it.

"Buffy, *move it!*" Xander yelled, his voice full of terror. She started to jump in response, but someone else was suddenly there—*Angel!*—grabbing her by the forearm and yanking her sideways so hard that her teeth clicked. A good thing, too; she felt the creature's snout brush her and got a triple dose of adrenaline that catapulted her sideways and fully out of range before its mouth shut where she'd just been. And still—not a sound other than that low, eerie grumble, as if the creature understood that, at least for right now, it had to be quiet in order to ensure its own safety. But that was impossible, wasn't it?

There was no time to ponder the thought. The dinosaur careened to the other side of the wide alley and rebounded off the wall there, leaving a shower of bricks and exposed mortar as it scrambled to keep its balance. Buffy pulled away from Angel and was after it in a heartbeat, but she still wasn't fast enough. Horrified, she realized it was going to reach the nearly defenseless Oz long before either she or Angel could get there and stop it. The T. Rex went into a sort of crouch and she saw Oz raise his two-by-four in a defiant fighting stance—

Desperate, Buffy swung her pipe as hard as she could against the side of a steel Dumpster next to her.

The noise was horrendous, like a cannonball landing on the roof of a metal building, piercing enough to

make Buffy's teeth vibrate and the infant dinosaur instinctively cower like a startled dog. It spun and bared
its teeth defensively, then took a lumbering step toward her, the prelude to another charge. She braced,
then forced herself to keep her eye on the creature
when a door to her left abruptly pushed open, spilling
a neat square of cool fluorescent light between her and
the T. Rex.

"What the—*hey!*" a man's voice cut in. Buffy allowed herself a split-second blink to look at the guy and
saw that he'd come out of the back of some unidentifi-
able storefront. Their unexpected visitor's voice ended
in nearly a scream as his eyes adjusted to the lower light
and he realized exactly what he was seeing. *"Get it
away from me!"* he shouted, trying to back-pedal.

Too late. The hapless man started to cry out again,
then the T. Rex's head shot forward and its jaws
snapped together. The guy's head and a good portion of
his shoulders disappeared as the dinosaur's razor-edged
teeth severed through bone and cartilage and it reared
back and started to lift its head to swallow its meal.

Oz wasn't one to let a diversion like this go to waste
and he dodged sideways in the opposite direction. He'd
taken no more than four steps when the tottering torso-
remains of what Buffy was determined was going to be
Baby Dino's last meal suddenly exploded into dust. At
the same time, a sharp puff of the familiar brown powder erupted from both sides of the creature's mouth; in
response, it threw its head forward and sneezed as
though it were no more dangerous than the family cat.

"Imagine that," Buffy heard Oz say as he put more
distance between him and the T. Rex.

"Not the method I normally reserve for vampires,"
Buffy observed, mentally noting to check the store later

for the vampire's handiwork. "But that works, too." Before the dinosaur could recover from its surprise, Buffy sprinted forward and leaped for the fire escape a few feet over its head.

"Buffy, are you *crazy?*" shrieked Xander, but the T. Rex had already seen her. She caught the rough metalwork one-handed and hung there for a single eternal second, saw both Xander and Oz rush in and whale at the T. Rex's hindquarters in an effort to pull its attention away from her. Angel stayed where he was, crouched and ready, perhaps, to place himself between her and it when the time was right. But her friends' ground attack was no good. Oz and Xander might as well have been mosquitoes dive-bombing the hide of an elephant for all the thing acknowledged their presence. The power inside it, that dark, driven intelligence, knew and recognized Buffy, wanted *her* so much that it never noticed Angel at all and barely looked backward at the other two teenagers.

But that glance downward, that *one* glance, was all Buffy needed. By the time the dinosaur brought its oversize head back up to face her, she was on the forward swing like a monkey in a tree—

—and she rammed the length of pipe into its eye and deep into its brain.

This time it did roar, a bellow of pain and rage that so far overshadowed her earlier whack against the Dumpster that her strength then seemed only pathetic now. Blood, lots of it, and shot through with streamers of abnormal light, pulsed out of the hole where its eye had been and only a few inches of the pipe was still visible. Enraged, the T. Rex dove for her yet couldn't see well enough to find its target. With both hands now free, Buffy clawed at the steel grid work of the stairs, but she didn't quite get her legs up in time to avoid getting cracked by the good side of the dinosaur's head. She took the blow on her side, then lost her grip and fell, rolling automatically and feeling the concrete burn away at her knees, elbows and palms. Weaponless, she was still right back on her feet, scanning the alley frantically. There was something a couple of yards to her right that might be useful, but—

She heard Angel growl as the baby T. Rex leaned toward her and roared again, but the dinosaur's sound ended in midnote and its remaining glowing eye burned a sudden, hot white-gold, the surge of a life force fighting to keep itself going. The possessed creature took a single, shuddering step forward, then collapsed in the middle of the alley as the light in its eye fizzled out.

Silence.

The four of them inched toward it, and Angel gave a cautious prod at one of the dinosaur's hind legs with the toe of his shoe. Nothing moved or twitched. "Dead," he said simply.

"I like a good joke as much as the next clown," Xander said in a wheezy voice, "but I just can't think of any right now."

"Not seeing the humor either," Oz said.

Both guys were still gripping their two-by-fours, but the pipe Buffy had used was completely inside the T. Rex's skull, driven the rest of the way by its own crash to the ground. "Okay," she said, and was surprised to realize she was panting, proof of the fear she hadn't allowed herself to acknowledge. "Angel's right. It's dead. I . . . think."

"Can a demon-infested T. Rex play possum?" Xander asked, staring down at it.

"I'm going to guess not," Oz answered.

"Is this a demon or a dinosaur?" Angel asked, puzzled. "Dinosaurs don't exist anymore."

For a moment Buffy actually seemed amused. "Of course they don't. Neither do vampires, demons, shapeshifters, or any of the other nasties here on the Hellmouth."

Xander shuddered as they studied it for a few more seconds. "Doesn't look like it's going to go 'poof' and disappear, does it?"

"Ditto," said Oz.

"We'll drag it over there," Buffy said decisively and pointed to a relatively empty spot between a high pile of broken wooden pallets and a half-dozen garbage cans. "Maybe Giles can think of something and we'll just come back later and deal with it then." Angel and the other two looked at her doubtfully, but she sucked in her breath and gamely wrapped her bruised and bloodied hands around one of the baby dinosaur's heavy-boned ankles. The skin felt clammy and warm, totally gross. "Gag me," she muttered.

Xander and Oz nervously grabbed the other ankle and Angel took hold of its tail, and, grimacing, they began hauling the creature toward the area Buffy had chosen. There was nothing light about the T. Rex and they found themselves dragging a good three hundred or so pounds down the pavement. "Too bad this thing isn't edible," Xander huffed. "Feed a lot of mouths on this sucker!"

"Who says it isn't?" Oz asked blandly.

"Ewww?" Buffy pointed out.

"Kidding," he said.

"Let's hide this thing as best we can, then head for the library," she said. "Bring Giles up to speed and see if there's something in those books of his to give us a clue."

"I'm supposed to be at the Bronze with Devon to

talk to Alysa Bardrick," Oz said. "I'll meet you there after?"

Buffy nodded. "Cool. And anyway, we should make sure the other forces o'night around here aren't out of control." After a few more uncomfortable minutes of jostling, shoving and grunting, at last they had the small, dead dinosaur jammed as far out of sight as they could manage.

"You know," Oz commented as they finished, "I could swear this thing was, like, trying to *go* somewhere."

Buffy raised an eyebrow. "What makes you say that?"

He shrugged. "The way it moved . . . just a feeling, I guess. Animal instinct."

"How about guessing what we're going to do if someone finds this thing before we figure out how to get rid of it?" Xander demanded as he wiped sweat off his forehead. "How the hell are we going to explain it?"

"We aren't," Buffy said flatly. She gestured at them to follow her and they headed quickly out of the alley. "We won't be here to worry about it."

Angel looked at her, then back at where they'd stashed the dead mini-dinosaur. "I assume you're going to tell me what's going on."

"Of course."

"Later," she heard Oz say. She glanced over and saw him head out. After a moment, the three of them did the same, their task a stroll-patrol while Oz turned toward the Bronze. For once, Xander was quiet, and Buffy smiled a little, wondering if he was going over their dino-battle and thinking longingly of the bazookas at the Armory.

"So what—" Angel began.

"In a minute," she said quietly as Xander drifted a few yards ahead. "First . . . I hear you've met the new band manager."

Angel shrugged, but didn't say anything. Typical.

"I was getting the lowdown on her from Willow," she continued. "Seems kind of . . . strange, the way she wants to get everyone in on it, don't you think?"

Another noncommittal shrug.

"I mean, why would she, you know? Unless she was involved in something else."

Still nothing. Buffy tried again.

"You know, I've heard stories about people being sold and stuff across the border—"

"I get the hint, Buffy," Angel said. "I'll ask around."

Buffy smiled.

"Giles, what's the matter with it?" Willow cried as she backed hastily to the other side of the library table. "Is the cage going to hold?"

"Get back!" Giles poked again through the mesh of the steel door holding the Timimus at bay, intentionally jabbing the metal tip of his fencing sword into the flesh of the dinosaur's left shoulder. It screamed in anger— *screeeee! screeeee!*—and didn't calm down at all, but at least it backed away from the door, momentarily abandoning its sudden assault.

"Maybe it's hungry," Willow suggested nervously. "Maybe we should feed it." The beast's eyes—windows to the soul?—were lit so brilliantly they looked like circles of red-gold fire.

"Somehow I don't think doing something that's likely to increase its energy level *and* size is really the answer to our dilemma," Giles said as he stared at the dinosaur. "Despite a lack of sustenance, its demon force seems to be making it grow quite rapidly."

"But maybe it's angry because it hasn't eaten," Willow said. "We could get some lettuce and carrots from the cafeteria—"

"I really don't believe it's a vegetarian, do you?"

Willow swallowed. "Well, no bunnies or rats, or . . . whatever. That's all I'm saying."

"No *anything*. It doesn't need our help." Giles paused. "It appears to have calmed down a bit, don't you think?"

"Only if you can consider spastic snarling calm." Willow stared at it thoughtfully. "You know, it really did seem ticked off. And look at its eyes—don't they look a whole lot brighter than before?"

"Yes," Giles agreed, peering at the creature. "I believe you're right." He studied it for another moment, then frowned. "Quite so. . . ."

"What?" she asked as he folded his arms. "Why do you have that frowny face? Frowny faces aren't good. Especially on you."

"I'm just . . . concerned, that's all." The librarian's eyes narrowed in concentration. "Increased aggression, the brightness of its eyes, the unaccountable growth. We've assumed there's a demonic presence involved, of course, but I just hope it's not psychically linked to something else over which we have no control."

"Like . . . *another* dinosaur?" Willow shuddered.

"We need to research this some more," Giles said instead of answering. He tapped his chin distractedly. "There are some much older books I haven't checked yet. I thought they were out of date, but—"

"I don't think evil gets old," Willow said. "It just gets more experienced."

"Unfortunately that's all too true," Giles agreed. He

backed away from the cage, then went behind the counter and began rummaging. After a few minutes he stood, holding up a book and wiping away a smudge of dust on one cheek. The Timimus had finally stopped its screaming . . . for now. Instead of pacing, it crouched quietly a few feet from the door and watched them with those dreadfully radiant eyes. "Here's a start," Giles said triumphantly. "I've been trying to find a connection between dinosaurs and demons and coming up blank. Perhaps, however, the bridge is something that resembles both, such as a dragon."

"Let me see that," Willow said and reached over the counter for the book. When he gave it to her, she thumbed quickly through it, then went back to the computer. "No—wait. It's just another reference to Ladon, that Greek thing you were talking about."

"Then there has to be more," Giles said. Willow saw him disappear below the countertop once more and heard scraping and bumping as he moved things around, and a quiet double sneeze courtesy of the dust he was stirring up. "Perhaps in here," he said as he stood again. "I haven't thought of this volume in months." The book he grasped this time was even older than the previous one, its indigo-dyed leather cover held together by frayed and ancient straps. But when he scanned through the first few pages, he only looked more puzzled. "This refers to Ladon as something else again," he said. "It says Ladon is a dragon demon 'which has been trying for millennia to get all four of its spirits into four suitable hosts on earth.' "

"Better four than a hundred," Willow said brightly.

"Four is more than enough," Giles reminded her as he scowled at the book in his hands. "We need to put serious effort toward discovering exactly what we're dealing with here and how disastrous the results might be, preferably before morning. I'm starting to suspect something far worse than we thought, and I would much prefer us to solve it on paper before Buffy, Oz, and Xander find themselves dealing with it in the flesh."

Chapter 10

"DUDE, YOU LOOK LIKE YOU GOT DRAGGED DOWN THE road by a pack of dirty wild dogs," Devon said.

"Might as well have," Oz mumbled, but thankfully Devon didn't hear him above the group playing on the stage and the babble of voices in the Bronze. If only the singer had any idea. Oz ran a hand idly through his spiky hair, then found his palm filled with grit and a few splinters left over from the two-by-four he'd been swinging in the alley. Good thing it was dark in here. He knew he should clean up before Alysa Bardrick got here for their meeting, one which Oz wasn't even sure he wanted to attend anymore.

Tired, still feeling the effects of the back-alley battle, Oz let himself drop onto a chair for a moment. Decisions, decisions. A day or two ago it had all seemed so black and white. Now someone had gone and thrown his life into that 256-shades-of-gray mode and he was trying to find the answer somewhere between the tones.

"So what's the word?" Devon asked, grabbing a chair and spinning it around to where he could face Oz. "You think we ought to sign up with this woman?"

"I haven't decided yet," Oz answered honestly. "This could change everything. We'd probably have to quit school, pack it up and head to L.A. Mondo-chango influence, man."

Devon winced. "Drop out? Man, my parents would entirely freak. Why can't we just keep on doing it like we are—weekends and stuff, except have her arrange the gigs?"

Oz rubbed his knuckles thoughtfully, finding a dozen skinned places. "I'm thinking Alysa's going to want an all or nothing deal."

Devon frowned, then his gaze cut over Oz's shoulder. "Well, here she comes. I guess it's time we find out."

Oz turned and saw Alysa picking her way through the jumble of people, tables and chairs. She wore another sleek black outfit, this time a slightly shimmery pantsuit and long jacket, probably made by some designer that Cordelia could have named in an instant. When Alysa saw them watching her, she smiled a greeting but Oz could tell by the way this one, like her previous ones, didn't reach her eyes that she was all business, no emotional involvement with the clients. She had about as much warmth as the heavily industrial song being played by the band on stage tonight.

"Good evening," she said as she reached them. There was another chair at the table but she ignored it, seeming to prefer a power stance in front of them. She definitely liked being in charge. "I liked what I heard last night, so I've brought the contracts," she said and slid a leather-covered folder onto the table. "The one for Dingoes covers all the band members for a four-year term.

There are separate ones for Xander and Willow, and I included one for Angel in case you can convince him to change his mind. I had to leave their last names blank, but they can fill them in."

Devon blinked at her uncertainly as Oz watched her pull out a meticulously neat pile of paperwork. Four years? And Willow, Angel and Xander . . . a contract for a roadie? He'd never heard of such a thing. "The rest of the gang isn't around right now," Oz said slowly. "I guess we didn't realize you'd be bringing this stuff. They didn't know they should be here."

Alysa nodded. "Well, I thought I'd include it in case they were. But their parts can wait. Here's the band contract." She pushed a stapled stack of papers toward him and reached into her purse for a pen. "We can get that signed—page eight—and out of the way tonight."

Oz sat back. "Actually, we can't."

Alysa's eyes darkened although she managed to keep her expression pleasant. "Is there a problem?"

Oz glanced at Devon, willing him to be silent. "Just that we haven't had a chance to talk to Mitch about any of this, and since he's an equal part of the band, we can't decide for him."

Alysa's eyebrows raised. "Mitch? Who's that?"

"He writes all the lyrics for the songs," Oz said smoothly. "Doesn't play anything, so that's why you've never seen him on stage with us."

Alysa frowned. "May I ask why you haven't mentioned this before?"

Oz shrugged, while Devon kept carefully quiet. "Like I said, we didn't know you'd be bringing contracts. Mitch is on vacation with his parents. Cancun or something."

Alysa blinked slowly, like a cat sleepily considering

the next best way to deal with a troublesome mouse. "Cancun. In the middle of a school semester."

Devon leaned forward and shrugged carelessly. "Rich people," he said. "They kind of go when and where they want."

Their wannabe band manager pressed her lips together, as though holding back a sarcastic comment. Instead, she leaned over and swept up the contracts, then tucked them back into the folder with her pen. "All right. But I'll tell you right now that we need to wrap this up by tomorrow afternoon. I don't have any more time to invest in this without knowing I'm going to get a return on it."

"He won't be back in town until late tomorrow night," Oz said blandly, despite the warning bells in his head.

This time he saw Alysa outright scowl before she dropped a mask over the expression. "All right," she said again. "Monday then. But it'll have to be during the day."

Oz considered this. "Can you come to Sunnydale High? I could meet you after school. In the library— that'd be cool."

She paused, then nodded. "Fine. *But,*" Alysa added as she tucked the folder beneath one arm and spun on her heel, "that's absolutely the end of your time limit." She stared at the two of them for a moment, then her gaze slid to the stage area, where a group called Broken Mirror was pounding out rock 'n' roll with an overly heavy hand on the bass. Oz didn't really think they were that great. "You know, Saturday night is the prime spot," she said casually. "Extremely well paid. Did you know Broken Mirror is one of my clients? A month from now it could be Dingoes up there instead of them." She gave them a final sharklike smile.

Oz and Devon sat there for a few minutes and considered this, watching as she strode out of the Bronze. There was a briskness to her walk, an *anger*, that hadn't been there when she'd first come in. They'd ticked her off by yanking away the band reins and putting them into the hands of someone she'd never met.

And never will.

"Mitch?" Devon asked now. "So what the hell was *that?*"

Oz stood and pushed the chair away, kind of enjoying the scraping sound it made across the beat-up floor. It made him feel reconnected to solid earth. "A stall," he told Devon. "A phantom writer to give us a little more time to think about what it is we're getting into, and just how deep we want to go."

Willow hugged herself and listened in dismay as Oz gave her and Giles a rundown about the T. Rex that he, Buffy and Xander had killed in the alley by the Bronze. "Buffy said she'd come by and tell you everything," he said to Giles, "but we haven't had a chance to talk to either Kevin or Daniel yet. She and Angel are probably still on patrol. I was ... done sooner than I thought. Did you guys find out any info?"

Willow shook her head tiredly. "Not much. A couple of references to ancient mythology and dragons, but nothing we can pinpoint yet."

"We're still searching," Giles said, and inclined his chin toward another stack of waiting books. "It's just a matter of time."

Willow nodded in agreement, then studied Oz. "Anything else?"

"Not on the dinosaur scene," he said. He glanced at Giles, but the librarian had **already tur**ned back to his demonology books. When **he** spoke again, he'd dropped his voice to where only she could hear. "But we did have that meeting with Alysa Bardrick." He went on to fill her in.

"Wow," Willow marveled afterward. "She wants *everyone* to sign contracts? She sure wants to move, like . . . *fast*. And legal. What did you do?"

"Stalled," Oz told her. "I said we had to talk to someone else and I wouldn't be able to tell her anything until Monday afternoon. She's going to come by here."

Willow thought about this. "Here at the library? Do you think that's a good idea? I mean, what with the Timimus . . . ?"

"At least it'll give us a few more days to think it over," Oz said. "We can get this whole dino-deal out of the way and do something about that Timimus."

She chewed her bottom lip for a second and stared at the computer. "You know," she said softly, "why don't I do a little digging around?"

Oz looked at her speculatively. "On Alysa?"

Willow nodded. "I'm demon-researching, but I can do the Alysa hunt in a couple of sub-windows, see what I can see."

He nodded. "Yeah, maybe that's a good idea." She could hear the exhaustion in his voice when he continued. "I'm gonna head home and get some shut-eye. If you're here when Buffy comes by, tell her I'll meet her early in the morning and we'll head over to Kevin's, see if we can find out just what he and Daniel have been conjuring up."

Conjuring, Willow thought. Interesting choice of words, and not something that should be done if a person—an amateur—didn't know exactly what they were doing. "All right." She saw Oz glance over at Giles again, but the older man was deeply absorbed in his books. Her boyfriend gave her a little grin, then leaned over and kissed her, ever so quick, on the lips before leaving.

She sat staring after him for a little while longer, then set a couple of power searches going in the background while she mulled over the whole conjuring thing and thought again about Kevin and Daniel. As with so much of what spewed out of Sunnydale, there was undeniably something magical at work in this, but it was dark and ugly and ought to have been cut off at the neck a long, long time ago.

By the time Buffy and Angel made it to the library, Willow had gone home and only Giles remained, burning the proverbial candle over his musty old books. He barely acknowledged them as they pushed through the library doors.

"Nice to see you all were concerned about my welfare," Buffy said. "Being as the main foe tonight had an appetite a bit larger than the average bloodsucker."

Giles didn't look up. "Oz was here," he said. "He told us all about it."

Buffy looked around. "Xander was dead on his feet. We sent him home. Willow—"

"Went home," Giles told her, finally raising his nose from whatever he was reading. "And Oz said he'd meet you in the morning to go talk to Kevin Sanderson. How was patrol?"

"Amazingly vamp-free," Buffy told him and looked at Angel. "We're thinking the word's out that something bigger's visiting and sees them as fair game for dinner."

"Ah." Giles finally seemed interested. "So whatever is behind all this is something quite intimidating."

"You still don't know?" Buffy demanded.

"No. But we have to be getting closer."

Angel raised one eyebrow. "Why is that?"

Giles looked at them both grimly. "Because, quite frankly, we're running out of places to look."

"Hey, man. It's Devon."

Oz squinted at the telephone, then glanced at the clock. He was going to get up in another half-hour anyway, but a call from the singer at six in the morning? His first impulse was to ask "Who are you and what have you done with Devon?" Instead he scrubbed at the sleep in his eyes and asked, "What's up?"

Either Devon was wired from being up all night, or he was majorly pissed about something. The answer came in only a few more words. "You remember that Friday–Saturday gig we had set up in Newport next weekend? The high-dollar one we've been waiting on for three months?" Devon ground his teeth. "Well, we lost it."

Oz frowned. "Lost it how?"

"I called the club manager last night to double-check on their speaker setup, see if we needed to add anything to their equipment list. He said he was going to call me today and cancel anyway, because he'd lined up a different band, said it was some 'hot little outfit called Shy.' "

"Hold it," Oz said. "Didn't he sign our contract?"

"Yeah, and I called him on it!" Oz could picture Devon waving his hands in the air. "Basically, he said too damned bad. He'd gotten the offer from Shy's manager late last night and he took it. The jerk told me to go hire a lawyer. Hell, he knows we don't have deep enough pockets for that kind of stuff."

Oz's eyes narrowed in the predawn darkness. An offer late Saturday night? He'd bet anything—

"Did he say who Shy's manager is?"

"Oh yeah," Devon said. "Wouldn't you know it? Alysa Bardrick." He was silent for a moment. "What I can't decide is did she step in here to push her own client, or did she do this because she found out it was us who had the booking for that date?"

Oz didn't answer, but he was pretty sure that both he and Devon knew the answer to that one.

No bright California sun this time; Sunday A.M. was overcast and chilly, even though it probably never would get around to really raining. Buffy hugged herself beneath her sweater, then glanced at Oz; he looked as tired as she felt—dark circles under his eyes, a smattering of bruises here and there. Still, he gave her a hopeful grin when he caught her eye. "So, do you think it's too early?" she asked.

Oz shook his head. "Nah. Those eager student types—they're always up at the crack of dawn. Even if Kevin's not awake, his parents probably are. We'll just try looking pathetic and desperate enough so they're willing to wake him up."

Buffy chuckled. Desperate for class notes? Notes, not, but they definitely had the desperate part down. And getting more so by the hour. "Got it."

This morning Kevin Sanderson's house seemed gloomier than it had on their previous visit, the yellow brick darker and more subdued, the row of bushes more like a mini-wall than ornamentation. Even the empty hanging baskets were wrong somehow, as though something—even plastic blooms—should have been stuffed in them to create an illusion of cheerfulness. The whole effect made Buffy shiver again, compounding the grayness of the day and making her wish even harder for sunshine.

And when Oz knocked, Buffy knew right away that they were off to a bad start by the way the footsteps inside pounded hurriedly toward the entrance.

Mrs. Sanderson yanked open the front door. The look on her face was full of hope, then her expression immediately crashed when she saw it was them. "Oh!" she said. "I'm—I'm sorry. I thought it would be my son."

Buffy stepped forward. "Kevin's not home? Do you know where he is?"

Mrs. Sanderson shook her head as her husband moved into place behind her. Mr. Sanderson looked much more haggard than his wife and Buffy recalled her comments yesterday about his feeble health. His weaker constitution was obviously standing up poorly against the stressful situation. "He didn't come home last night," Kevin's father rasped. "A Saturday night, a teenage boy . . . we expected him to be late. But he's never stayed out all night before without calling."

"He's not that kind of boy," Mrs. Sanderson added, and Buffy wondered if she was telling them that, or reminding herself and her husband. "We got the number for Daniel Addison from information, but no one answers." She looked at her husband, her eyes wide and filled with fright. "No one's answered all *night.*"

Mr. Sanderson stared at the floor for a second, then lifted his head. His eyes were reddened and sunk deep into his skull. "Maybe they got involved in some paleontology project and lost track of the time," he suggested. "They probably decided not to wake us up by calling really late. After being up half the night, they probably slept in." The older man looked at his watch. "But if he's not home by noon, I'm calling the police," he said decisively.

"Oh, surely it won't come to that," Mrs. Sanderson

protested. "You know how Kev gets overwhelmed by anything to do with dinosaurs. More than likely, it's just a new project." She glanced at Buffy and Oz, and Buffy could tell the woman was looking for support.

"Overwhelmed," Buffy said. "Yeah, that's probably it."

Oz looked at her sharply, then gave the Sandersons a pleasant nod. "Well, we'll check back with you later," he offered.

"Okay," Mrs. Sanderson replied, a little too brightly. "You do that, and when he gets home, I'll tell him you came by. Oz, wasn't it?"

Oz nodded. "Yeah, that's me."

The older woman nodded her head jerkily. "You two just can't seem to get together with my Kevin, can you?"

"Oh, we will," Buffy assured her as she and Oz turned and headed off. "Sooner or later . . . we'll catch up with him."

"So," Oz said when they were out of earshot and they'd seen the front door of the Sanderson house close, "what do you think? Vamp attack?"

"I don't know," Buffy admitted. They made their way back to Oz's van slowly, neither really knowing where to go next. "A lot of people here in Sunnydale have a sort of . . . *feel* for what goes on behind the scenes. I mean, most don't go walking around outside by themselves at night just because they kind of instinctively know they shouldn't. Kevin's so new . . . maybe he doesn't have the Sunnydale safety radar yet. I guess it could have gone down that way." But with everything that had happened, she wasn't really convinced and she was sure Oz wasn't either.

Oz nodded. "Or he could be at the museum," he suggested. "His parents said there's no answer at Daniel's, and we didn't try the museum last night. Why don't we give it a shot this morning? It'll be open by ten."

Buffy nodded, then squinted unhappily at the sky. "Jeez, with these clouds it could be ten or it could be four. Yuck. I'd much rather have the sunshine."

Oz nodded. "In Sunnydale, sunshine is definitely an advantage."

"Yeah," Buffy agreed, and shot a final, glum look overhead. "Let's just hope it's shining on the museum by the time we get there."

"Am I right in detecting a really overwhelming sense of big-time screw-up here?" Buffy asked Oz under her breath as he pulled over to the curb and cut the engine.

The grounds in front of the Sunnydale Museum of Natural History, usually so spacious and uncrowded, seemed to be filled with people. All of them were of that same not-good variety who tended to wield, where they weren't pointing television videos and cameras at everything, guns, badges, and billy clubs. Added to that were several police cars with flashing lights, an ambulance that hadn't bothered to turn its lights on at all, and the most dreaded minivan of all—the one with the circular words SUNNYDALE COUNTY MEDICAL EXAMINER stenciled on each side.

"Oh, yeah," Oz whispered back. "Definitely in the big bad domain. Now what?"

"Now we get closer," Buffy decided. "Keep our mouths shut and do the 'little pitchers with big ears' thing."

Oz scowled. "Always hated that saying."

"Me, too. Come on." They climbed out of the van and Buffy led the way around the worst of the crowd with Oz right behind her, deftly avoiding the cameras and looking like nothing more than a couple of curious teenagers. She paused now and then, gazing off into space and going for the airheaded blond look that nearly guaranteed no one would pay attention to her and her companion. It didn't take long for them to work their way up toward the front, not far from where several police officers and a couple of white-suited techs milled around the morgue van as if they had nothing better to do. The back doors were open and Buffy could see a mound inside covered by a sheet that was splotched with dark circles, spots that looked black in the shadowy interior.

Rather than linger like vultures, the two drifted away from the opened doors and closer to the knot of city personnel, straining to hear anything they could. As they did, Buffy saw one of the techs climb back inside the van and retrieve a plastic bag, then return with it to talk to one of the cops.

"His I.D.'s in here," the tech said. When the officer looked pointedly at the bloody contents and made no move to take the bag, the tech shrugged and split it open with gloved hands. He dug around in it for a few seconds, then brought out a fabric wallet splattered with plenty of red. Buffy couldn't help flinching at the unexpected ripping sound when the tech pulled apart the velcro-bound flaps and peered at what was inside. "Couldn't tell it by what's left," the tech told the policeman with a grimace, "but according to this he's not much more than a kid—only twenty-two years old. Says his name is Daniel Addison."

Oz's face went white as Buffy sucked in a lungful of air and whispered "Uh-oh."

The cop who'd refused Daniel's personal effects looked over at them and frowned faintly. Buffy made a show of appearing vacant and twirling the end of a lock of her hair, and after a second, he returned his attention to the tech. "Any idea what happened in there?"

The white-jacketed guy shrugged. "Not a clue. My first guess would be some kind of animal, but this is a museum, not a zoo. Everything in there is already dead and stuffed. This has gotta be the work of a psycho or something—wouldn't be the first one in this town."

A second cop pulled a notebook out of his pocket and began scribbling in it. "That's certainly true," he said. Buffy thought she caught a note of disgust in his voice as he looked around at the reporters just now starting to pack up and leave. "And you know by twelve o'clock this'll be all over the afternoon news." He exhaled. "Give me the kid's address off of that I.D., would you? I don't know what he was into or what he was doing in the museum, but I guess we're the lucky ones who get to hunt down his next of kin before they find out on the tube that he got famous."

Chapter 11

"Okay," Oz said. "We've been hanging here for nearly two hours, waiting for everyone to leave, and we've tried calling Giles three times with no luck. I think this is about as good as it's going to get." He peered around the corner of the museum. "They've got a sign on the front door that says it's closed for the day," he told Buffy. "But there are still people going in and out. If we want to get in there without tripping an alarm, we need to do it now, before the rest of the cleanup crew leaves and powers up the security system."

"No time like the now time," Buffy muttered.

He saw her glance down the long side of the building, then he spied a recessed doorway, almost invisible behind a Dumpster. "How about over there?" he suggested.

"The garbage exit," Buffy said with pseudo-brightness as they hurried over to it. "Always my favorite option." Nevertheless, she wrapped one hand around the knob and turned it experimentally; it was locked, of course. She gave a final, quick look around, then twisted hard. There was the faint sound of metal bending inside the mechanism, then the steel-plated door obligingly swung outward.

"At least it's quiet," Oz said. "In the horror movies, the doors always squeal." Buffy shot him a don't-go-there look and he shrugged. "Trivia."

"I can do without, thank you," she said. She motioned him to stay put, then slipped inside the square of darkness. After a second she poked her head back out and waved at him to follow. "All clear."

He decided it wasn't wise to remind her that they said that a lot in the movies, too, usually before some drooling monster leaped out and began slashing at the bubble-brained blond. Instead he stepped through the doorway and carefully drew it shut behind them, making sure it didn't drift open again on its own. If the security force engaged the alarm system, would the broken lock show up on their computer? Nothing to be done about that now.

Buffy had been right. This was some kind of maintenance area at the back of the museum, full of trash bins and boxes, piles of cardboard and papers stacked and tied for future recycling. Off to one side was a trash compactor and the room smelled of overripe fruit and vaguely rotten vegetables—the lingering scent of a thousand discarded meals from the small cafeteria Oz remembered was on the second floor. He followed Buffy as she hunted around the room until she found the way out. No lock here, he noted, but who wanted to break into the trash room, anyway?

But the hallway outside was another matter. While it was dimly lit, they had to back up and push themselves against the wall when they realized it led directly to the main foyer and the front entrance beyond that—the same entrance that was being closed up, as they watched, by one of the museum's security guards.

"How many guards do you think they have?" Oz whispered.

Buffy shook her head. "It's a big place. They could be cheap and have one . . . or they could have as many as two per floor."

"So how are we going to find our way around here? We can't exactly ask for information."

Buffy considered this, her gaze tracking the guard as he walked to a desk at the front left corner of the foyer, the one where tours and school field trips went to check in. "There," she said, pointing.

Oz nodded and they watched the uniformed man pick up a clipboard and make a couple of notations on it, check his watch, then drop the clipboard and head down the hallway. When he was out of sight, Oz crept forward and slipped behind the desk as Buffy kept watch at the juncture of the main foyer and the hall down which the security guard had vanished; half a minute later, Oz hurried back to meet her, a blue plastic notebook clutched in one hand.

"Floor plans," he announced with a grin.

Buffy pointed to one of the restrooms a few feet away; they zipped over to it and ducked inside. "Let's scan through this, see if we can figure out where Daniel Addison's office or desk might be."

"I remember one of the cops outside mentioning a lab on the third floor," Oz said. "Why else would they be talking about it if it's not where Daniel was found?"

Buffy nodded and flipped through the pages in the notebook until she found what she was hunting for. "All right," she said, marking out her thoughts with a finger as she talked. "We duck out of here and go for the stairs right behind the guard's desk. Watch out for him, because he might already be on his way back. Up to the third floor, and when we come out, go straight until about halfway down the hall, then turn left. That should lead us right into the lab area." The lighting in the bathroom was low, down to little more than emergency night levels. She squinted at the page. "I can't tell if it's a locked area or not, but I'm betting it is. Whatever it is, we'll deal. Let's go."

Crouching behind her, Oz waited while she pushed open the door of the restroom just enough to make sure the guard wasn't around, then they hustled out and hugged the wall. As they scurried along the hall and up the wide staircase, always on the lookout, Oz couldn't decide if he felt like a convict trying to escape, a mouse avoiding a cat, or a spy in one of the James Bond movies that seemed to be so plentiful inside Xander's brain nowadays. He wished he had something like that going on inside his own brain right now. The fantasy world of high-tech espionage seemed truly preferable to the words that kept running through his mind. . . .

. . . *I guess we're the lucky ones who get to hunt down his next of kin before they find out on the tube that he got famous,* uttered by the cop outside who at this very moment was likely delivering the horrible news to relatives of the late Daniel Addison. Who would that be—mother and father? A fiancée? This, of course, made another question scream inside his head: Where was Kevin Sanderson? Was he dead, too? If he was, it was solely because he'd followed someone who'd promised, among other things, to show him the way to something he wanted more than anything else in the world. While Oz knew nothing about the goals of budding paleontologists, it wasn't hard to equate this with his own desires about Dingoes; from there, it was just a step over to the black and white signature block being pushed by the hard-nosed Alysa Bardrick.

Despite the high stress level trying to distract his thoughts, the trek to the third floor was easy enough. Perhaps there really was only one guard for the entire museum or, at best, two. Two made more sense because it would give each man some cover to take needed breaks, plus split up the not inconsiderable job of inspecting all three floors, not to mention there was probably at least one level of basement storage running beneath the building. They'd have to be careful not to get tripped up and find themselves watching one guy walk away but not realizing another had just stepped in place behind them.

"There," Buffy said suddenly. They'd just come out of the stairway and, after checking, started down the hallway; even though her voice was barely above a whisper, the heavy silence of the building made it sound huge in his ears. "See the crime tape? That has to be it."

He nodded and they ducked between the strips of black and yellow plastic crisscrossing the open doorway. Crime scene or not, this wasn't like on television; someone had already been dispatched to wipe away at least the worst of the blood and gore. It'd been a hurried job, though, and they could see splatters here and there, smeared circles where the rag hadn't been rinsed enough, thick, unpleasant-looking droplets hanging off the edges of some of the metal lab tables. There was way too much stuff in here for a rush cleaning crew to tackle and do a decent job of it. Oz and Buffy stepped carefully, avoiding still damp areas of the floor as Buffy inspected everything.

"What are we looking for?" Oz asked in a low voice.

Buffy shrugged. "Beats me. But I'll know it when I see it."

He shot a glance over his shoulder, trying to estimate when the guard would make his next rounds. "Well, we need to— Hey, look," he said suddenly. "The biggest piece of evidence and everyone missed it because they didn't know what it was."

Buffy leaned forward. "What is it?"

"Eggs," Oz said softly. *"Hatched* eggs." He paused for a second, and when he spoke again his voice was shaking slightly. "I think we could be in Big Trouble City here."

She still couldn't quite see what Oz was indicating because of the shadows cast by the dim lighting. "Why?"

He turned to face her, then stepped to the side. Finally she could see the ruins of a small cage behind him, metal bars that looked strong and sturdy bent aside and twisted like they'd been nothing tougher than picture wire. "Because," he whispered, "there are *three* of them!"

For a few, overlong seconds, he could tell that Buffy wasn't able to process this. Three eggs ... but they'd killed one infant dinosaur in the alley by the Bronze, and they had one locked up at the library with Giles. That ought to leave just—the unidentified creature that had obviously killed Daniel Addison. They hadn't expected it to be easy, but Oz was about to break worse news.

"Look closer," he said urgently. "These shells are all from the same kind of egg—they were overlapped in the fossil base. That means they're all the same kind of dinosaur." His eyes were wide. *"Two* more, Buff. Probably both like the one we fought outside the Bronze. Two more like the T. Rex."

She started to protest, then he saw by her face that she realized he was right. The Timimus at the library was different, older than these other ones by several days. It must've been the first experiment by Kevin and Daniel, the prototype. When their efforts had succeeded and the creature had escaped, they'd gone for bigger and better results. Boy, had they ever.

Oz cleared his throat as quietly as he could. "Now what?"

But Buffy still looked as stunned as he felt. "I'm not . . . sure," she admitted. "It can't still be in here, can it? I mean, the place was infested with authority earlier. They probably searched it from roof to basement. It worries me that we don't know where Kevin is, but maybe Daniel decided to do this experiment without him. For all we know, he could already be at home." She bit her lower lip thoughtfully. "Let's find a phone," she said finally. "Maybe off in one of the lounges or something, and then try Giles again. See if he and the others have come up with anything since yesterday."

Oz nodded and they began to pick their way out of the laboratory area. They were only a few steps from the doorway when something caught Oz's eye, a notebook set on top of a pile of others. The place was so full of binders, journals, and more notebooks that it wasn't surprising the cops hadn't noticed it. "Wait," he said. He snatched it up and flipped through it to make sure. "This is Kevin's," he told Buffy. "I remember him writing in it in class."

"Is there anything useful in it?" she asked. "Like whatever gave him the oh-so-brilliant idea of bringing a dinosaur back from the extinct?"

"Oh, I think it's pretty clear where that idea came from," Oz muttered.

"Daniel Addison."

"Yeah." He scanned the pages anyway, going for the

last of the entries. "The question is, where did *he* get it?"

Buffy opened her mouth to say something, then Oz saw her tense. "Guard!" she suddenly whispered.

Oz shoved the notebook into the oversize pocket of his shirt, then darted between two of the lab tables, pushing himself as far back and down into the darkness as he could, hoping it was enough. Buffy went for an alcove at the side of a double line of shelves loaded with specimen jars and labeled bits of fossilized bone. He knew they mustn't get caught here. It would raise too many questions they wouldn't be able to answer, not to mention tie them up in endless hours of bureaucratic baloney. In the meantime, somewhere out there wasn't one, but *two* dinosaurs, and if the evidence left behind in the mini-nest was to be believed, they were, as he had said, looking at two more T. Rex babies.

Footsteps, growing in Oz's hearing, the kiss of rubber soles against the tiled flooring, the step of a man with nothing to hide and very little to worry about—except as he neared the lab. A terrible crime had been discovered here earlier, and so of course he would check this area a little more closely. But would he cross the crime tape, violate the edict of the police to get a close-up fix for his curiosity?

The footsteps stopped and Oz could hear the man's breathing, little bellows of tense air just outside the doorway as the beam of a flashlight shone inside, then danced around the far reaches of the room. The guy outside sounded a little breathless and heavy, not at all in top shape, but did he see something interesting? Something *irresistible?* Was he willing to limbo himself through the barrier in front of the door?

Another twenty, then thirty seconds, but . . . no. The

footsteps picked up again and continued down the hallway, finally fading away altogether. If Oz was remembering Buffy's description of the floor plan correctly, this meant the guard would turn right and go through the Director's Gallery, then he could either examine the huge chunk of space dedicated to North American mammals and the smaller section covering marine life, or just turn right again and head down the stairs past those two areas. Unless he had to check the Chaparral first, in which case he'd end up going down the same staircase Oz and Buffy had climbed to get up to the lab. It was going to be tricky to get out of here.

He still had the floor plan notebook and Oz glanced at it now to make sure he was pinpointing their position on the third floor. Got it. If they came out of the lab and turned left, the way that the guard had gone, they'd find the entrance to another restroom and lounge. Maybe Buffy was right and there would be a phone inside it, a public pay thing that wouldn't set off a light somewhere on a guard's console. He could keep a lookout while she was doing that, and he'd go through Kevin's notebook some more to see if he could find the core thing that had started this entire Cretaceous mess.

When they were absolutely sure the security guard had moved on, Buffy motioned at Oz to follow her and they scurried out of the laboratory and made for the lounge right next to it.

When the telephone rang, Giles knew it couldn't be anyone else but Buffy or one of her friends. Who else would dial in here on a Sunday? Still, the requirement for decorum remained. It would be just his luck to find Principal Snyder on the other end if he spoke with too much familiarity.

"Library," he said as pleasantly as he could into the receiver. "Mr. Giles speaking. May—"

"Giles, it's me. We've been calling for *hours!*"

It was, indeed, Buffy, although her voice was hushed and her words were quick, as though she were hiding. While the idea wasn't at all comforting, Giles was not surprised.

"Sorry, I've been back in the stacks, but I'm glad you called. I was concerned. Where are you?"

"Oz and I are at the museum," she said in a hushed voice. "It's closed for the day. Daniel Addison is dead."

Giles scowled. "Killed by a dinosaur?"

"Well, we've got the usual 'animal attack' explanation, but that's stretching it a bit when you consider the murder took place inside a building full of dead things—or *supposedly* dead things. I don't guess you've come up with any great secrets of the universe, have you?"

"It's not particularly a revelation, but we have unearthed something that might be of interest," he told her, dragging on the telephone cord until he could reach the pile of books he had left open on the table. On the top of the stack was the old one with the indigo leather cover that he'd found stashed beneath the counter, and he held it with one hand while he searched for the passage he remembered. "There's a reference to a dragon demon called Ladon whose goal is to find hosts for each of the four parts of its spirit."

On the other end, Buffy was silent for a moment. "Ladon, huh? I guess that would fit," she said. "Except . . . what's the point? And how did this whole thing start to begin with? Wait. Oz wants to talk to you."

"All right." Giles heard Buffy and Oz exchange a

hasty, muffled sentence or two, then Oz was speaking. Giles could picture him leaning into the phone with that same sort of intelligent intensity he always displayed in person.

"I think I found the why in the equation," Oz told him. "In Kevin Sanderson's notes, one of the last entries he wrote in here. It says Daniel Addison found a notebook when he was unpacking a museum storage crate. It doesn't go into a lot of detail, but does the name Gibor Nuriel mean anything to you?"

"Nothing at all," Giles responded. Still, he hastily wrote the name on a piece of paper. "Should it?" He heard pages being turned for a second or two, then Oz continued.

"Kevin didn't list a date, but I get the impression Nuriel was a paleontologist who worked for the museum decades ago. It was his field notebook that Daniel found and according to Kevin, it had some kind of ritual in it that appeals to something called 'Ladonithia.' "

Giles started. "Ladonithia? Willow found a reference to that but it went nowhere. Perhaps that pathway isn't such a dead end after all. What else do you have?"

"Not much," Oz noted. "The real jackpot would be to find the notebook Daniel Addison used, the one belonging to that Professor Nuriel. Of course, we haven't found Kevin, either."

"And Daniel Addison is dead," Giles said thoughtfully. "That's not good."

"No, it's not." Oz paused. "Here's Buffy."

Giles heard a note of desperation in Buffy's voice when she was back on the line. "We found three eggs in the museum lab, Giles. *Hatched* eggs, all stuck in the same chunk of rock. That means there are two more dinosaur 'babies' somewhere just like the one we aced last night." Her inhalation was clear. "And they're a day older and who knows how much bigger. Get it?"

"I'm afraid so. Willow, of course, is continuing to research but—"

"Do I really need to remind you that we could at any time mutate into dino food?"

"I am all too aware of that, I'm afraid." The librarian glanced at the clock, saw that it was already past one in the afternoon, and tried not to dwell on his memories of how quickly the Timimus hidden in the back was growing. "I expect Willow will be here at any moment," he said. "Perhaps you should come back to the library until we find out more?"

"First I think we should go through the museum to make sure nothing is still hanging around," Buffy said. "Obviously no one saw anything on the street, but the cops didn't find anything inside either. It's a big place." She paused. "Pretty smart dinosaurs, don't you think?"

"Perhaps," Giles said softly, "it's a smart *demon*."

"That too. It wouldn't be the first time." There was another pause as Oz said something in the background. "Okay, here's Plan A. We run through all three floors of the museum and the basement, if we can find a way down there without the guards catching us. Then right before we leave, we'll call you again—figure in an hour or so. By then you'll have the answer to everything, right?"

"Certainly," Giles said dryly. "Uh, Buffy?"

"Yeah?"

"What's Plan B?"

She didn't answer for a moment. Then, "Well, it's not exactly all laid out, but it has a lot to do with running really fast and not getting eaten."

"Excellent idea."

* * *

Giles was just about to break down and dial Willow's home number when she hurried into the library with Xander. "Where have you been?" he admonished. "Buffy and Oz are inside the museum, and Daniel Addison is dead—found murdered there this morning."

Xander grimaced. "Dino-bite?"

Giles started to retort, then gave up. "Yes, more than likely."

Willow's jaw dropped open. "Does that mean they're in the museum with another dinosaur? Right *now?*" She looked appalled.

"Did you find anything else?" Giles asked, intentionally by-passing the question. "I went through the volumes here but didn't have any luck."

The redheaded teenager blinked, then made an effort to focus as she nodded. "Definite pay dirt, though it took me all this time. Take a look." She swung her book bag onto the table and dug through it until she pulled out a stapled sheaf of computer print-outs. "This is what I finally came up with between the Internet and some vague references in a couple of my Wiccan books."

Giles was puzzled. "In your Wiccan books? You mean conjuring spells?"

Willow shook her head. "No. I had to backtrack and search in an entirely different direction. Believe it or not, I started with protection spells I found—stuff to guard against the spirit demon Ladonithia. It's old stuff and was buried pretty deep." She glanced at Xander, then back at the librarian. "But I have to tell you, none of it seems really strong considering what it's going up against."

Giles pulled off his glasses and chewed on the end of one earpiece. "There's that reference to Ladonithia again," he noted.

Willow began flipping rapidly through the sheets of paper. "Yeah," she said. "But once I got on the right track, the info was all there. I just couldn't find it right off because the web site had it posted as graphics instead of text. It verifies that 'Ladon' and 'Ladonithia' more or less refer to the same thing. The suffix 'ithia' was just something added over time, kind of fancying it up."

"Let me see," Giles said, leaning forward. He picked up the papers, reading aloud from the printed picture of a scroll where Willow indicated with a forefinger. " 'The four-headed Ladonithia is the netherworld's demon parallel to the mythical Greek dragon, Ladon, and as such, while its host body can be destroyed, Ladonithia's essence can never truly be vanquished. It sleeps deep in the underworld and will awaken only when called to the presence of a suitable host by the proper ritual, and the host itself must be a creature comparable in figure if not necessarily in size. Even then, Ladonithia is so powerful that it can only release its spirits one at a time, each into a *separate* host. Once it is able to instill all four spirits into hosts, Ladonithia must then meld all four entities into one simultaneously so that it can be freed, at last, from its underworld prison. When this happens, the unstoppable demon will attain its original gargantuan size and strength and will roam the world devouring the bodies and souls of mortals.' "

Willow's face was pale. "Did you see the woodcut image of it? Pretty beastly."

Giles frowned as he examined the printed image, an ancient-looking and not very detailed rendition of a flying dragonish creature with four horned heads atop muscular necks.

"Wings," Willow noted unhappily. "It has *wings*."

But Xander raised his chin confidently. "It doesn't matter," he said. "Its buddy system idea is a goner, cuz we toasted one of the hosts last night."

"Okay . . . so we've killed one of the hosts," Willow acknowledged. "Now what happens?"

"What's this 'we' stuff?" Xander asked huffily. "I don't recall you being in the 'we' group."

"Wait," Giles murmured. "Let me read a little more . . ." He scanned the page, then tapped it when he found what he was searching for. "Here it is. 'The spirit from a dead host transports back to share the original host—' "

"Exactly!" Willow said enthusiastically. "That explains this one's temper tantrum last night!" She turned to stare at the Timimus in the weapons cage, and it glared back at her. "It was being, like . . . invaded or something, when you guys blasted the other one by the Bronze!"

"—until another host can be found." Giles frowned as Willow's words sunk into his brain. "That doesn't bode well for its reaction when Buffy and Oz find the next one, does it?"

"Assuming they don't get chomped on," Xander said carelessly.

"Xander!" Giles snapped.

"What?" He blinked, oblivious to the color draining from Willow's cheeks. "They're fighting something with three-inch long razor sharp teeth, remember?"

"Xander, shut up," Giles said, with uncharacteristic coarseness.

The young man started to wisecrack, then ducked his head and at least looked ashamed when he saw Willow's expression. "Oops. Sorry." He was silent for a second. "They'll be fine. You'll see."

Giles glared at him, then went back to the notes Willow had brought. "'To return the demon to its slumber in the underworld for at least another threescore years,'" he read, "'all hosts must be defeated, and the original host must be destroyed only *after* its spirit is reunited with its three kindred.'"

"Not good," Willow said in a raspy voice. "I mean, look at it now. What's it going to be like soaking up a double dose of what it got last night?"

"Why can't we just kill it now?" Xander suggested.

"It doesn't say," Giles told her after a few more moments of scanning the text. "But my best guess would be that to do so severs the ties between it and its sibling spirits. Perhaps the spirit or spirits in it then transfer to them, and this is the only way to guarantee that you have all four in the same place . . . thus a fair shot at returning the beast to the underworld. It seems best to assume the original host is the controlling factor."

"So," Willow mused, "we would've all been better off if Buffy had just killed the thing the night she found it. *Before* any more eggs were hatched."

"What's that threescore part?" Xander asked suddenly. "Some kind of football score?"

"A unit of time, Xander," Giles said in annoyance. "Twenty years—"

"You *have* heard of 'fourscore and seven years ago,' right?" Willow stared hard at her friend.

"It's . . . familiar." He looked at her, then Giles. "What—did I miss something?"

"Never mind," Giles muttered. He grimaced, forcing himself past another bout of Xander-related amazement. "Twenty is a score. If I'm interpreting this correctly, the demon can attempt to free itself approximately every sixty years." He looked questioningly at Willow.

She nodded and brought out some more printed pages, some from other parts of the web site she'd discovered, more from completely different ones. "I came up with dates where there were instances of weird stuff happening over the last several hundred years, most recently around dinosaur dig sites but before that, it was out west. A lot of it was tied up with legends and stories about creatures that could have been dragons. Back then they probably just didn't know what they were looking at."

Giles thumbed through the stack. "And the last time was . . . ?"

"You got it," Willow said. "Just about sixty years ago."

"Which," Giles pointed out, "would coordinate precisely with what Oz told me on the telephone about something he read in Kevin Sanderson's notebook. Here, I wrote it down." He showed her and Xander the scribbles he'd made about Professor Gibor Nuriel, but Willow's indrawn breath made him realize they were on to something before she even read the remainder of his writing.

"I saw that name," she exclaimed. She scrambled to go through the computer pages until she found one detailing an old newspaper clipping. "This says he was killed in 1939 while on an expedition in Texas. His tent blew up from an unknown cause. All his personal effects were returned to the museum."

"Yes!" Giles said excitedly. "That would explain it. Oz said that according to Kevin's notes, Daniel had found the paleontologist's notebook while unpacking a storage crate."

"And if you go farther back, like I did, you'll find another wacked-out incident about sixty years before that." She showed them yet another section. Willow began reading the short recounting, written in the stylized writing of the late 1800s, aloud. "This is part of the record of a pterodactyl skeleton discovered, again, in Big Bend, Texas," she told them. "It says a drifter claimed to have seen a tribe of traveling gypsies performing a 'suspicious ritual' over a pile of bones late one night, then some kind of creature—presumably the pterodactyl—rose up and tried to fly. But because the beast had only a single huge wing, it succeeded only in dragging itself away." Willow looked at them. "According to this, the sheriff formed a posse the next morning and it was hunted down and shot, the remains burned."

"Amazing." Giles tapped another sheet of paper. "It was happening even back then. Presumably, each time the first host was killed, it shut down the process. But ours . . ." He glanced at the book cage, then thought better of it in hindsight. "If you read further in the text, it says that Ladonithia offers to fulfill a wish for the person who helps it return to Earth, but like the snake figure in the Garden of Eden, its motives are dishonest and the promise is a lie. If we tried, I suppose we could backtrack this demon's attempts to enter the world all the way through recorded time, just by correctly interpreting the appropriate myths and legends."

"Oh, definitely," Willow told him. "We—"

"I hate to poop on your parade," Xander interrupted, "but how does any of this past history stuff help Buffy and Oz in the here and now?"

"As we well know, on the Hellmouth the past is not necessarily dead," Giles said. "And Buffy and Oz need to know the current facts. If these creatures have some kind of homing instinct toward the main host, that information will likely assist Buffy and Oz in tracking and eliminating them before the beasts find their way out of the museum."

"Whoa," Xander said. "Just . . . *whoa.* Them? Creatures? As in plural? You mean it's already got all the dino-baby bodies it needs? When did this happen?"

Giles blinked, then realized that in all the excitement over Willow's discoveries, he'd neglected to mention the hatched nest. "As far as Buffy could tell, Daniel and Kevin seemed to have hatched three dinosaurs at once—"

"Oh, don't tell me," Xander moaned. "Two more like the one outside the Bronze, right?"

"I'm afraid so."

"I'm thinking a career as a barehanded traveling alligator tamer would be a good change of pace right about now," Xander said, sounding anything but enthusiastic. "Please don't say you want me to go find our pals at the museum and pass along these little news tidbits."

Giles pushed his glasses firmly in place on his nose. "That's precisely what you must do. They're in far too much danger for us to simply wait until they call again."

"I'll go with you," Willow said. "There's safety in numbers, remember? We can watch each other's backs."

"Oh, sure," Xander said bitingly as he picked up the sweater he'd thrown across the chair a few minutes ago. "Think of it as an adventure, something amazing that you can tell your grandkids fifty years from now." His mouth twisted as Giles saw the teen give him a final, dark look. "Because we just know that all this vampire and monster business isn't going to follow us around for the rest of our lives . . . don't we, Giles?"

God forgive him. As the librarian watched the two teenagers file out of the library, he couldn't bring himself to honestly answer that.

Chapter 12

"OKAY," BUFFY SAID. THEY WERE BACK DOWN ON THE main floor just outside the museum's small, locked souvenir shop. "We've covered both the upper floors and the door to the basement is dead-bolted. If we make a final round here, I'd say we can head on out. You're sure we shouldn't force that basement door?"

Oz shook his head. "Bad move. I saw the connection to the security system at the top. My guess is not only will it bring the guards down on us, it's probably wired to the police station besides."

Buffy looked around thoughtfully. "Well, I suppose if we can't go in, nothing can come out, either. We might trip the alarm when we leave, but we'll be gone anyway."

Oz nodded. "So which way now?"

"That way," she said, pointing up and to the right. "We'll just make a big circle and end up back here. Then we can go back to that maintenance room and get out the same way we came in."

"Sounds like a plan to me," Oz agreed. "Lead on."

Buffy didn't need any more prompting; she was as anxious to get this over with as Oz. But when they turned into the short hallway, they found themselves facing two different sections, both long and dim.

"Split up?" Oz asked. "Behind door one, Gems and Minerals. Door two, American History."

"No way are we separating," Buffy said firmly. "That would be way too far into the danger range." They hugged the wall as she tried to decide which of the long areas in front might be more interesting to a baby dinosaur. Oz didn't help matters by motioning to a sign overhead and a few feet directly down the hallway: AFRICAN MAMMALS. Damn, another choice. Did dino-babies like to hunt? Could be, but the odds were they'd favor live meat over dusty, taxidermied parts. She started to mouth off about this, then saw something on her own that added even further to their decision dilemma. On their left, down and across the pathway at the back portion of the main foyer that housed the two huge dinosaur skulls, was a smaller, more discreet directory sign. White block letters on a black background with a couple of arrows: NORTH AMERICAN MAMMALS, then FOSSILS AND DINOSAURS. Wasn't that just peachy.

"What's that?" Oz asked softly.

Buffy followed his finger to where he was pointing at something on the floor. At first, she didn't see anything in the dimness, then her eyes did a force fit to the reduced lighting at shoe level. There, at the juncture where the wall's wide baseboard met the floor beneath the directory sign, was—

"A pen?"

Oz cast a look toward the foyer to make sure the

guard wasn't around, then hurried over and picked it up. "Exactly."

Buffy followed him over, then raised one eyebrow. "And your point would be?"

Oz's expression never changed. "Just your average everyday ink pen." He lifted it to eye level and let it dangle there, holding it by the very top with two fingers. "With blood on it."

Buffy squinted at it, and yes—he was right. There it was, looking black in the poor lighting, all over the pen. "Guess they don't sell bloody writing tools in the gift shop, huh? What do you think?" she asked. "Daniel's? Or Kevin's?"

Oz shrugged, glanced to the side, then slipped the pen into a trash container by the wall. "What'll it be— fossils and dinosaurs?"

Buffy gritted her teeth. "What else?" She eased around him and led the way. A quick glance into the fossils section showed nothing but a long, large room filled with glass-fronted shelves against the walls and display cases in the center of the floor, all glowing with muted light. A pretty clear view down to the end, and it would've been hard for something as big as the creatures they were looking for to hide comfortably in here. There was an exit at the far end, but she'd investigate that later if they found nothing in the next room.

The dinosaur exhibit was something else again. The entry was a high, arched doorway over which hung a brightly colored banner proclaiming WELCOME TO PALEO-VIEW! They started to go through, then stopped. Buffy's mouth twisted in annoyance. "Great. Could this be any *more* helpful?"

Facing them was a room longer and easily twice as wide as the expansive fossil room next door. As with the rest of the main floor, the ceiling stretched some twenty feet overhead, but the effect was anything but airy. Instead, the prehistoric jungle motif—and really, had she expected anything else?—made it seem nearly claustrophobic. Greenery, some silk, some real, was abundant on all sides, while still running on low volume in the background was the theme that apparently carried the exhibit throughout the day. Hidden fans moved air through the room and made it seem like gentle breezes eased through the foliage. Even the hard granite blocks of the floor were a mixture of green hues to go along with the theme, but there was no need to try to hide their footsteps here; the sound of soft roars, grunts and who knew what else would give them excellent cover. But it, as well as all the tropical-looking greenery, would also give the things they hunted the same advantage.

No wonder nothing had gotten out of the museum. This was the perfect place for a baby dinosaur to hide.

"Why is it so humid?" Buffy asked quietly.

"To add to that authentic jungle feeling," Oz answered. He glanced around. "They probably shut the humidifiers down at night to keep the exhibits from rotting out. Good job on the models."

Buffy scowled a little, but he only shrugged. "Some of them sure are realistic," she noted nervously. "Never thought a museum exhibit would make me nervous."

Oz gave her a dry look. "Surprising, considering what I heard about Xander and that Incan mummy princess."

Buffy's gaze flicked around the massive room, searching for telltale movement between the rustling oversize ferns and the fake dinosaurs. "True. But somehow I feel a bit outclassed this time."

"Maybe in size," Oz said. "But not in brain power."

Buffy wasn't comforted. "Who knows? Don't forget that Giles said we might be dealing with something that has the smarts of a demon, not a dinosaur."

Oz's face remained impassive. "Could be. If so, this particular one isn't having much luck."

True again, but didn't everyone learn as they went on? The way Buffy saw it, Ladon or Ladonithia, just kept trying by making more dinosaur copies of itself. She swallowed and squared her shoulders; she dreaded going deeper into this shadowy, spooky exhibit hall, but it was time to move on to see what they could find. While the scared part of her hoped it would be nothing, the logical part knew that if they didn't find it here, they'd have to hunt it somewhere else, so what was the difference?

Oh . . . normal lighting for one. And twentieth-century noises, like cars and people and anything but the low growling and snarling that seemed to surround her and Oz on every side in this huge room. And weapons—*yeah, weapons would be good.*

"Wait," Oz said in a low voice. He'd stuffed the floor plan into his pocket and he pulled it out now. "What happens if we do find something? Let's backtrack and go here first."

He pointed at one of the pages and Buffy followed his finger. "North American Cultures?"

"With benefits." He shoved the book back into his pocket. "Stuff like spears and axes. We'll pick up a few things, then come back in through the rotunda entrance at the far end."

Buffy sniffed. "What? And not charge our beasts empty-handed? Why does this sound like a much better plan?" Glib comment or not, she could have hugged him.

Together they backed out of the dinosaur entrance,

then crept back toward the fossil room. "Down there," Oz said. "Then turn right and go through the mammals, circle around that way. We'll get to check the whole exhibit and pick whatever we need."

She nodded and let Oz lead the way this time. He seemed to have a knack for reading the museum map and finding his way around in here, while she was doing pretty well at picking up on when the guards walked their rounds. As Oz guided them deftly into a room filled with Native American exhibits and relics, she could only hope she'd do as well when it came to their prehistoric foes.

"Jackpot," he said in a low voice.

Oz stopped her with a hand on her arm and pointed to an array of objects high on the wall, but still within reach if they stood on some of the exhibit cases. "Try not to break anything," he said in a pseudo-whisper. "Cracking glass guarantees an alarm."

Buffy nodded. "Got it," she said, and scurried forward with him right behind her. What they could take was limited to what they could comfortably hold and actually use, so instead of long spears, Buffy opted for four wicked-looking tomahawks, ones with good, heavy edges. They could each carry one, plus have another tucked into their waistbands. The tomahawks, she figured, would be much more effective than spears. Once a spear was thrown or stuck into their target, that was probably the end of its usefulness, plus she wasn't sure of the strength of these ancient, wooden-handled ones. Ignoring several bows and arrows, she also chose a couple of long, antique-looking knives. Even if the blades weren't sharp, the points could still deliver a mortal blow, and she thought it was doubtful that the strings on the bows would hold up if she actually tried to fire an arrow. The arrows themselves just seemed puny when she considered the target.

"We're set," she whispered to Oz. "I'm ready if you are."

Oz looked like he wanted to comment—maybe say something like "Ready for what, our final glory?"—but he only nodded and moved in front of her, guiding her up and through the rest of the exhibit to where the spacious rotunda branched out from the room's back exit. There, a quarter of the way around on their left, was the smaller rear entrance to the dinosaur room. Dim, vaguely golden light spilled from the doorway, the toned-down version of the daytime's full tropical effect. Oz's face was pale in the low light and they could both hear the muted sounds of the faked dinosaur growls and grunts, the electronic chittering of small animals for which Buffy had no name, and the noises of insects that were thought to have lived at the same time as the dinosaurs. Didn't they say cockroaches had been around for millions upon millions of years? The thought made Buffy shudder as they ducked inside, and she wished desperately that the staff had simply shut the sound effects off entirely when the museum closed.

"Whoa." Oz breathed beside her. Buffy glanced at him, then followed his gaze to something huge and dark hanging above their heads. The thing up there, poised in a downward swoop, was so realistic it nearly made her cringe. Despite the darker area near the ceiling, she could still see the meticulously created veining in the enormous wings of the reproduction of a savage pterodactyl.

"Could've done without that," Buffy muttered. Thank God Kevin and Daniel hadn't gotten hold of any pterodactyl eggs. As the Slayer she could do a lot of things, but she still hadn't mastered the fine art of flying.

"Lot of ground to cover in here," Oz said quietly. "And a lot of noise."

Buffy peered past him. Green and black shadows filled the room, and between the close, damp atmosphere and the breezes ruffling the leaves of the interspersed real and fake plants, the place seemed way too alive, like something could easily blend in . . . and would she even notice? "Yeah," she started to say—

Something moved between a couple of the exhibits farther up on the right, about a third of the way into the room. For the briefest of seconds, she saw a shadow, bigger and darker than the rest, slide across the dark green floor.

"Time to rock?"

"Oh, yeah," Buffy said. "I think it just went behind that . . . bunch of ugly, bird-faced things over there."

"Oviraptors," Oz said matter-of-factly.

"Over-whatevers. Let's go."

The two of them ran forward in a half-crouch that still let them move quickly, hugging the line of an imitation rock wall that separated the Oviraptor exhibit from the designated walkway. Oversize leaves fluttered around them but Buffy couldn't tell if they were supposed to or not. It was like being in the middle of a forest at twilight, one filled with movement and whispers. Was that odd snuffling sound really just part of the museum's programmed sound effects, or was it something else entirely?

"Up there," Oz said. "On an angle to the right—see between the Carnotaurus and the Cynognathus?"

"Again?"

"The big thing on the right with lots of teeth and stupid little horns, and the fuzzy things on the left that look like mutated tigers."

Buffy squinted, trying to pinpoint what he was talking about. "Oh . . . yeah. I see it now. Great." What he was talking about wasn't particularly big, but it was undeniably their boy. Or maybe it was a girl. Did it really matter? She scowled and stayed where she was. "But where's the other one?" she asked Oz softly. "There should be two."

"I dunno. Maybe it's moved on, maybe it's right around the corner." He was silent for a moment. "Buffy, how the hell are we going to do this?"

She gripped one of her tomahawks, wanting the weight of the primitive weapon to somehow make her feel better. No such luck. "With this, I guess," she said. "We just are. And there's no time like the now time." Yipes! Hadn't she said that the last time they'd faced a dinosaur? She hated déjà vu.

Backing up her statement, she fixed her sight on that bulky shadow and skittered forward. She could sense Oz as he followed her, although she couldn't quite hear him. It wasn't just the noise of the fans and the sound effects still softly pumping through the dinosaur exhibits that blotted out his movements, but his own unconsciously wolflike tendencies. He probably didn't even realize the way every gesture, every step that he took, resembled the stealthy creatures whose legacy was now a hidden part of his own makeup.

But as well as Oz moved, her own sure actions must not have been nearly as quiet. They didn't even get to the juncture of where the wall ended before they heard a low, warning growl that was frighteningly different from the noises coming from the speaker—sounds that instantly seemed pathetic when compared to the real thing. Buffy forced herself to keep going when her legs wanted to freeze, putting a mental override on the flight impulse that shot through every nerve in her body. She'd faced few things in her time as the Slayer that threatened to so completely overwhelm her.

Another throaty rumble came out of the greenery in the exhibits ahead, then the creature they sought stalked through a curtain of vines hanging from the ceiling and stepped into the aisle in front of them.

Neither Buffy nor Oz said anything. Buffy's mind went blank, and if she'd been drowning—which she knew from experience—she might have seen her life flash before her eyes. As it was, she heard the air expel from her lungs at the same time that Oz inhaled sharply; funny how people showed fear in individual ways. It didn't matter, though. At this point, all choices had been taken out of their hands.

The Tyrannosaurus Rex that stood and snapped at the air a few yards away was more of a toddler than the baby they'd vanquished in the alley the night before. It was taller by at least a foot and had a lot more meat on its bones—a result of the passage of only one night? Buffy didn't want to think that its healthy roundness had anything to do with a diet of Daniel and Kevin, but she couldn't get the idea to go away once it surfaced. It looked at them with the same glittery golden gaze that its sibling had possessed. There was a hotter quality to this one's eyes, though, something reminiscent of the hellish glow that they'd seen in the eyes of the Timimus that night in the library, when this whole mess had started with her capture of that birdlike creature. She hoped that radiance didn't mean it was any more intelligent, but the way their luck was running, it probably did. As if it could read her thoughts, it suddenly bobbed its head up and down, like an angry bird. Its movements were fluid and strong, with no hint of awkwardness or hesitation.

"My, my," Buffy finally managed, never taking her gaze from it. "What big teeth you have."

"What big *everything* you have," Oz said very quietly. "It might be just wild speculation on my part, but I'm thinking that junior at the Bronze might have been the runt of the litter."

"Well, that's good, right?" Buffy tried her best to sound encouraged. "That means the other one is probably no bigger than this, yes?" Out of the corner of her eye, she saw one side of Oz's mouth twist.

"Nice try." He peered at it, obviously fascinated in spite of their predicament. "You know, the brow ridges on its head are awfully prominent. I'd say they look a lot more like demon horns than dinosaur—"

Dino Baby charged.

This time, the flight instinct took over both Buffy and Oz. She went one way, while he leaped in the other direction, and for a moment the small T. Rex faltered, unable to decide which prey was the more worthy. For all his natural stealth, however, Oz was not as swift as Buffy, and since he was the slower of the two, the young dinosaur ultimately chose him. It twisted sideways and lunged as Oz leaped over the mock-stone wall and into the Oviraptor exhibit, coming down in a roll that sent him into a knot of foliage next to a grouping of the crested, pale models on a fake hill, none of which was very big. Buffy skidded to a stop and tried to reverse direction to head back toward Oz, and found herself facing the same problem the T. Rex had just discovered: Despite colors chosen to carefully blend it in with the jungle theme, the floor was still slick granite tile and quick maneuvering was damned near impossible. Both Buffy and the T. Rex slipped and went down, though Buffy seemed to land a lot on the lighter side.

The dinosaur's left leg went forward and under it—nature had never intended for this creation to run on polished granite tiles—and it lost its balance. When it fell, its bottom jaw came down hard on the stone wall; no doubt the floor vibrated all the way up to the guards' desk by the main foyer. The wall, it seemed, wasn't stone, but it wasn't Styrofoam either—maybe only chunks of painted, dried plaster or molded globs of hardened plastic. Still, whatever it was constructed of apparently hurt because the creature gave a not-so-quiet roar of pain as the stuff cracked and dug into the flesh of its face. So much for stealth.

Sprawled painfully on her elbows, Buffy managed to haul herself to her feet before the dinosaur could find any traction. Its own drool had served to make its position even worse. While the powerful back legs and toes tipped with long, curved claws scrabbled at the floor and its tiny front legs clutched uselessly at the air, the T. Rex's head was still pointed in the direction it had last seen Oz run. Beneath the heavy, malformed ridges of its brow, the thing's eyes burned with malevolence and the desire to kill.

Hefting one of the tomahawks, Buffy ran toward the dinosaur before she could change her mind, her only thought that she should strike, as hard as she could, at its neck. This was something she'd never imagined she'd encounter. Did it even have an artery close enough to the skin surface for her to reach with this dull-edged weapon? Memories of the nice piece of pipe she'd found in the alley came back, and in hindsight she wished she had grabbed one of those spears she'd seen a few minutes ago. Despite their wimpy wooden shafts, she might've had more of a chance at victory with something long and pointed. Even with it struggling on the floor, swinging at the dinosaur's neck with the short-handled tomahawk was going to put her precariously close to the thing's monstrous jaws.

But there was just no other way.

She came down just behind the baby dinosaur's right shoulder and slipped in the more than generous amounts of dino-saliva. No wonder the beast couldn't regain its footing. *Ick.* Was this natural, or was it just the idea of human flesh that made the dinosaur, or maybe the demon spirit inside it, salivate in anticipation? Buffy had hoped to bring the tomahawk down with both hands, as hard as she could, into that really good soft spot right below the line of its jaw, dig in nice and deep and hope there was a big artery waiting down there. But the goo on the floor threw everything out of whack. She managed to keep her grip on the tomahawk's base but her other hand automatically slapped downward to break her fall at the same time that her right knee rammed into the T. Rex's shoulder.

So much for its not noticing her.

Forgetting about Oz, it twisted around and tried to bite at her, and the blow that Buffy wanted to land beneath its jaw ended up slamming into its snout instead. The blade surprised her by cutting skin, but then it came back and nearly hit her in the face. There wasn't much padding on the dinosaur's nose and it had hit bone and bounced. The low roar the T. Rex had maintained so far changed to a bellow of outraged pain that was unmistakably not something on the museum's tape. Long and loud, it carried a pulsing undercurrent that made Buffy grit her teeth without realizing it.

Her target bucked, tried to bite again and missed, then got one knee under itself, the prelude to getting upright. Not good. Buffy much preferred it to continue flopping around on the floor like a giant fish. She barely avoided its teeth and flailed at it again with the tomahawk, her swing awkward and uncontrolled. Even so, she had the satisfaction of feeling her weapon *thunk* solidly into the excessively protruding brow ridge above the baby dinosaur's right eye. She would have been a lot happier had she taken out the eye itself, but sometimes a girl had to be satisfied with what she got . . . and was that fear she heard in its next bellow?

The T. Rex wrenched its head away from the pain and Buffy lost her grip on the tomahawk. It was kind of like trying to stand on wet ice, but she managed to scramble upright, then squashed her instinctive urge to aim a hard roundhouse kick at the dinosaur's head. It would be a weak blow and comparatively speaking, the mouth thing here was a lot bigger than a bloodsucker and she really didn't want to lose her leg if it managed to bite her. Unfortunately, dino-toddler was also finally getting its balance and rising; in a few more seconds she'd be facing something that was a good foot or two taller than she was and probably two hundred pounds heavier. She'd fought a few chunky vamps along the way, but none of them had teeth like this baby.

Then it was up and leaning toward her, and despite its size it had an almost fascinating reptilian grace, a fluidity to its movements that vaguely resembled those of a lizard. Instead of going for the other tomahawk, Buffy chose the long, pointed knives she'd picked up, one for each hand. She felt and smelled its breath, a nauseating mixture of blood and meat, and tried to block the instantaneous memory of the comment by the lab tech outside regarding Daniel Addison—*"What's left of him, anyway . . ."* When the dinosaur's mouth yawned wide, instead of stabbing at the bony jaw, Buffy darted forward and shoved the first of the knives up and into the roof of its mouth as hard as she could. In a split second that felt like forever, she felt the flesh catch, then rip for at least ten or eleven inches; then it hit something, maybe a protrusion of bone, and she yanked her hand out of the thing's mouth and left the knife behind, jammed firmly in place.

The T. Rex reared backward and screamed, a horrendous noise that sounded more like a train engine than an animal. More proof that she'd scored a victory was the blood blanketing her hand and running down her forearm, adding to the slippery mix on the floor. Buffy switched her remaining knife to her right hand, still determined to go after that elusive neck artery, when Oz hurtled at the dinosaur from the other side. With a snarl that was eerily like the wolf into which he transformed for part of every month, her co-hunter brought one of his tomahawks around and buried it deeply into the big muscle just above the knee joint in the creature's left leg.

This time, the roar of the T. Rex was a blast of thunder as it buckled and went down on that side, its heavy leg knocking Oz back a good ten feet as it fell. Buffy wasn't fooled, though. Oz had hurt it, sure, but no way would his blow be enough to keep it down and guarantee they'd win this fight. Somewhere in the background Buffy thought she heard someone other than Oz shouting: the guards, no doubt drawn to the battle by the noise and now seeing something they couldn't begin to comprehend. Did museum guards have guns? Now *that—*

"Freeze right where you are!" a man shouted from behind her.

—answered her question.

Freeze? Not likely, not when Dino Baby was doing a one-legged sprawl and crawl across the floor, so desperate was it to have her for its next meal. She still had half her stash of weapons, one of each; now she just had to decide how to use them.

"Buffy, look out!"

There was a crash and part of one of the exhibits fell over, no doubt caused by a flick of their disguised demon foe's tail. The creature's ploy to startle the guard and make him fire at her worked, but instinct made her duck in response to Oz's yell and also saved her butt. She heard something kind of like a big firecracker exploding, and while it was probably not at all true, Buffy could've sworn she felt one of the guard's bullets whiz over her head. And, of course, it completely missed the T. Rex squirming on the floor.

Skipping back until she was out of tooth range, she whirled. "What are you shooting at *me* for, you moron! Shoot the *dinosaur!*"

"Nice try," the guard snapped. "Just put your hands in the air and back away from the exhibit." His voice shook as he jerked his head at Oz. "You, too, kid. Jimmy, find the volume on the speakers and turn that crap off."

Turn the volume off—who *cared?* Buffy started to retort, then realized that from where the two guards were standing, on the other side of the walled mutated tiger exhibit, they literally couldn't see the T. Rex on the floor. To make things worse, the creature had stopped its movement; now it was just lying there quietly, eyes glowing with hate while its chest rose and fell with plenty of life still left in it. Oh yeah, the demon controlling the animal was cunning, enough so that it would keep the T. Rex down and quiet and make Buffy and Oz the only thing on which the guards would focus. Very tricky . . . and dangerously intelligent.

Suddenly the sound effects disappeared and everything went silent. From where she and Oz stood, the T. Rex's head was pointed toward them and Buffy could see the dinosaur's carefully regulated breathing, slow and even, virtually soundless. "I got it, Scott," the second guard said as he hurried back to his partner. "Damn, these kids sure made a mess. Hey, you think they're the ones who killed that guy up in the labs?" He sounded absolutely thrilled at the idea. *Hey, boss, look at us! We caught the murderers!*

"Maybe," said the first guard, his eyes narrowing. "You go around the other side, see what kind of damage they've done and make sure they don't have any more weapons."

"Don't do that!" Buffy said in alarm.

"You just keep your mouth shut, missy," the second guard, Jimmy, grunted. "You're in enough trouble already."

"But it's not safe," Oz put in. "There's a—"

"Shut *up*," Scott barked as Jimmy took off in another direction. "I don't want to hear another sound from either of you until the cops get here. I mean it. And you can just put that knife and whatever it is in your belt there on the floor right now."

Buffy saw movement between the greenery lining the walkway and her heart beat faster. "Wait—"

Jimmy's words cut her off as he stepped into view and strolled toward her, Oz, and the downed baby T. Rex. His .38 was drawn and leveled. "Aw, Scott, you oughta see what these kids have done. There's goop and red paint all over everything and—" He frowned as he spotted the small dinosaur sprawled across the pathway. "Hey, I didn't know we had an exhibit with something like *this* in it."

"Don't come any closer!" Oz warned. Buffy saw her friend take a step backward, knew he was trying to force the T. Rex's attention to stay on him. At the same time that Scott threatened them again—

"I thought I told you to keep quiet!"

—their demon-infested dino lurched up on its good leg and with a throaty bellow, launched itself at Jimmy.

The result was damned near chaos.

Jimmy got off only one shot as Buffy and Oz threw themselves down. There was no way either of them could have gotten to the guard in time to help him anyway. Half of his face and skull disappeared in a burst of blood, bone and gray matter as the dinosaur's teeth-studded jaws snapped shut around it, then pulled back. For a second Jimmy's body twitched, then it collapsed at the same time that Scott scrambled forward and began firing wildly.

Jimmy's first and only shot had to have hit pay dirt—there was no chance it couldn't have—but there just wasn't any way to tell if Scott's trigger-happiness was actually helping any. *Bang bang bang bang*—one after another, with him screaming as loudly as he could and the dinosaur roaring at the same time, until Buffy thought her eardrums were going to burst. And more noise—was it her own shouting, and maybe Oz's, too? She couldn't tell.

And suddenly, the worst of it stopped.

There was still some yelling, a bit, perhaps, from everyone there. Yet the thing that stood out above all of it was a terribly . . . empty clicking sound.

Still hugging the floor, she twisted until she could see Scott. The guard was standing there, mouth half slack and eyes glazed as he stared at the T. Rex baby and squeezed the trigger of his now spent .38, again and again and again.

"Uh-oh," Buffy said.

She catapulted herself off the floor and tackled the guard just as the dinosaur, bleeding from at least a half-dozen bullet wounds, reeled toward him. Her body slam took him sideways and out of munching range, but she knew instantly that it wasn't going to do any good. He'd come out of his shock trance, but for some reason the fool was fighting her, trying to get back toward the dinosaur and face down the thing with his bare hands like someone had given him a shot of Rambo-itis.

Her knife was gone, as was her tomahawk—lost somewhere between first bite and the ensuing spray of gunfire. Buffy couldn't see Oz, but she was betting he'd done the smart thing and beat tracks within the dense greenery at the base of an exhibit housing a couple of huge dinosaurs that looked like hairless, thirty-foot ducks with dumb expressions and ridges on top of their heads and backs. She got up and managed to drag the guard back a couple more feet, but it was the dinosaur blood that ultimately cinched it; she was covered in the stuff and before she could do anything about it, her hold on Scott slipped from his waist all the way down to nothing more secure than one ankle.

"*No!*" she shrieked as he kicked away from her. "Don't—"

Too late.

Scott was a big guy, definitely on the side of chunky. Maybe he was a wannabe weightlifter and that—or maybe it was steroids—was what made him think he could take down the creature snarling at him. Buffy tried to save him a second time, but she failed. She just couldn't get up enough speed to close the distance before the T. Rex closed on Scott. The guard stood before the dinosaur with an insane grin on his face and his hands bunched in fists in front of him, and all he got in return was a third of his torso ripped out from under him before he could aim a single swing at the unimaginable thing that caused his death.

For a second all Buffy wanted to do was squeeze her eyes shut and block out the horrid sight. If she lived beyond this afternoon, would she forever remember the sight of this man's intestines slipping to the floor while his body tottered upright for far too long?

Time—again, if she lived that long—would tell. Right now the odds had dropped out of their favor and once again it was two weaponless humans against one nearly unstoppable demon-possessed monstrosity. So far the score, dinosaur: two and humans: zero, wasn't good.

But it had to be hurting, had to be getting weaker. The blood that covered its green and gold hide wasn't all the guards'. So far it'd been stabbed, hacked, and shot. At first Buffy had thought that the knife she'd left inside its mouth had probably only broken in the soft tissue and pissed it off, but every time it roared another pulse of scarlet gushed from between its back teeth. The question was did it come from the shallow but painful slash inside its mouth, or from some deeper, unseen damage done by Scott's bullets? Either way, the T. Rex was still upright, and still on the attack. But all of the dangerous beauty had been stripped away from it, and while the creature that staggered in front of them now was undeniably deadly and vicious, in some ways it was also pathetic, like a miserable, dying animal that desperately needed to be put out of its misery.

And that was exactly what Buffy planned on doing.

It didn't matter that she was defenseless as well as weaponless; at an angle behind the T. Rex was a towering stash of dozens of sharp implements in the form of the dinosaur that Oz had described as having "stupid little horns"—a Carnotaurus. It was big and butt-ugly, doing as much justice to evil-looking as a tyrannosaur did. What made this exhibit a lot more helpful, however, was the way that the creature's head, while fully molded out and painted, began to morph at neck and shoulder level until it slipped into bare skeleton. And hey, hey—weren't those nice sharp ribs over there going to come in handy?

She feinted to the right, yelling the entire time. "Oz, get its attention! Make it look at you!"

Ever cooperative, her friend popped up out of the fake bushes and waved his arms wildly at the small T. Rex, reminding her absurdly of one of those flip-up targets at a carnival game. "Hey, ugly!" Oz shouted at it. "Over here!"

With her start to the right, then Oz's sudden appearance, the undersize dinosaur pitched awkwardly in that direction, its small, mean gaze now focused on Oz. As he hastily backed away, keeping an eye on what was behind him to avoid a trap, Buffy darted around the T. Rex's other side and ran over to the Carnotaurus skeleton. The thing loomed over her, nearly thirty feet long and easily four times the size of the creature she and Oz were battling, but at least this one was conveniently dead.

Knowing she was probably going to bring the entire exhibit down and hoping it wouldn't crush her when it fell, Buffy reached up and yanked on one of the rib bones. It was surprisingly—and thankfully—heavy, but it was also sturdily stuck in place. She heard the Tyrannosaurus toddler roar as it tried to drag itself after Oz, then heard him yell at it in return as he ran between the overlong legs of the exhibit's spotlighted animal and a waist-high sign labeling it as an Hypacrosaurus.

Teeth grinding with effort, Buffy yanked on the rib bone again and heard the metal supports comprising the skeleton groan. She was getting there. All it would take was one good inside kick, *right*—

—*there,* at the brace by the outside back leg, and this sucker was coming down.

She kept hold of her chosen rib as the Carnotaurus skeleton crashed to the floor, trying to guide most of it away from her and causing another mad cacophony of sound to add to the noise that had, it seemed, been going on around her and Oz for hours. Bone-shaped pieces dropped in every direction, a strange parody of a rainstorm. Still fighting with its injured leg, the T. Rex had pulled itself after Oz until her friend had the wall behind him. If Buffy didn't do something quick, he'd be forced to retreat toward the back exit and risk being followed by the tyrannosaur.

But the noise that the Carnotaurus exhibit made when it hit bottom was enough to turn the demonized dinosaur's head back toward Buffy and instantly change its direction. "Just can't make up your mind, can you?" she said, then grunted and yanked once more on the rib in her hand. Stuck in a chunk of spine, it resisted at first, then finally came free not a second too soon. Hobbled or not, the T. Rex was almost on top of her head before she was able to swing the fake rib bone around in a powerful two-handed arc. The end of the pseudo-bone was ragged and sharp from where she'd broken it loose from the heavy base; it caught the snapping dinosaur across the upper chest and penetrated, leaving a gaping, gushing wound as Buffy dragged it hard all the way across.

It was undoubtedly a mortal wound, even if the dinosaur wasn't yet ready to give up its quest for the death of these two troublesome humans. This time its scream was oddly high-pitched—either it knew it was running out of time or the pain was just too much for it to deal with. Crimson blood sheeted the entire front of the animal until it coated the floor and made it look like the T. Rex was flailing for purchase in the most gruesome lake imaginable. Without warning it tried to bite at her and Buffy swayed backward, overbalancing on the treacherously slick floor. She slipped and went down and the motion actually helped her, getting her head out of the same spot where Baby Dino's blood-flecked teeth crashed neatly together a millisecond later. When Buffy got a firm enough footing, she came up again, hard, swinging her bone-weapon in a neat semicircle across the area directly under the Tyrannosaurus's jaw line.

There was no roar of pain.

This time, there wasn't any sound at all.

With its airway and main artery severed, the creature wobbled soundlessly where it stood for an overlong ten seconds, opening and closing its mouth as if it couldn't believe what had just happened. More blood—Buffy had never seen anything bleed this much—fountained from the upper part of the wound, spraying everything in its way. Buffy felt a line of it cross her face, warm, wet and utterly disgusting—and hey, wasn't that going to be the final doom for her nice yellow top? Speaking of yellow, all the pizzazz had left their demon-dino's eyes, fading right in front of her as she watched from a cautious two yards away and Oz crept up from the other side.

Finally the thing lay lifeless in front of them.

"Piece of cake," Buffy said, but she sure didn't mean it.

Oz, covered in grit and with a bruise along one pale cheekbone, raised an eyebrow. "I'm glad you think so," he said gently. "But . . . where's the other one?"

Chapter 13

Willow thought her heart was going to explode when they suddenly ran into Buffy and Oz in front of the Stegosaurus exhibit inside the museum.

Everyone sucked in air and for a moment, no one said anything. She and Xander could only stare at their friends, trying to comprehend how Buffy could have so much blood dripping off her, Oz's dirty and bruised face, the fear etched in both their expressions.

Xander was the first one able to speak. "Are you guys all right?" he demanded. There was a strident edge to his voice as he stepped forward. "What happened? Where are the big scary extinct things with bigger, scarier teeth?" His gaze raked Buffy, and Willow knew she and Oz were wondering the same thing: *Whose blood was it?*

"Buffy?" Willow knew she sounded desperate, but that was okay. It wasn't a crime to be petrified for your best buddy.

"ffy blinked. "Oh . . . sorry . . . dinosaurs. Yeah."

She glanced wearily at Oz, and his nervous look back into the shadows of the dinosaur exhibit room confirmed Willow's worst fears. "One down, one to go. I don't think it's in the museum, though."

Willow thought that was a gutsy thing to say, considering the grimaces on both their faces. "How can you be so sure?"

"We're not," Buffy admitted. "But with the racket we just made, I think the other one would've come to join in the fight, tried to finish us off." She looked a little sick. "There were two museum guards and it . . . killed them both."

Willow's mouth twisted. "Oh."

Oz's eyes suddenly sharpened. "Hey, how did you guys get in here and find us?"

"A back door," Xander answered. "Wide open to some kind of trash area."

Buffy's brows drew together. "You say the door was open?"

"Totally," Willow said. "Anyone could've walked in . . . or out."

Oz folded his arms. "I definitely shut that."

Buffy started to say something else, then Willow saw her tilt her head, as if she were listening to sounds they couldn't hear.

"Sirens," Buffy said a moment later. "One of the guards said something about the police coming. We need to get out of here pronto."

The rest of them nodded and turned to follow her out, then Willow stumbled. The toe of her shoe had tangled in a small pile of items shoved beneath a clot of the imitation flora that had been sloppily dragged over a portion of the fake stone wall in an obvious attempt to hide something. "Wait a sec," she said. "What's this?"

Oz slipped up next to her, then knelt and pushed aside the semi-crushed silk leaves. "School junk. I think someone dumped their backpack." He frowned as he flipped open one of the notebooks and found a page covered in algebra. "This is Kevin Sanderson's stuff. I recognize the handwriting."

Buffy leaned in. "You know, we never did find the owner of the bloody pen."

"Sounds like the name of a mystery novel," Xander said. *The Owner of the Bloody Pen.* A novel of mystery and suspe—"

"Xander, be quiet," Willow said. "Bloody pen?"

Oz nodded, then poked through the jumble of things on the floor again, pointing at a couple of items—a gray plastic calculator, a bottle of white correction fluid—that were smudged with dried red. "I'm thinking it was Kevin's."

"So he's hurt," Willow said.

"It can't be too bad," Buffy said. "We didn't find his body, and we've seen what these things can do to the puny human form when they get serious about it."

"I don't get it. Why would he dump everything out here?" Xander asked. "If he didn't want it anymore, why not just drop the whole thing?"

No one said anything for a few moments while they considered this, then Willow's gaze focused on something a few feet inside the exhibit. Dismay settled over her. "Because," she said slowly, "he needed the backpack to carry something."

Buffy frowned. "Like what?"

Willow lifted her finger and pointed to a section along the floor of the exhibit that had been broken out of a Stegosaurus nest. "Eggs."

* * *

Kevin felt like he was moving on fast forward through dense fog.

What had happened here? He thought that, given enough time, he might be able to piece the events together, lay them all out in a sort of flow chart that would chronicle, if not actually explain, the ruin of his life that had started with Daniel Addison walking into Mr. Regis's classroom. There was so much that needed to be recorded, but he had lost his notebook somewhere . . . maybe he could get a new one and start fresh. Yeah, that would be good. Because other people needed to know about this, and all it would take for him to get it down was a few sheets of paper, a pen, and . . .

Silence.

Now that was key, because he simply didn't have that luxury anymore. In the course of his life, during difficult school projects, complex calculations or the heavy duty problem-solving and speculation that sometimes turned up in the higher levels of the studies to which he'd become exposed, Kevin had always pictured a sort of private, empty . . . *space* inside his brain. Nothing big, no idiotic airhead concept; it was more like an available file drawer, a little quiet area free of clutter and reserved for clearheaded thinking, the kind of deliberation that an intelligent person sometimes needed to get, or perhaps keep, themselves out of a jam.

Well, something had moved into that space.

We will go to the school, Kevin.

It was a . . . *presence* in his mind, constant and inescapable, a shadow that had blasted through the dubious and far-too-fragile barrier of his skin, blood and bone on some kind of sub-DNA level. And it had happened so damned fast—or at least it seemed that way. Trying to look back on it, Kevin knew that realistically time had flowed at a normal, logical pace, the same way it always did in the everyday world. He was the one who had lost his grip on reality and his position in the universe, and while that hold might have started to decline with Daniel's first suggestion about using Nuriel's incantation on Wednesday evening, things hadn't really gone into full slip-and-slide mode until he and Daniel had revitalized the three Tyrannosaurus Rex eggs yesterday.

What were the clichés? The blink of an eye, the turning of a key . . . or the millisecond that it took for one person to make a life-altering decision. That single, stupidly blurted sentence of his to Daniel—

"I have more eggs."

—had changed everything.

Where had it gone wrong, really wrong? Beyond the fact that Daniel had gotten involved with something unnatural and incomprehensible, where had he hit the point of no return, that oh-so-critical instant? Kevin thought he had to be the one to take the credit for that, with those damned eggs of his. A second, stunning success with the incantation, and then . . .

Disaster.

There was no other word for it. Three beautiful, healthy T. Rex hatchlings, safely contained within the metal cage that Daniel had carefully set up—a cage that became immediately too small and far too weak as they watched, hour by hour, the infant dinosaurs grow at an abnormal and terrifying rate. And Daniel hadn't helped matters by feeding the babies a constant diet of white mice. Thinking back on it, Kevin thought he could recall seeing Daniel occasionally get that same vaguely dreamy expression on his face that Kevin no doubt now had on his own during the times that the thing inside his head began to speak. Daniel had probably been hearing his own version of the voice for days, perhaps since the initial time he'd used the incantation from Gibor Nuriel's notebook to coax into existence the first living dinosaur hatchling the world had seen in uncounted millennia.

As for Daniel himself . . . Kevin wanted to remember how it had happened, or why, but his efforts were futile. Surrounding Daniel's death were too many blank spots for him to navigate, as if the essence that permeated his brain had gone in there with a can of black paint and sprayed blinding spots on the things it did not wish him to see. What was left was the fragmented image of Daniel with big holes in it, the stained glass window that represented the young man's life but which now had hundreds of missing sections. Did he really remember Daniel *intentionally* opening the door to the overcrowded cage? After that, Kevin recalled rushes of red and the sense of something unaccountably growing right before his eyes as he cowered in a corner in the lab. After that . . . well, he just had no idea.

The back of Sunnydale High School, a janitorial entrance by the boiler room and a general supply area, suddenly appeared in front of him and the thing that was quietly, dangerously keeping pace with him. Was this what his life had come to? Back entrances, blood, and hiding. But no . . . the thing that lived inside him, the force that guided him, had promised otherwise in a cooing, seductive voice.

Look at what you will gain by following my instructions. Fame, freedom from this nothing little town and a return to your beloved city, a spectacular career . . . everything you want so badly.

And so he had obeyed, even though he didn't always

remember exactly how he did the things the voice wanted, or why it wanted him to do them to begin with. *Like now.* Somehow he had made a path through the shadows of twilight in Sunnydale for himself and the three hundred-plus pound tyrannosaur that had seemingly exploded from a hatchling that Kevin had actually thought was "cute" when he'd first seen it fight free of its splintered shell. Admittedly any idea as to how the things the voice continued to promise would actually come about had vanished, but he was still lucid enough to wonder what he was supposed to do at the high school library, or why it would want him to take the young dinosaur there in the first place.

That is not your concern. All you need do is obey.

And so he did, because he must, even though in his soul he thought that the voice was probably lying to him. Had it promised Daniel—the now *dead* Daniel—these same things? Still, resistance was unthinkable. Whatever possessed Kevin now was strong and unstoppable, and his single, pathetic attempt at disobedience had resulted in a screaming inside his skull that made him want to rip his eyes out to stop the pain and the noise. Perhaps, he thought foggily, if he just gave it whatever it wanted, it would be done with him and simply go away.

And for some reason not shared with Kevin, it wanted to be in the Sunnydale High School library.

So be it. Kevin checked the janitorial door and found it unlocked, then pushed it wide so that the dinosaur could follow him into the building, like an absurdly oversize pet without a leash. Inside was a hallway, a lot darker and grubbier than the bright California decor so prevalent in the remainder of the school. In Chicago, school buildings were locked up tight after school hours, and the grounds were closed, the better to keep out loiterers, drug dealers and to discourage considerably less desirable behavior. Apparently they had no such concerns in this sunny southern California town.

It seemed like it only took seconds to get the T. Rex out of there and into the main system of halls. Thankfully there was no one around. A good thing, since he didn't have clue one how he'd explain or deal with a surprise visitor, but he had a very good idea how the dinosaur would. A few turns, a couple of dead ends, and he ended up standing with the beast in front of the main entrance on the end of the building that he was pretty sure housed the library. The fact was, Kevin wasn't that good at finding his way around the building yet and it looked like starting at this entrance, the one he used every morning, was going to be the only way he'd be able to locate it.

The library! the voice inside his head thundered.

"R–right," he said shakily. Kevin got his bearings and took two steps forward, then a man came around the corner at a juncture midway down the hall. The teenager instantly recognized the glasses and tweed jacket look, a countenance that reminded him a lot of his dad: Mr. Giles, the school librarian.

Their eyes met and they both froze, then the older man's gaze cut to the hulking form of the adolescent Tyrannosaurus Rex standing nearly beside him. An entire range of emotions flashed across the librarian's face—fear, dismay, regret—but oddly enough, he didn't seem surprised.

"Kevin Sanderson, I presume," he said. He didn't come any closer.

Kevin nodded, then suddenly he didn't know what to say. *Yeah, that's me, and hey, wouldja look at what I made!* just didn't ring right. How had Mr. Giles known who he was?

"I'd like you to move away from the dinosaur," Giles said before Kevin could think of an answer to that. "I don't believe it's safe."

Safe? Kevin frowned. Of course it wasn't safe. Look at what one of its siblings had done to Daniel. *That was its nest mate, right? The one that didn't escape last night? Or was it this one . . . or a pair of them, working together?* He wasn't sure of anything anymore. There was something in his memory about one going with him and the other staying behind at the museum to deal with some problem there, another exit through a maintenance area and then coming over here, but it was all jumbled up, mixed with intermittent flashes of Daniel and blood, plus . . . *pain?* Yeah, he'd gotten hurt or something, scratched or knocked aside by one of the hatchlings when Daniel had opened the door on the cage and the dinosaurs inside had broken it apart in their frenzy to be free. There was a gouge, not too awfully deep but enough to bleed, on his left forearm. Or was this injury from the bizarre set of horns growing out of the T. Rex's skull, protuberances that had nothing to do with the skeletal structure of this species of dinosaur? Had it pushed him somehow, nudged him in the direction in which it wanted him to go? Be that as it may, Kevin had gotten blood all over his stuff before he'd emptied the backpack and—

"Oh, no," he said and held up his pack, his thoughts suddenly clearing up. "Look. I have dinosaur eggs— Stegosaurus, actually. We have to hatch them."

But the librarian shook his head. "No, Kevin," he said. He seemed to be enunciating his words very carefully, as if he were speaking to someone he thought couldn't quite get the meaning of something vitally important. "Believe me, that's the *last* thing we must do."

Kevin frowned. "But why——"

The T. Rex beside him suddenly roared. Kevin dropped the backpack to the floor and clapped his hands over his ears as he sank into a cringe under the onslaught of enraged sound right next to his eardrums. Then the voice that had been inside his head for what seemed like centuries, was simply . . . *gone*. No warning, no explanation. Kevin had just enough time to feel a great sense of loneliness as the thing that was supposed to guide him to his destiny pulled out and abandoned him—

—before the young tyrannosaur closed its teeth across his neck and upper body.

"I think we need to get back to the library right away," Willow told Buffy as they quickly made their way out of the museum. "I found out major stuff last night, and since you and Oz only tangled with one of the dinosaurs, the last one might be on its way back to the school. Where's the van?"

Between the still heavy cloud cover and the waning afternoon, the side alley was in the dark for the moment. Still, she saw her boyfriend point toward the street just beyond the front of the building, where they could see the bubble lights of several police cars flashing. It wouldn't be long before the whole place was investigated. "Parked across the street," Oz said. "Conveniently located between two police cars."

"Looks like Oz's Public Transportation System just went off-limits," Xander said.

Buffy scowled. "Then we use old-fashioned foot power. The library is good, but we need to be somewhere—*any*where—else before the cops find the bodies of the guards and the dead dinosaur."

As Buffy led the way, Xander, Willow, and Oz fell in step behind her. Oz was only a shape beside Willow as they moved through the darkness, but she sensed his confusion even before he touched her arm. "You said the last T. Rex might head for the school. Why would it do that?"

"Maybe to get to the other one," Buffy suggested, and Willow had to hand it to her friend—she was definitely thinking along demon lines. "Remember you said you thought the one in the alley was trying to get somewhere?"

"Yeah," Oz said. "It did feel that way."

"Exactly," Willow said. "It—"

"—wants to do this mind-meld thing," Xander jumped in. "Like the Vulcans in *Star Trek!*" They turned the corner and thankfully left the museum, with its growing infection of visiting law enforcement, behind.

"Somehow I don't think it's going to be very Vulcan-like," Willow said. "The way we figure it, it's a dragon demon from the underworld, really ugly and really huge, that has to find four hosts that kind of look like itself to put its spirits into."

"Possession," Buffy said promptly. "But what then? Try to free the other ones so they can cause chaos and destruction?" She shook her head in disgust. "How typical."

"Not quite," Xander told her. "Four hosts—dinosaurs—then they all get to one place so they can do the mind dance thing all over again, the other three with the *first* one. See, it seems that the power behind El Numero Uno is too big for one little body, so he can only get out in pieces. But then he can put all of those pieces *together.*"

"It's the greed thing," Willow said a little breathlessly. "Bigger, better . . . *hungrier.*" Almost everyone here was a little bit taller and longer-legged than Willow, and while they seemed to be moving at a comfortable trot, once again she found herself doing the extra effort duty. Only a couple more blocks to go. "If it gets itself all into one form, then it's free to go into munchmode."

"So even though we've now killed two of them," Oz said, "you're saying it can try again?"

Scowling, Buffy jerked to a stop. "Wait a minute. This means if we kill one, its spirit still bounces back and forth between the demon in the underworld and an egg somewhere up here, like, forever?"

She wanted to get back to the library and Giles, but Willow was still grateful for a chance to catch her breath. "No. The . . . displaced spirit goes back into that first host, where it waits for the chance to . . ." She frowned. "I don't know—hatch again, I suppose. The only way to win is to kill the other three hosts, *then* destroy the original one."

"Got it," Oz said. "Because now it's kind of a container for all four spirits at once."

"Exactly."

"So that kills it," Buffy said, starting to move again.

"Oh, no. This is the Hellmouth. Nothing around here ever seems to *really* die." Willow looked meaningfully at Buffy. "It just goes back to sleep for another sixty years."

"We won the battle, but not the war," Oz said.

"Great," Buffy muttered. "I get to fight this thing again when I'm nearly eighty years old."

"If you live that long," Xander said offhandedly.

"Xander!" Willow exclaimed.

"What?" He frowned, then realization set in. "Oh . . . Hey, I didn't mean—"

"That's all right," Buffy interrupted with dripping sweetness. "It gives me something to look forward to."

"Well," Xander began, "Personally, I—"

"Let's plan birthday celebrations later," Willow interrupted. "Right now, Giles is alone in the library with that . . . *thing*." Her eyes suddenly widened. "Oh no! It's got *three* demon spirits inside it! I hope the cage in the library can hold it."

This put a little more zip into their steps. Now they could see the school kitty-corner across the street. Not much farther, and in the grayness of the afternoon, the windows to the library glowed softly behind drawn blinds. Crossing the street, the group finally broke into a run.

"There's still one thing that bothers me," Buffy said, her words jerking with each fast step. "How does it get the egg to host it or whatever to begin with?"

"A ritual," Xander told her. "So if you're right about this Kevin guy, he'll be the one to perform it."

"Yeah," Willow agreed as they finally reached the outside steps and headed up. Just ahead of her, Oz gave the double doors a push, then yanked himself upright instead of taking a step. Willow looked past her boyfriend and saw Kevin Sanderson lying on the floor in an amazingly bright puddle of blood. There was a big part of his body that was too mangled for her to comprehend—maybe even *gone*—but there was no mistaking the blond ponytail and the gold hoop still glittering in his left ear. His brown eyes were open and staring, as though he was surprised that something he'd loved so much had actually killed him.

"Or," Xander said as he stepped up behind them and saw what had brought Willow and Oz to a standstill, "the demon will find a way to use someone else."

And farther down the hall, muffled by the closed doors to the library, they heard Giles cry out just before something unseen roared.

Then . . . silence.

Chapter 14

"GILES!" BUFFY YELLED, BUT SHE AND THE OTHERS hadn't taken ten steps before the third of the Tyrannosaurus Rex siblings lumbered into view from the corridor that led to Giles and the library.

Everything—human and otherwise—froze.

Buffy didn't know if a dinosaur could look startled, but this one certainly did. Once separated, the demon spirits apparently existed completely independent of one another, and obviously the one controlling this hatchling had been confident its brother or sister would put her and Oz out of the picture.

"Guess it just isn't your lucky day," she muttered beneath her breath. From the library, Giles shouted again, then she heard the Timimus screech wildly. Damn, in the wake of the toothy monsters they'd been dealing with, she'd forgotten all about that thing. It was also the "oldest" of the dinosaurs. Just how big had it grown, and more importantly, *what was it doing to Giles?* Maybe her own luck wasn't that hot either.

And now here was this razor-mouthed killing machine, at least seven feet tall and with several hundred pounds of muscle, standing between a weaponless her—and why was *that* always happening?—and the library. To make everything really go weird, the thing about the horns that Oz had mentioned in the museum had been all too true, and it seemed that each successive dino-sibling was looking more like Papa Demon; in fact, this one had pointed, very un-dinosaurlike eight-inch horns sprouting from the bony ridges over its eyes. Like a purebred T. Rex wouldn't have been hard enough to kill.

"Buffy," Willow said urgently. "Giles is in there *alone!*"

She didn't want to leave her friends, but she couldn't let Giles down, either. "I'll distract it," she said in a low voice. "Get it to chase me away from the library. You guys act like you're going with me, then cut back and help Giles."

"I'm going with Buffy," Oz said, never taking his gaze off the T. Rex swaying from side to side several yards away. It looked huge and dangerous, like it was evaluating them and might go from poised to charging at any second. "When you get to the library, remember you can't kill the Timimus until this one's dead. Jump the gun and we could be in deep trouble."

"Wait a minute," Xander protested. "I saw the look on your face when bad boy here popped up, and I know this is the biggest one yet. What are you going to—"

"Whatever we can," Buffy said. "Trap it—maybe in the gym, or the auditorium."

Willow inhaled raggedly. "Just stay out of the way of its teeth!"

"Gladly," Oz replied.

Buffy ran a hand across her mouth. "When we're done, we'll come back to the library and help you."

Xander and Willow exchanged glances. "Listen . . ." Xander began.

But Oz's eyes glittered as he stared at the T. Rex. "Don't worry about us," he interrupted. "We can handle it."

The low, wolflike tone of his voice made them glance sharply at him to make sure he wasn't unexpectedly changing. But he was all right. "Okay," Buffy said, because she had no choice. "Then . . . *go!*"

All four of them moved at once, with Buffy and Oz staying on the right-hand side where they could veer away at the last second. They sounded like a pack of wild animals; surely nothing human or remotely intelligent had ever charged something this big and deadly, and screamed, hooted, whistled and flailed their arms at it to make it come after them. The predator instinct in the T. Rex prevailed and it charged without hesitation, the long, heavy claws of its back toes leaving deep furrows in the linoleum as it scrabbled for purchase.

They were fortunate. While she and Oz would never make it to the hallway, between them and the dinosaur was the door to one of the classrooms. Buffy and Oz careened through it with barely enough space for safety between them and the creature's heavy, snapping jaws as it followed. Only the fact that it was reaching already, its neck stretched to the limit of it being able to maintain balance and still stay upright, kept them out of range. Banking on the T. Rex's attention being focused on her and Oz, Willow and Xander dropped and dove to the left, trying to make themselves as small as possible, a couple of nothing little specks along the floor that the beast would never notice. It worked, and for just an instant, as she and Oz fled, Buffy's head and heart were simultaneously filled with elation that her plan had succeeded, and terror for what her friends might have to face in the library without her there to help them.

Then Xander and Willow were up on their feet and headed toward the library to save the Watcher.

There was something inside him, an interloper of some kind. And Giles desperately wanted it out.

Was this, he wondered vaguely, what it felt like to be a vampire? What it felt like to be Angel? No, surely not; normal vampires reveled in their evilness, enjoyed it, *spread* it. Because of his circumstances, his unparalleled possession of a soul, Angel fought his own dark nature at every turn. But at least he had some measure of control over himself.

Unlike Giles.

He'd fought it, yes, and he was probably stronger than the hapless teenagers the demon had used and so carelessly disposed of. Older, wiser, stronger . . . but he was still only human, and the hammering and screaming inside his head was beating him down. He could no longer tell if the noise was inside his skull or out. Why had they not thought of this, realized that the Ladonithia demon would, of course, have to communicate somehow with a human in the physical realm to accomplish its goal? He knew what it wanted. Oh yes. Ten minutes ago, he'd picked up the Stegosaurus eggs for it, feeling like a paralyzed bystander watching dumbly as his own body moved jerkily down the hallway and retrieved the backpack that unfortunate boy had dropped right before his death.

Then the demon had wanted him to do something with those eggs, but Giles was not a greedy man, less self-centered than the younger people, and the demon could find nothing with which to tempt him. So far Giles had resisted with every bit of strength he had, but he was losing the battle. The clamor inside his brain was hellish, a cacophony of sound never meant to be heard by human beings, consciously or subconsciously. It was like music stripped of all its beauty, a demonic orchestra hammering out sound using instruments too terrible to describe.

Against his will, against everything that he was, Giles had watched his own traitorous hands remove the heavy, fossilized eggs from Kevin Sanderson's backpack and line them up along the library's counter.

There were three of them, that magical number again. Perhaps this was the demon's way of insuring a place for each of its spirits should the dinosaur that had killed Kevin perish at the hands of Buffy and her friends—if they themselves hadn't already fallen under the ferocious onslaught of another beast at the museum. There was something else it wanted him to do, something worse, but so far, Giles wasn't cooperating. He knew it had to do with revitalizing the eggs, but he wouldn't stop fighting the thing inside his mind long enough to let it tell him. That was the only way he could, so far, prevent it from getting its message across.

But he was tired, and he was weakening.

The librarian gritted his teeth and pushed himself away from the counter, heard fragments of sentences jitter inside his mind as he did so—

whatever you want
obey me
incantation
free me

He slapped his hands over his ears and spun, got a flicker of misplaced déjà vu as the recollection of Kevin doing the same thing twisted through him. *"No!"* he shouted, as much to resist as to hear something, *any*thing, besides the presence roaring in between his ears and the Timimus screeching hysterically from the cage a few feet away. "I will *not* do this!"

The voice boomed then, and agony razored through everything he could feel: his head, his chest, his hands, surely his eardrums were just going to explode right now. Giles screamed and dropped to his knees, hoped he could still remember to breathe but thinking he might be better off if he didn't. Horrified, he felt himself surrender and his mouth opened, ready to say the twisted words of the spell speeding through his thoughts: *Hear this call, spirits of Ladonithia Awaken and return from your abyss to—*

"Giles?"

Momentarily derailed, Giles felt the demon retreat in surprise. It would no doubt only be for a precious few seconds, but at least his mind was his own again, blissfully clear of everything but the throbbing memory of his previous agony.

"Angel," he gasped. "Thank God!"

Scowling, the tall, youthful-looking vampire strode to where Giles was kneeling and pulled him to his feet. "I came by to see if Buffy was around," he said. "Looks like it's a good thing I did." His sharp gaze took in everything at once: Giles's trembling body, the fossilized eggs on the counter top, the frenzied Timimus inside the weapons cage and which was now slamming itself against the door, bigger since yesterday by at least seventy-five pounds. "I don't think that's going to hold it much longer," he shouted above the dinosaur's shrieks. "We should get out of here!"

Obey me.

"Arghgh!" Giles reached up and yanked on his own hair, as hard as he could, hoping the physical pain would give him just a tad more time. "Angel," he screamed, "that creature, that *demon* . . . it's *inside* my— It's trying . . . to make me—"

OBEY ME!

Giles had no choice. It was as though his pain sensors had reached out and shut off the neural pathways that ran from his own brain to his mouth, rerouting everything into the demon's control. He hated himself but still he heard the dreaded words start to come out as he turned his back to Angel and faced the waiting eggs:

"Hear this call, spirits of Ladonithia," he rasped. "Awaken and return from your abyss to—"

A hand reached out and spun him, then the hard front of Angel's knuckles connected with his jaw and everything went blissfully, quietly, black.

"Angel?"

He whirled, automatically feeling guilty although he knew he had done nothing wrong. There was something about Willow's voice, especially when it sounded like it did now—half a question, half an *I-don't-believe-I-saw-what-I-just-saw* statement—that fired up the guilt factor of the human soul inside him to the tenth power. Didn't it just figure that she and Xander would arrive in time to see him punch Giles's lights out?

But he had no time for regrets, and he turned back and knelt next to Giles. "There's something wrong with him," he told them.

"He's unconscious?" Xander asked sarcastically.

He gave Xander a sharp glance. "I hit him because

he was delirious," he said. "Trying to say some kind of incantation. I was afraid *not* to knock him out."

A mixture of fear and relief flashed across Willow's features as she hurried forward. "So Oz was right. The demon will just use someone else." She ran a hand across her forehead while Xander just stood there with a guarded expression on his face. "It's a good thing you were here to stop him."

Angel checked Giles again—"sleeping" soundly—then stood. "What's going on here? What's that thing in the weapons cage? That doesn't look like what we fought in the alley by the Bronze."

"It's a Timimus," Xander said, as if Angel was supposed to instantly know what he was talking about.

"A what?" Several centuries old and he could still sound like an idiotic kid. How humiliating.

"A Timi—another kind of dinosaur."

Angel grimaced and stared from the two teenagers to the squawking, frantic creature pacing around the cage. "Another one. So what do we do with it?" he asked instead.

Xander shot the dinosaur an uneasy glance. "Since the tranquilizer gun is in there with him, I'd vote for using the tried and true caveman method of a club to the head, but for now . . . nothing. We have to wait until Oz and Buffy kill the T. Rex."

"Another one?"

Willow nodded, her movements jerky. "It's the demon," she explained. "It took us a while to identify it, but we finally figured out that it has four spirits. They all have to be inside this one before—"

At their feet, Giles groaned.

"Good," Angel said, relieved. "I really hated hitting him."

"I can't believe I'm saying this, but I think you have to hit him again," Willow said.

"What?"

Giles groaned once more and his eyelids fluttered. Willow gestured at the Watcher urgently when the older man's hands trembled against the floor, instinctively searching for something to hold as he tried to clear his head. "Don't let him wake up, Angel. The demon'll get inside his head again. It's better if we don't even give it the chance."

"Well, I'm out of its playing field, but why won't it just take over you?" he protested. "Or Xander?"

Willow's eyes narrowed and she sent a hot glare toward the dinosaur. "It *tried.* It . . . touched me or something, inside my head, right when I was coming in."

"Was that what that was?" Xander asked. "I felt it, too—nasty. I thought I was having a brain freeze."

"Why didn't it work?" Angel demanded.

"I made protection charms for us this morning," Willow answered, tugging on a cord around her neck. "Using hair, some herbs, a carnation and a little incantation." Distressed, she glanced at the awakening librarian. "I guess I should've made one for Giles, too."

Before Angel could comment on this, the older man groaned again. "Ladonithia . . ." he said thickly from his spot on the floor. Giles's eyes, Angel saw, were rolled so far back in their sockets that almost nothing but the whites showed, far too close to zombie-ized for comfort. "Eggs . . . must hatch them—" Suddenly the librarian tried to stand. Angel put out one hand to stop him and was nearly knocked off balance by a surprising show of strength.

"Angel!" Willow cried. "*Do* something!"

"Like what?" he yelled right back as Giles surged upright and tried to claw free.

"I *told* you. Just—"

Angel popped poor Giles in the nose. Again.

"Dammit," he said as he watched the librarian crumple into a silent heap on the floor. He scowled and turned back toward Willow and Xander. "I can't just keep beating on him, you know. He's only human."

"I know," Willow said. "But we have to keep him down, otherwise he'll make more dinosaurs and free the demon's other spirits."

Angel threw up his hands. "Okay, I'm lost here. I've got the dinosaur part, and even the demon part, but I'm knocking Giles out because he can *make* dinosaurs?"

"It's too complicated to explain right now," Xander said. "Can't you just trust us?"

A corner of Angel's mouth turned up in a smirk. "Her . . . maybe. But you?"

Willow exhaled in exasperation. "Would you two please stop sniping at each other like an old married couple? This is *serious!*"

Good point. Abandoning the argument, Angel glared in the direction of the caged demon-dinosaur. The thing was big, like an oversize lizard with a weird parrot's head and beak. He thought he'd seen it all until now. Boy, was it ugly. "Why don't we just kill it?"

Xander shook his head. "Believe me, there's nothing I'd like better than to ice this reptile and go help the others. But we can't, not until the fourth and final spirit is back in its body."

"So what you're saying is that there's three demon spirits in it now, but there's more to come?"

Willow nodded. "Another one in the T. Rex. And the instant it dies, this thing—" She pointed at the Timimus. "—is going to go even more ballistic than it already is." Her eyes were wide and scared. "That's why we don't have any choice but to stay here, and also why we can't just get rid of it."

The T. Rex—oh yeah. He'd gotten sidetracked. Oddly, the—what had Xander called it?—Timimus, that was it, despite its nerve-wracking screeching and constant movement, seemed alert and vaguely intelligent. It had to be the demons inside it, Angel decided. It was trying to comprehend what they were doing, trying to wait them out and get another crack at Giles. *Or maybe it senses me.* "So I can't let Giles wake up or he'll get possessed, and we can't kill the thing that's trying to do the possessing." He scowled. "So what are we supposed to do with this thing in the meantime? Stand here and look at it?"

"Have faith," Willow said with false brightness. "Any second now, Buffy and Oz will send their share of dino-meat back into Extinct Land."

"And how will we know when this happens?"

"This thing will get . . . meaner," she said reluctantly.

"Yeah," Xander put in. "As in a lot more hyper and ticked off when the fourth spirit comes back to roost in Papa Dino."

Angel's mouth twisted. "Buffy and Oz—you're sure they can handle it?"

"Positive," Willow said.

Even so, Angel felt his gut twist in silent fear, because Buffy's two best friends looked anything but convinced.

Chapter 15

"IT'S GAINING ON US!"

There was no hiding the apprehension in Buffy's voice, and no reason to want to. Whether the dinosaur chasing them could sense fear or not wasn't going to make them run any faster. There were at top limit now, careening through classrooms, down hallways, even blasting through stairways that they'd hoped—uselessly—would slow the creature down.

No such luck.

But Oz had a plan.

Buffy's legs were longer, so she'd been leading, constantly looking over her shoulder to make sure Oz hadn't been turned into a dino-tidbit. But her choices were random and spontaneous, and she was hesitating at turns. No good. As capable and strong as Buffy was, this was a game of animal against animal rather than Slayer against vampire. A second here and there could end up getting one or both of them killed.

Oz had no intention of letting that happen.

The full moon was weeks away, but his werewolf instincts were still there, etched into every cell of his body. To a normal human, it might have seemed as though he'd been running for years, but not Oz. Like a wolf, he felt that he could lope for hours without stopping or tiring, until his prey either dropped at his feet from exhaustion or was run into a trap.

The young Tyrannosaurus Rex hunting them didn't know it, but that's exactly what Oz was going to do.

Deep in his nose, floating below the remnants of industrial cleaning fluids, the leftover scents of a thousand kids and lockers filled with dirty athletic shoes and forgotten lunches, Oz smelled chemically treated water. He lengthened his stride, pulling ahead of Buffy. "Follow me," he yelled.

She didn't protest as he angled around to the right and bolted into the gray-walled stairwell that led to the lower level. They clawed their way through the metal door, then Oz slammed it shut with all of his strength. It caught and latched just as Baby Dino's snout hammered into it, and the dinosaur bellowed in anger. The door wouldn't hold it for long, but it would stop the creature for the precious half-minute it would take the beast to break the steel hinges.

"Okay, I'm open to suggestion," Buffy said.

"I'm on it," Oz told her as he motioned for her to follow him down and around the landing, then they dashed out of the stairwell. One flight above them, metal groaned as the door caved in. "Come on! This way!"

"Are you sure we shouldn't stop and fight?" Buffy yelled as she bolted after him, their sneakers squealing against the tiled floor of the long hallway now in front of them.

"Not yet!" And ahead, finally, was exactly what Oz had been aiming for all along—

The double doors that led to the swimming pool.

The two of them burst through and the doors swung shut. They skidded to a stop with the deep end of the Olympic-size swimming pool glistening only a few yards away and the air saturated with the smell of chlorine.

Oz spun to face Buffy. "The chemicals will make it hard for the dinosaur to catch our scent so it won't be picking up that we're actually behind it when it comes in," he told her quickly. "At least not until it's too late." He chanced a quick glance out the wire-meshed windows of the doors and saw the T. Rex lumber awkwardly out of the stairwell, then hesitate. But even if the scent glands were messed up, there was nothing wrong with its eyesight this close. It spotted the movement of Oz's head through the glass instantly and scrabbled for footing, working itself up into a full charge.

There wasn't any more time. Oz leapt to the side and grabbed a thick coil of blue plastic pool hose lying amid a pile of pool poles and nets. Holding one end, he let the coil untangle itself, a good fifty feet long, as he pitched the other end of it to Buffy. The Slayer caught it reflexively.

"Wrap your end around the balance rail over there and hold on," Oz told her. *"Hurry!"* As Buffy moved to the rail, Oz did the same. They could hear the dinosaur thundering down the hallway toward them, getting closer and closer. Beneath their feet, the floor vibrated. "When that thing hits the door," he said urgently, "we're going to pull this hose up tight and trip it. We *have* to get it into the pool, and once we do, we have to *keep* it there until it drowns."

"Won't it just swim?" Buffy demanded.

"No." Oz's voice rose to a shout as he tried to be heard above the noise of the approaching dinosaur. "I don't think it can without forelegs!"

"I hope you're right!" Buffy yelled as the T. Rex blasted through the doors. It hit them so hard that one slammed back and cracked against the wall. The other simply broke away from its hinges and fell inward with a crash. The creature's own speed kept it going, and when Oz yelled "Now!"—Buffy yanked upward on the hose, catching the dinosaur above its knee joints and below belly level, toppling it forward. The T. Rex couldn't keep its balance; it went down hard enough to ripple the water in the pool, then slid rapidly forward on its chin. A smear of blood stained the tiled floor beneath its jaw and its powerful back legs raked and clawed, finding even less traction on the tiles in here than in the hallways elsewhere. It reached the edge of the pool and went over, skidded into the water with a loud, unpleasant splash and a louder, water-filled roar of surprise.

"Keep it in the deep end of the water!" Oz yelled as he snagged a pool pole of his own. "Do whatever you have to, but don't let it get to the shallow end or it'll get out!"

Bellowing, the dinosaur lurched upward from the water and collided with the other edge of the swimming pool. Oz didn't want to contemplate the power in back legs that could propel it that far above a surface that was a good five feet higher than its head. If they were lucky, it would never even know that such a thing as the "shallow end" existed.

Buffy grabbed a wall brush with a wide metal end and swung it like a baseball bat, letting it go at the last second. It sailed end over end and the tip of the brush *thunked* into one side of the dinosaur's head; the creature went back under with a half squeal, half gargle. When it came up again a long few seconds later, there was considerably less height in its spring, and Oz was betting that it took a lot of energy to propel that much weight up and down. Although the claws on its short forelegs left heavy gouges in the ceramic edges of the pool, there wasn't enough size in those tiny limbs to enable it to drag itself out. Sputtering and choking, its bellows were starting to sound weaker and clogged with liquid. Success was surely in sight, and Buffy snatched up something else—a cleaning net—as it churned toward her side of the pool. She darted forward and slammed it down on top of its head, making it instinctively yank away from the edge of the pool once more. Another splash and again it dropped beneath the surface of the water.

But when it propelled itself upward a third time, it was clear that its zigzag pattern was taking it toward the shallow part of the pool.

"No!" Oz barked. "Keep it out of that end!"

He and Buffy ran along the pool's edges with it, one on either side of it. Only a few yards away floated the nylon rope that divided the two ends of the pool, held aloft by evenly spaced buoys. If it got much closer, the young dinosaur's head would be above water again and it would be literally able to walk right out of the pool . . . and they'd be doomed.

"I don't think the safety rope's going to stop it!" Buffy shouted. Her face grim, Buffy swung at the T. Rex's emerging head again, then was rewarded when the net at the end of her flexible pole looped over its snout and hooked neatly over one of its unnatural horns. The netting ripped and stuck wetly over the beast's eyes, but the square metal frame dug solidly into the flesh of its face and embedded itself beneath its heavy jaw. Looking victorious, she threw her weight in the other direction and tried to drag it back toward the deeper water. "Gotcha, you big, ugly—*aghhhh!*"

It yanked Buffy into the pool.

"Buffy!" Oz yelled, as if she could actually hear him underwater.

Buffy's head came out of the water and Oz motioned frantically at her with the pool brush he'd picked up. "Grab the other end of this! Watch out for its teeth!"

But the T. Rex was more concerned with survival than the splashing Slayer a few yards away. The net Buffy had looped over its mouth was still there, solidly stuck, and the metal frame had just enough leverage to hold the heavy jaws shut; now when the creature tried to leap up for air, it could no longer breathe through its mouth. The dinosaur's attempt to take in air through its nose wasn't enough; it sucked in chlorinated water instead, then went back under.

Still, it came up again, and this time Oz couldn't believe the images his eyes were feeding his brain. Instead of swimming toward the pool brush he was pushing at her, Buffy inhaled deeply, lunged forward and wrapped her hands around the beast's heavy horns, then hauled its head beneath the water.

The water churned wildly as the half-T. Rex, half-demon rolled and twisted, all direction lost as it fought to breathe in an airless environment. It got its nostrils a few inches above the surface a final time and Oz caught a flash of wet blond hair as the Slayer pulled downward yet again, throwing everything she had into the effort.

Then it was over.

Abruptly all the waves went out of the water and for

a long moment the surface of the swimming pool was almost calm, the perfect picture of what it should be. "Buffy?" Oz strained to see if anything moved below the murky, oblong shape floating a few feet underwater.

Nothing.

"Buffy!" He dropped the brush he was still holding and took a step toward the edge of the pool, then jumped back as his friend surged upward only a couple of feet away. Oz knelt and offered a hand to help her out of the pool, then they stood and stared at the water as it shimmered and finally went quiet. Five seconds passed, then ten, as the final ripples eased the creature's corpse slowly toward the shallow end. Finally, head down and still, the tyrannosaur's body stopped, a long, dark golden shape just below the surface.

Buffy stared hard at it. "I wonder if it's playing dead."

"I don't think so," Oz said. "But sometimes drowned people come back if they get pulled out in time. Maybe there's an air pocket or something in their lungs that keeps them from totally giving up the ghost. If it comes back . . ." He didn't need to finish.

Buffy nodded, and together they stood and watched the lethal thing drifting silently in the pool, wondering how Willow and Xander were doing with Giles in the library.

"I am *not* going to knock him out a third time," Angel announced. "He could end up with a concussion or something else humanlike."

Unfortunately, Willow knew this could very well be true. But what to do in the meantime? "Here," she said suddenly. She hurried over to the computer and pulled the power cord from the back of the CPU, then unplugged it at the outlet. "Tie him up."

"How is that going to keep him quiet?" Xander asked.

For a moment she was lost. Then she ran behind the library counter and started rummaging around. "Aha!" she exclaimed as she waved a roll of packing tape above her head. "This'll do the trick!"

"I should've just taken him out of here," she heard Angel mutter as he wound the heavy power cord around the still unconscious Giles's wrists.

"Hello?" Xander cut in. "Big T. Rex out there running arou—"

Inside the weapons cage, the Timimus went absolutely berserk.

It slammed itself against the cage door with enough force to make all three of them jump. Its screeches filled the room and razored into Willow's eardrums; beside her, Xander and Angel looked none too pleased about the noise assault on their ears, as well. Worse yet, the creature's behavior was like a trigger in Giles. While Willow struggled to find the end of the tape on the roll in her hands, the librarian's return to awareness this time was anything but gentle. His eyes opened wide and his back jerked upright; then the incantation they so had not wanted to hear started tumbling from his lips.

"Hear this call, spirits of Ladonithia," he intoned. His words were full of clear, British snap. "Awaken and return from your abyss to this frozen host, first of four, to then combine, and grant to he who resurrects you—"

Willow finally found the end, yanked out a strip, and slapped it over his mouth.

Giles struggled mightily, bucking and twisting in Angel's grip and throwing his head furiously from side to side, trying to rub his face against his jacket, against Angel's hands, anything to get the tape off his mouth. With Angel holding him down, Willow finally had to wind the tape all the way around his head and overlap the ends, just to be sure the man couldn't find a way to be free of it.

Xander made a face at the hair twisted up and stuck beneath the packing tape. "Man," he said above the screaming of the dinosaur, "that's gonna hurt when he goes to take it off."

A few feet away the Timimus rammed the door to the weapons cage, then charged it again. Willow winced as she saw the metal door shudder beneath the nonstop onslaught. "He's never going to get the chance if we don't kill that thing!"

"I thought you said we couldn't," Angel yelled.

"We only had to wait until the last of the spirits came back home to roost!" she shouted back. Even this close to Angel, and hollering, it was hard to be heard over the creature's racket. "By the way it's acting, I'd say Buffy and Oz went, saw, and conquered!"

"That," Buffy said from the doorway, "is *exactly* what we did."

Her friends whirled and gaped at her as she strode over to where Giles twisted on the floor, still fighting to escape his bonds. Water dripped from her hair and her clothes were plastered to her body, but none of that mattered. She wasn't hurt, they weren't hurt, but Giles . . . Seeing him like this made Buffy suddenly furious. She'd thought all these dino-battles had exhausted her, drained her strength all the way to the bone—not to mention ruined her clothes—but when she looked down at her Watcher, all her stubbornness and will and natural fight came back somehow, as if she were a battery plugged into a big recharger.

Buffy turned her head and glared at the beaked dinosaur raging inside the weapons cage. She couldn't say she'd never felt such hate for anything since coming to Sunnydale, but boy . . . it was mighty, mighty close. Giles was in mental agony at her feet, out of control and taken over by that disgusting, birdbrained, hideous thing over there, a beast that didn't even have the decency to look like any proper dinosaur she'd ever seen.

"So we're planning to rip that thing apart with our bare hands or what?" Xander asked, forcing her thoughts back to their situation. "Being as how we have all these weapons at our disposal."

Buffy's scowl deepened. Good point there. The weapons cage had definitely been a poor choice of prisons for the Timimus, but then they hadn't known the nasty beastie was going to grow like a weed and turn its crankometer up to killer disposition.

But five seconds later, on the heels of yet another attack on the door and the sound of a huge, metallic crash, Buffy and the others realized that the Timimus no longer stood between them and the cabinet where Giles kept all Buffy's best demon- and vampire-slaying paraphernalia.

Because nothing at all stood between the Timimus and them anymore.

For one slow-motion moment, the dinosaur simply stood there and looked, well, *stupid*—like the oversize and mostly thoughtless animal it was supposed to be. Unfortunately, even predators with walnut-size brains had well-honed attack instincts, and this one now had all four parts of a single demonic entity raging inside it. The cage door had fallen knob down and now the dinosaur leaped forward and landed on it, wobbling there as if it were trying to understand the requirements for balancing on this strange surface. Then its eyes focused on Angel, who had dropped into a protective crouch in front of the utterly helpless Giles, and it started forward on legs that were long and slender, but incredibly powerful. Once it stepped off the cage door and realized that the entire floor didn't bounce back and forth like the door had, Buffy saw the muscles in its legs tense for a leap. It was going to charge Angel, she realized, because as far as it was concerned, he was the one thing that stood between it and the only human within range who could complete the incantation it so desperately desired.

"HEY!" she screamed as loud as she could. She waved her arms frantically and was rewarded when the Timimus reflexively turned its thin face toward her and froze. Unarmed, she still took a couple of steps toward it, faking a challenge, to try to keep its attention. As Xander and Willow slowly backed away, she was thankful to see that at least this thing wasn't as big as the Tyrannosaurus.

"Excuse me," Xander said in a pseudo-whisper, "but what's the deal with the, uh, moving bumps on its shoulders?"

Bumps? Oh yeah, there they were, three pulsing areas around its neck, rippling and swelling, growing with every passing second. The last T. Rex had sprouted demon horns. Maybe this one was trying to mutate, too?

"Angel," Buffy said quietly, never taking her gaze off the dinosaur, "we have to move fast before this thing grows more heads. Get Giles out of here."

Angel didn't argue, but when he bent to pick up the librarian, the Timimus's head swung back in his direction and Buffy knew Angel didn't have time. This creature simply wasn't going to be bothered with her. It just wanted Giles.

With an ear-splitting screech, it headed toward the

two men, muscular legs clambering among the chairs and stacks of books in its way. But Angel wasn't slow. He'd known the attack was coming. He hooked one hand firmly under the collar of Giles's jacket and yanked him around the side of the library counter, then practically threw him in back of it. When he turned back the Timimus was nearly on top of him, with Buffy right behind it.

The dinosaur lunged at Angel's head, trying to snap at him like a giant parrot. Angel dodged out of the way, but Buffy knew he wouldn't be able to keep it up. Vampire or not, this creature was designed for just this type of attack, with a body built like an oversized ostrich and all the heavy muscle that went with it. And if it actually managed to connect with that sharp snout . . . well, Angel was going to lose a lot of undead flesh.

Things started flying through the air at its head. Willow and Xander were frantically lobbing books at it. The Timimus ignored them and swooped at Angel again, then started to go for the third try. Before it could dart forward, Buffy blindsided it with one of the wooden library chairs.

The Timimus screeched, swung around and bit at her but missed, and in those few seconds she saw Angel drop below the library counter. There was the sound of books crashing to the floor, then he reappeared with a small, metal table held aloft like a gladiator's shield. "I can hold it now!" he shouted. "Go!" He gestured at the cage. To make sure it didn't track her progress, Angel grabbed a pencil cup off the counter and threw it at the Timimus to regain its attention. The cup hit the thing just above its right shoulder with a noisy clatter and a couple of sharp pokes thanks to the letter opener and a pair of scissors. The beast squawked in surprise and swung back toward him, then got beaned by another book tossed by Xander on the right. Between the four of them, the creature must've felt like the bull's-eye in a game of darts.

Buffy grabbed her chance, spun, and bolted for the weapons cage.

She was there in five running steps and she leaped neatly over the fallen door rather than stepping on it, afraid it would make noise and the Timimus would realize something was up. When she jerked open the cabinet door, she had a moment of indecision that felt like forever. What would be the best tool to kill this beast? But her uncertainty was gone as quickly as it had come. If humans had lived at the same time as this rather small dinosaur, her ancestors might have used a club to take it down. She, however, was a modern woman, and had no time for such crude methods.

Buffy reached inside and snatched up the crossbow.

Angel, Xander, and Willow were shouting and the Timimus was shrieking, but Buffy suddenly felt a fine sense of calm spread through her body. This was her world, not the dinosaur's. It didn't belong here, but she did, and so did Angel, and Giles, and all the people she cared about. She would handle this dino-demon once and for all.

She stepped out of the cage and onto the door, not caring anymore if she made noise. A few yards away, Angel's metal shield was pocked with dents and gouges, and the Timimus was wearing him down, not at all affected by the flying books.

"Pardon me, bird-face," Buffy said. Her voice never rose above conversational level, but despite the barrage of noise in the room, the Timimus still heard her, still picked up something . . . *different* in her tone. It abandoned its attack on Angel and whirled, long tail dragging across the fronts of lower level shelves and sending books and papers sailing in every direction. Already seven or eight inches tall, the three incomplete growths around the base of its neck waved in the air like blind snakes, but its main head came up and stopped as it stared at her, perhaps trying to process what it was seeing.

"Angel," Buffy said softly.

Her vampire boyfriend ducked below the counter——

——and Buffy fired her arrow.

The tip hit the Timimus at the front lower corner of its eye and kept going right on through its skull. When the arrow smashed into the wall behind the counter, it carried bits of dinosaur skin, bone and blood with it, leaving a gory pattern on the paint. For a second the Timimus just stood there, paralyzed, then it sank to the floor with a sort of slow-motion grace, like a gigantic, gently collapsing swan.

Angel peered cautiously above the counter. "Helluva shot," he said with admiration.

Buffy edged toward the downed dinosaur, automatically loading another arrow into the crossbow, just in case. Xander and Willow also inched in, their faces washed in fear. When Buffy was about three feet away, the dinosaur opened its mouth and gave a terrible, unearthly squeal. She tensed and brought up the crossbow once more——

But the dinosaur exploded into a cloud of glowing brick-colored dust.

"Well," Angel said, staring. "No matter where we come from, it seems like we all look like that in the end, doesn't it?"

Buffy started to answer, but Willow cut her off,

her face suddenly shock-white beneath her red hair. "Buffy—*where's Oz?*"

"Right here," he said from a few feet away. He stalked into the room, then stopped and studied the glittering reddish-gold powder that had settled over a good portion of it.

"I'm thinking Hoover," Xander said.

Buffy ignored him. "The T. Rex?"

Oz shrugged. "I gave it three minutes to make sure it stayed dead."

Willow looked nervous. "Three minutes isn't very long. Maybe a few more—"

"Nah," Buffy said with a grin. "That's really all a dead demon is worth."

Epilogue

"Man," Xander said, "you should've seen the look on Coach Lannes's face when he saw all that red crap in the pool. If people had rations of being pissed, he's used up his until the year 2020."

They'd spent the night cleaning up the library as best they could, and now, while Angel carefully stayed in the library's deeper shadows, Buffy and the rest of the Slayerettes were lounging here and there around the room during a free midmorning period. Buffy nodded, considering Xander's description. "So it was just like in here," she said. "Lots of red—"

"Dust," Willow finished for her. "It got into *everything*. Coach Lannes said the entire pool has to be drained and the motor on the pool filter has to be replaced. If he catches who did it . . ." She shrugged.

Xander leaned forward. "I distinctly heard him mention something about giving the perpetrator blue pool hose as intestines. They're blaming the whole thing—

the pool, the library, the broken doors here and there—on vandals."

Buffy couldn't help grinning. "So I think it's safe to assume that the T. Rex bodies we left in the alley by the Bronze and in the museum are also dustized?"

Angel crossed his arms. "Yeah. No one ever mentioned finding anything in the alley, but there was a piece in the paper this morning about 'evidence' vanishing in the murder investigation at the museum. I'm thinking it's a dead dinosaur disappearance."

"The guards and Kevin are being tied into Daniel Addison's death," Xander told them. "According to the news, the cops are blaming them all on an animal attack, a continuation of the pet disappearances last week."

Buffy nodded, trying to stay focused despite noticing that, always on the quiet side, Oz seemed even more so today. "What do you think, Oz?" Buffy asked.

He blinked. "About?"

She shrugged. "About why this whole thing started, or how. I mean, there has to be some motivation behind it, doesn't there? Kevin Sanderson and Daniel Addison were just normal guys interested in guylike stuff—"

"Beg to differ," Xander interrupted with a wave. "Cars, girls, baseball. That's guylike stuff. Lizards? Not."

"Depends on the guy," Willow said.

"Maybe," Xander allowed. "But dinosaurs shouldn't be obsession-worthy. Girls and cars, on the other hand—"

"Not necessarily," Willow cut in. She leaned over and looked at something in front of Oz and he pushed it toward her. Buffy recognized the notebook Oz had picked up in the museum, and when Willow curiously flipped it open, it was filled with tight, neat handwriting.

"Kevin Sanderson's," Oz explained for the benefit of the others.

"Did you read it?" asked Buffy.

He nodded, his eyes hooded. "As far as I could make out, Kevin was following Daniel's lead, and Daniel was following the demon's. I never got my hands on the original notebook described in here, the one Daniel found somewhere in the museum, so I don't know what went on sixty years ago. But going from what Kevin wrote, I'm guessing the demon promises fame and fortune or something like that to whomever he can get his hooks into. It's either an outright liar or likes to do the nasty irony thing."

Giles stepped out of the library office and moved to join them. "Then Daniel Addison was a prime target for it," he said. "If recollection serves, I believe his records related something about his being unwilling to think for himself."

"'Unwilling to work to succeed,'" Willow corrected, obviously quoting from memory. "And ... no, he didn't much think for himself."

"So the demon moved in to help," Buffy said. Saddened, she shook her head.

"Yeah," Xander commented. "And wasn't it just mondo disastrous when he let someone else's brain do the thinking part for him."

"It wasn't so much thinking *for* Daniel as making a bunch of hyped-up promises about all the great stuff that would happen to him if he did what the demon wanted," Oz said. "Kevin's notebook records more about what was going on with Daniel than with him, but I'm guessing Ladonithia switched its attentions over to Kevin."

"Who was another great victim," Willow said. "Just moved here, no friends, trying to start everything over. It was easy for the demon to make promises that it never intended to keep. It was just using Daniel—then Kevin—to get released."

Giles nodded. "As an adult, I wasn't so easily directed, so I barely heard any such fantasizing." No one said anything for a few moments, so Buffy glanced knowingly at Angel. He gave her a tiny nod, then made a noise and straightened up on his chair.

"Hey, Oz," the vampire began, "you remember I was there when that band manager woman talked up to us in the Bronze?" Oz nodded. "Well, I, uh . . . did a little checking here and there, hung out a little at Willy's and asked a few people I know who know other people." Angel looked at his hands uncomfortably. "There's some stuff I thought you ought to get the lowdown on."

For a long second Oz didn't say anything, then he sighed. "Spill."

Angel shrugged, and Buffy knew he was making an effort to appear more nonchalant than he was. He really didn't want to be involved in this, and he wasn't at all pleased with what he was about to tell. "She's taken over the management of a lot of bands the last two or three years," he said finally. "Young ones, like you and Dingoes. I called in a few favors, and . . ." Angel's voice trailed off.

"And?" Oz prompted.

"It's not a very impressive record," Angel admitted. "None of her bands seems to have gotten very far. They're all still playing the low club circuit, and some of them have been with her for years."

Oz raised an eyebrow. "So you're saying she can't get the big-time club gigs?"

Angel rubbed his hands together, looking quietly uncomfortable. "I don't know if she can't, or just won't. Some of the band members . . . well, a lot of them . . .

seem to have gotten so miserable that they're into drugs now. Her deal is insisting that they can't manage their finances so she takes all their earnings, claiming it's going for expenses and that she's investing the rest. Word is she supplies a lot of the drugs just to keep them cooperative. Most of them haven't seen a dime in next to forever."

"Oh," Xander said. "This is so not good. Sure doesn't sound like a nominee for Band Manager of the Year award." He looked disappointed, and Buffy remembered that Alysa Bardrick had supposedly offered him a space along with the others.

Angel nodded. "It's a pretty reckless lifestyle, a lot of wildness and, from what I heard, not a whole bunch of happiness. Her career guidance skills seem to be seriously lacking, although she certainly has a lot of . . . clients."

Oz stared at the tabletop without saying anything for a few moments. "I guess I knew it was going sour." He shot a glance at his girlfriend. "Willow did some virtual checking. The info wasn't stellar."

Willow looked at him sympathetically. "Yeah. Alysa wasn't lying to me in the Bronze. She doesn't have a web page or any advertising on the net, but I found a few anonymous postings here and there, in band-related user groups. There was a definite fear factor thing going on. One even said signing up with her was like getting drafted into a Third World army . . . for life. You gave it all and got zip in return."

"They sound more like slaves," Buffy said thoughtfully. "Or prisoners."

"That could very well be close to the truth." Giles's voice was quiet as he joined the conversation. "If she appropriates the entirety of their income, they're probably dependent on her for the most basic necessities. Food, clothes, shelter and . . . well, who knows what else. Likely anything she can use to keep them tied to her."

"Boy," Buffy said. She looked at Giles briefly, then let her gaze slide toward the notebook on the table, because she didn't want him to see the gratefulness in her eyes. "You really have to choose those mentor-types carefully."

"Yeah," Oz said, staring off into space. "Yeah, you do."

The day had gone amazingly fast—too fast, in fact. For Oz, school usually dragged; the information the teachers offered was too easily absorbed by his brain and, more often than not, very uninteresting in general. Apparently the universe was conspiring against him today; he dreaded having to deal with this afternoon's responsibilities. It seemed the Powers That Be had decreed that the clock should move along at ten times its normal speed, solely for the purpose of tormenting him. He wasn't looking forward to it.

Then it was his last period, and then even *that* was over and done with, while around him most of the other students had at least one final hour or so of education. Not him, though. Now nothing stood between him and his future.

Except, maybe, Alysa Bardrick.

She was waiting in the library when he got there, looking tall, thin and impatient, her sleek black outfit not much different from the nighttime attire he'd seen her wear at the Bronze. It was completely out of place here at the school. Waiting on the library table was a thick sheaf of papers—the same pile of contracts, no doubt, for him and the other members of Dingoes, as well as for Xander and Willow. There was probably one for Angel, too, if Alysa could convince him to sign away a chunk of his existence, along with the rest of his friends.

"Hello, Oz," Alysa said.

"Hi." He came in, hiding his reluctance, pulled out one of the chairs at the library table, and dropped onto it. "How are you?"

"I've brought all the contracts," she said, ignoring his attempt to be polite. "You'll see that everything is in order. If you'll just sign on page eight, we can start pulling everything into place." The older woman looked at him expectantly. "Where are the others?"

Oz caught a glimpse of Giles on the other side of the library's open office door. Giles knew about Alysa's appointment with him, of course, and after the information that Angel had dropped on their heads this morning, Oz couldn't blame the guy for wanting to hang around, just in case. This woman could no doubt spin a whole bunch of new definitions for the word "devious."

"Well?" Alysa said, arching one eyebrow.

"They aren't coming," he said.

For a moment she didn't say anything, then the band manager folded her arms, looking stiff and vaguely volatile. "I see," she said in a bristly voice. "I take it, then, that you and your friends are still unsure about my services?"

"Actually," Oz said, "I think we're pretty clear on all accounts." And it was true; he'd talked things over with Devon and the others at lunch, giving them the scoop on what it would probably mean to let her put Dingoes Ate My Baby on her client list. Ultimately everyone was totally okay with Oz's decision. In fact, Devon had pretty much shrugged it off and said better luck next time. His parents, he'd told Oz with a lopsided grin, would be just totally frosted if he dropped out of school and took off anyway. His cautious attempt at bringing up the subject the other night had resulted in no less than his dad threatening to sell Devon's car, and what kind of a band singer/senior could he be with no wheels? "We've decided to keep handling Dingoes ourselves," Oz finished.

He could've sworn Alysa Bardrick actually flinched when she heard this. "Really." She paused, searching for her next words. When they came, there was a tinge of frost in her tone, an undercurrent of threat that she'd kept well hidden until now. "That's most unfortunate. I saw a lot of potential in you and the others."

Oz looked at her blandly. "I'll bet you did."

A muscle twitched lightly at the side of her jaw. "Is there some particular reason for this, or has someone else given you . . . the wrong impression?"

A shadow disengaged itself from the side of a bookcase across the room and Angel moved to join them, his steps silent, his face brooding. "Seems to be a lot of that going around," he said in a low voice. Alysa started when she realized he was there, then her eyes narrowed as Angel continued. "Wrong impressions, that is."

"Uh-huh." Slowly building anger had drained the color from Alysa's face and her lips pressed together tightly, creating a blood-red slash across its bottom half. "And these wrong impressions would be coming from . . . where?"

"Oh," Angel said as he idly inspected his fingernails. "Here and there." He raised his eyes to meet hers without actually lifting his head. "Just . . . around."

Oz watched the play of emotions across the woman's face and tried to read them, knew he wasn't nearly as good at it as Angel was. In fact, he wasn't as good as

Angel was at a lot of things . . . like finding out information about someone before you damned near gave them everything that you were. Then again, he wasn't a couple of centuries old, either—*and I never will be*—so maybe he ought to cut himself a little slack.

"See," Oz finally said, "I figured it was a two-way thing. Sure, we do the music part of the deal, but you were also kind of applying for the job as our manager."

"I don't see what—"

"Your references sucked," Angel interrupted darkly. "In fact, I'd say calling them 'muddy' would be damned generous."

"Well," she said crisply, reaching for the papers. "There's certainly no sense in arguing. I have better things to do with my time than waste it trying to sign on a nobody high school band."

"Really," Angel said. He lifted one booted foot and rested it on the edge of the table, then stared at the polished wood. "Like what? Appointments to pick up a few . . . hard to find *substances* for your other band members, maybe?"

Alysa drew herself up. "Choose your words carefully, young man. In today's society, accusations aren't taken lightly without proof, you know."

Finally, the vampire looked up. His face was the epitome of innocence. "Accusations? I'm only speculating."

She gave Angel an icy glare, then turned back to Oz. "I'll give you one last chance," she said. "You and Dingoes could be on your way next week."

Oz frowned at her. "On our way to what? A carefully disguised form of captivity?"

For a fleeting moment, Alysa Bardrick looked shocked, as if no one had ever put it all together before. Then she recovered. "I'm not holding anyone. My clients can leave anytime they want." She gathered up the stack of contracts, then stuffed them back into her bag, carefully taking all evidence away with her. "Perhaps we'll meet again," she told Oz. She gifted Angel with a final glower, then stalked out.

"No," Oz said as the two of them watched her leave. He thought again of the dead Kevin Sanderson and the way he'd blindly followed the just as deceased Daniel Addison.

"I sure hope not."

"Boy, ain't this just the biggest mess you ever seen?" Bob Norrell complained. He and his coworker and best lunch buddy, Fred Vaughn, stood in the doorway to Daniel Addison's tiny office, staring at the chaos inside. Papers were strewn everywhere, file drawers had been pulled out and left on the floor, everything on the shelves had been taken down, examined, then pitched back up there any which way. "I'll tell you," Bob continued. "This has got to have been the worst week we've ever had in this place, and I've been here for almost twenty-three years. People murdered, big old bunch of red dirt showing up right in the middle of the dinosaur exhibit—it's gonna take days to clean that out. I don't know what the hell's going on around here anymore!"

The younger Fred just nodded, having learned a long time ago that it was best to simply agree with anything Bob Norrell said or pay the consequences. The older man could argue a point, even something about which he was obviously wrong, for three days, and damned near drive him insane over it. Fred had a young, pregnant bride at home who already did that; he didn't need it here at the museum, too. "You can say that again," he said.

"Well." Bob sighed. "Here we go." He gave the closet-size room a final, baleful look, then reached back and pulled up two flattened box forms, one for him and one for Fred. "Take this and let's get started. Like they said, pack it all up and put it down in the second level basement."

Fred began dutifully molding his hunk of cardboard into a recognizable box shape, tucking flaps here and there in the appropriate places. "Don't the cops want to look through all this stuff?"

Bob shrugged. "They already did. I'll give you one guess who made this mess."

Fred nodded again, then began scooping up papers and the little odds and ends that were thrown everywhere. There were blank spots on the dusty shelves where some of the more important fossils and bones had been removed; apparently the museum's administration had already claimed what they thought was important enough to recatalog or pass along to other people in the department. Everything else: storage. "What's this?" he said, and lifted a ragged, leather-covered notebook from under a stack of wrinkled computer print-outs. "Looks like it's been burned."

Bob peered over his shoulder, then made a *hmphing* sound. "No idea. It's old. Just shove it in a box with the rest of this garbage. We'll haul it downstairs and pack it away with the mice and who knows what else lives down there in the dark. Let someone else find it fifty or sixty years from now.

"When they do, *they* can figure it out."

About the Author

Yvonne Navarro is a Chicago-area novelist who has written a bunch of stuff, including novels, movie and television novelizations, and short stories. The Y2K bug hiccuped and allowed her to have two other novels published in the Year 2000 besides this one *(DeadTimes* and *That's Not My Name),* so *Buffy the Vampire Slayer: Paleo* is her eleventh published novel. She's also published a bunch of illustrations, although most of the time she draws people, not dinosaurs.

Her first published novel, *AfterAge,* was about the end of the world as orchestrated by vampires (surprise!) and was a finalist for the Bram Stoker Award. In her second novel, *deadrush,* she worked on zombies, and *deadrush* was also nominated for the Bram Stoker Award. *Final Impact* and its follow-up, *Red Shadows,* chronicle some really nifty people struggling to survive when the Earth is nearly destroyed by a celestial disaster. Yvonne wrote the novelizations of both *Species* and *Species II,* as well as

Buffy the Vampire Slayer: The Willow Files, Vol. I and *Aliens: Music of the Spears.* She also authored *The First Name Reverse Dictionary,* a reference book for writers.

Currently she's working on a supernatural thriller called *Mirror Me,* and still plans to someday write sequels to most of her previous solo novels. She also studies martial arts and loves Arizona, dogs, champagne, and dark chocolate. Visit her at www.para-net.com/~ynavarro, where you can read more of her stuff and see funny photos, plus find out how to get books autographed and keep up-to-date. Come visit!

"Wish me monsters."

—Buffy

Vampires, werewolves, witches, demons of nonspecific origin. All of them are drawn to the Hellmouth in Sunnydale, California. And all of them have met their fate at the hands—or stake—of Buffy the Vampire Slayer.

This volume catalogs and explores the mythological, literary, and cultural origins of the endless numbers of ghoulish creatures who have tried to take a piece of the Slayer in the first four years of the hit TV show.

THE MONSTER BOOK

by
Christopher Golden
Stephen R. Bissette
Thomas E. Sniegoski

AVAILABLE NOW FROM

POCKET BOOKS

3016

Everyone's got his demons....

ANGEL™

If it takes an eternity, he will make amends.

Original stories based
on the TV show
Created by Joss Whedon
& David Greenwalt

Available from Pocket Pulse
Published by Pocket Books

2311-01